Happy Ever After at Romansa Castle

THE CATCH UP

RAVEN MCALLAN

The Catch Up
ISBN # 978-1-80250-531-3
©Copyright Raven McAllan 2023
Cover Art by Kelly Martin ©Copyright March 2023
Interior text design by Claire Siemaszkiewicz
Totally Bound Publishing

This is a work of fiction. All characters, places and events are from the author's imagination and should not be confused with fact. Any resemblance to persons, living or dead, events or places is purely coincidental.

All rights reserved. No part of this publication may be reproduced in any material form, whether by printing, photocopying, scanning or otherwise without the written permission of the publisher, Totally Bound Publishing.

Applications should be addressed in the first instance, in writing, to Totally Bound Publishing. Unauthorised or restricted acts in relation to this publication may result in civil proceedings and/or criminal prosecution.

The author and illustrator have asserted their respective rights under the Copyright Designs and Patents Acts 1988 (as amended) to be identified as the author of this book and illustrator of the artwork.

Published in 2023 by Totally Bound Publishing, United Kingdom.

No part of this book may be reproduced, scanned, or distributed in any printed or electronic form without permission. Please do not participate in or encourage piracy of copyrighted materials in violation of the authors' rights. Purchase only authorised copies.

Totally Bound Publishing is an imprint of Totally Entwined Group Limited.

If you purchased this book without a cover you should be aware that this book is stolen property. It was reported as "unsold and destroyed" to the publisher and neither the author nor the publisher has received any payment for this "stripped book".

Totally Bound Publishing books by Raven McAllan

Single Books
Hong Kong Heat
Taken Identity
Fairground Attraction
The Duke's Temptation
The Viscount Meets his Match

Diomhair
Secrets Shared
Secrets Uncovered
Secrets Remembered
Secrets Dispatched
Secrets Learned
Secrets Dispelled

Daring Ladies
The Earl and The Courtesan

Castle on the Loch
Love by the Stroke of Midnight

Happy Ever After at Romansa Castle
The Fix Up
The Catch Up

Anthologies
Bully for You: Chasing Charlie

Collections
A Little Bit Cupid: For One Night Only

With Cassie O'Brien

The Scots and the Sassenachs
The Earl of Callander's Secret Bride
The Baron's Saving Grace
The Duke's Lost Love

THE CATCH UP

Dedication

To Ann,

my lovely editor.

Thank you for everything

Chapter One

Jan Fraser glanced idly out of the window of her twentieth-floor office and watched the scenery. Several Star Ferries moved across the busy Hong Kong harbour from the Central Piers to TST in Kowloon. From her vantage point they seemed like ants scurrying about their business. Not far from the shore a rubbish sampan snagged some weeds and a bag of goodness knows what from the murky water and a police boat went by on its way to some business or another.

She adored it. Every last, bustling, noisy inch of downtown as well as the tranquil hills and trails of the islands and New Territories.

Home. It was a satisfying thought, and one she gave thanks for on a regular basis.

It was no secret she loved her life as it was. Work, a great social circle, perfect—albeit tiny—house in Sai King, a lovely fishing village in the New Territories, and the knowledge of a holiday due to her. She relished the thought—and the joy—of getting out her suitcase and deciding which holiday clothes to pack. The downtime was well overdue.

All of which made her more determined to discover—why her? Why did life decide now was the time to throw some curveballs in her direction? Why had two things put spokes in her wheels?

The first, admittedly, was only an annoying gnat of a spoke. An ex who out of the blue was about to descend on her—or so he thought. Which would have been a not-so-pleasant surprise if his sister hadn't warned her. Not a long text. Just, '*Thomas in HK soon 4 filming. Arr Thurs. Sez will call u. Has yr wrk addy, not from me!*' The last three words had been highlighted *and* written out in full. As Ari was a supporter of 'text speak', it showed how she'd wanted to emphasise the fact.

His forthcoming presence was irritating, but not the end of the world. Surely she was far enough over him—as in, the other side of the world over him—to be cool, calm, collected and civilised if he did turn up? *Say 'hello, no thanks, I don't want a meal, or a drink, to go up the peak on the tram or take a trip to Disney World'. Don't add I'd rather swim with sharks or eat worms than spend my free time with you. Life is too short. Be polite and distant and hope I don't see him around the place. Be courteous and show him he means nothing to me anymore.* Even if the events that led up to them splitting still gave her the shakes.

Sod him. Why couldn't he accept I had the chance of a lifetime as well as him? That surely we could survive for six months apart, and if we couldn't it was as well to find out sooner rather than later? As it had happened, they hadn't needed to find out. Thomas had used the old chestnut 'if you loved me you'd come with me'. Jan had refrained from retorting 'if you loved me you'd accept how important my opportunity is as well', and instead said 'thanks but no thanks, I'm taking my chance of success as well'. In her mind his attitude had been selfishness in the extreme. It was her opinion that a relationship meant give and take, not one give and one take. Or at least not the same one doing all the taking and the other having to do all the giving.

Now it seemed he was about to appear in her life again.

Sod it. This time she'd be the selfish one, and if—*if*—they did meet up, it would be on her terms. She grimaced then smiled reluctantly. She was reading an awful lot into the fact an old...old what?... acquaintance—she refused to call him anything more intimate—was probably going to drop by to say hi. It could be no more than that.

What if it was, though. Argh. Enough. Jan gave herself a mental shake. Why worry about what might never happen?

If all that wasn't enough to keep her awake at nights, her boss had just dropped another bombshell on her. On a Friday afternoon no less. Just before they'd all departed the building for the weekend. No doubt on purpose. May could go home with a clear conscience, having discharged her duty. However, Jan thought savagely, not her. Bugger May. Now she, Jan, would spend all weekend trying to wriggle out of what was wanted from her.

And it was a bombshell she had an idea she couldn't really get out of. Not if she wanted to fulfil her job description properly. Mind you, if she were honest, would she really want to if it didn't mean the postponement of her holiday? Jan thought about that for a second or two and admitted to herself—reluctantly—probably not.

The door behind her opened and she turned to smile at May, her friend and boss, who waved a white hanky in the air.

"Is it safe to come in?"

Jan shook her head in amusement. "Yes, and you might well wave that. I could go off on you big time. Rotter."

"That's rotter, boss." May grinned. "Sorry, but who better to send? It is in your job description isn't it, even if not in so many words? I accept it means putting your holiday off for a few weeks, but A, we'll pay for all the extra expense, B, you were heading over there anyway, and C, you know darned well you're the one person who will break balls if need be."

"Sounds gruesome. And, *and,* note, I'm not due to be heading there until I've had a month in Portugal," Jan pointed out. "You're asking me to go to Scotland, the *west* of Scotland, in the main midge months. I've sold my midge net hat and run out of repellent. I'll be eaten alive."

May shook her head and laughed. "Buy a hat and repellent and put the cost on expenses. If we left it until after midge months, you'd have the hot humid summer here to contend with first."

"I'd be in Portugal. Hot and not humid." *Not like here.*

"Mosquitos."

"Vinho Verde."

"Sand flies, burnt nose, sweat rash."

"Nit-picker."

"I thought you said nose picker." May snorted. "I got over that ages ago. Well, three at least."

"Wow." Jan opened her eyes wide. "That long ago?"

"Still bite my nails, though."

"Who doesn't?" Jan looked at her own red—as in fire engine-coloured—nails. She didn't—often—and had discovered if she got her nails done she was less likely to put a finger in her mouth and nibble. "Seriously, though, it's not the time I'd prefer to spend around forest and water, posh hotel or not. After all, I doubt I'd be allowed to wear a midge net and smell of eau de citronella all the time." That, Jan admitted, was her preferred mode of dress during the height of the midge season. "With my trousers tucked into my socks and my hands up the sleeves of my jumper. I swear, the little blighters take one look at me, rub their wings or whatever together and think ooohhh dinner. And breakfast, lunch and all snacks in between." She scratched her arms. "Makes me itch just thinking about it."

May dipped her head. "Okay, point taken. You and midges do not go well together. But, Jan, we really do need you at the hotel." She was all seriousness now. "The new owner is adamant he wants our help to pitch it to the right people. He doesn't want to close it to the public—well, not all the public—but there's a big, as in massive, superstar movie about to be filmed around there, and he needs advice on the best way to handle the situation. Not to antagonise anyone in any way. Especially the people who own some of the bungalows there. They're the biggest flies in the ointment."

"Close it for renovation," Jan said promptly. "Facilities and all. There, sorted. Portugal, here I come."

May laughed and shook her head. "Good try. He says not. There are a lot of people who own cottages and stuff in the grounds. He can't stop those people turning up. They'll presume they're free to use the facilities as normal. You can't be expected to accept there's no golf or gym or whatever when it's in the deeds of your house you have unlimited unrestricted use."

"Well, not if it's something dangerous that's closed, whatever."

"Nope, but it isn't, and they'd know that. Plus, to do the regular safety checks required they have to give a minimum of three months' notice to the punters. This place is *seriously* select."

"Hmm." Jan thought for a moment. It sounded intriguing, but she wasn't going to mildly give in and say okay. "I'd say he's got a problem if it's all true."

"It is. In the deeds. He's checked and so have our law people. Not a cat in you-know-where's chance of wriggling out of it. If anything is broken or whatever the hotel is liable, and it costs them money, not the house owners. The perks of paying top whack for rather gorgeous holiday homes."

"I can see that could be a problem." Jan stared out of the window and nodded as she thought furiously. A cruise ship was in the process of docking on the other side of the harbour and tugs and little boats were moving fussily around it. She never lost her sense of marvel at how busy the harbour was and how all the different types of craft managed to go about their business. A sampan dodged a tourist junk and she bet someone shook a fist in the bigger boat's direction. Jan smiled. How she wished she could hear the conversation going on there. Swearing was recognisable in any language.

May coughed. "Earth to Jan."

"Where exactly are we talking about?" Jan asked and dragged her mind back to the subject in question. "It might help to know that. After all, it could be on the east coast and nigh-on midgeless." She didn't think so for one minute, not the way May had been talking. "So?"

"That sadly is on a need-to-know basis," May replied in a regretful, 'sorry but it's not my doing' sort of way. "If you agree to head over and spend a month or two checking things out, giving advice and so on, I can, after you've signed a confidentiality clause, tell you where you'll be going. Not before and unless—" She broke off and held her hands up in the air. "I know, I know, it should be you know what you're letting yourself into before you agree, but this isn't my decision. I can tell you it's all above board and the directors are adamant they want you. As a colleague I say that, as a mate I agree I'd be as fed up as you are over it all and inclined to tell me and them—to F off. If a bit more politely."

Jan stared at May as she tried to remember something Arietta, her friend and warner of Thomas' imminent arrival in the city, had mentioned. Something about her—Arietta's—husband Moss possibly filming close to where they had a house in the west of Scotland and a lot of kerfuffle over it. Something to do with the film company not wanting there to be any chance of rubberneckers and the new owner of the nearby hotel adamant it couldn't shut its doors while the filmmakers faffed about in the extensive grounds. No contracts had been signed, including Moss', and everyone was getting, in Arietta's words, *"a wee bit antsy"*. Could it be that?

"Oh," Jan said much more nonchalantly than she felt, "Romansa Castle. Gaelic for romance. Moss Kirby's next movie. I heard there was a wee bit of a hoo-ha about if it was to be filmed there."

May jumped and stared at Jan for several seconds. "What are you? A super sleuth? Where did you get that info? That's supposed to be top secret. Both the hoo-ha and the place."

Shoot, I hope I haven't got Arietta in trouble. She didn't say it was for my ears only. Blast, damn and fig rolls. "Really? Since when? And I am right then." She said that as a statement, not a question.

"Since when what?" May prevaricated. "What do you mean?"

"Since when is it top secret," Jan replied in a patient way. "That wasn't mentioned. Just that the hotel felt it couldn't shut. The film company had discussed it with the previous owners, I believe. If I've got it right, they were offered a deal that the majority felt they couldn't turn down and then as the film company hadn't got anything signed, he...she...they said there was nothing to honour. Or something," she finished lamely. Moss had been a part owner and had been so disgusted by the mentality of some of his co-owners he'd sold his share willingly. He'd said he was relieved to let the whole sorry arguments and the stupid mess be sorted out by someone with more time. It might have been a house associated with his family, but any thoughts of hanging on to his bit of it were long gone. He'd still got his new home and a fair bit of land nearby where he and Jan had a gorgeous house and lived whenever possible and was happy with it. Weirdly, Arietta had informed Jan, the land Moss still owned was not the land the film company wanted to use. If it had been, life would perhaps have been simpler all round.

"So how are you in the know?" May persisted.

"I was brought up nearby when it was just a big posh house, though Mum and Dad moved from the area years ago." She grinned. "So have I."

May snorted. "You don't say. Go on."

"Well, I'm not really in the know, but know someone who knows someone from around there." A lame reply but the best she could come up with on the spur of the moment. "Sort of. I know a lot of knows but don't know a lot."

"A lot of knows there when there shouldn't be, eh?" May chuckled then sobered straight away. "Damn and blast." She sat down on Arietta's desk chair with a thump. The chair rocked, slid several feet backwards and spun around to face the wall. One of May's coveted Jimmy Choos flew off her foot and headed towards the ceiling.

With a leap that would have done justice to any rugby player, Jan caught it in mid-air and presented it to her friend with a grin. "Cinderella, your shoe."

May nodded regally. "Cinderella's would have stayed on," she pointed out as she stroked the soft leather a few times before she slid her foot back into it, and grinned. "Gah, I always forget your chair does that. Mine sticks."

"I make sure I do a full spin," Arietta said. "Might as well enjoy a wee burl around."

"Burl?"

"Spin. I forget you're not up to speed with your Scottish slang."

"I'm learning. Fair enough, but not now. Any more nuggets to share?"

Jan shook her head. "Don't think so."

"Then how about it? It's not compulsory, but—" May hesitated and worried her bottom lip with her teeth. A sure sign she was worried. "I honestly can't think of anyone better to go and advise them. Him. Or whoever. Plus, I've got a promise you can go first class both ways and to Portugal or wherever after the work part is done. If we do a good job, it could lead to a lot more prestigious contracts. Let's face it, we know we're good and doing well, but we can always try to do better." She winked. "Bigger bonuses."

Jan couldn't decide if she had made her mind up or it had been made up for her. Either way, it appeared her immediate future was settled. "If, just if, I head there and try and see what can be done, then I go on holiday straight after?" She could go to Europe on the same plane she'd booked—she'd decided to fly via the Netherlands—and head to Scotland instead of the Algarve. Work could sort out the logistics—and any extra flights and accommodation. Portugal in September instead of July and August would probably be a better temperature anyway. "Then back to my job here?"

"Of course," May said promptly. "Why, yes."

Too promptly? Hmm.

"Why do you not sound so sure?" Jan asked on impulse, and with growing suspicion noticed a look of guilt flash over May's face. "What aren't you telling me?"

"Nothing." May didn't sound very convincing.

"If you don't fess up, the next time you walk out of one of your Jimmy Choos I'll accidentally heave it out of the window, or down the loo."

"Cruel." May sighed and wriggled her feet deeper into her footwear as she tucked her legs under the chair. "Okay, they did sort of wonder if you'd sort of want to do an extended stint with them, still work for us but go on loan to them."

"What?" Jan's voice rose in a screech. "Stop over there and… Definitely no, no and no again. My home is here. I do not want to go back to Scotland to work for however long." Although if she could do part time there and the rest of the time in Hong Kong, she could be tempted. However, she had no intention of saying so. Not at that moment. It had been so long since she'd lived in Scotland she might find it wasn't to her liking anymore. "What a crackpot idea. I might be crap at what they want anyway. Next."

"All right, keep your hair on. I'll pass that on in politer terms. If you get everything sorted faster, then you can add the rest of the time onto your holiday. Don't be surprised if someone tries to persuade you, though. And before you ask, no, I don't know why you, etcetera. I mean, do they know your nasty habits?"

Jan laughed now the tense moment was over. "Rash statement, boss of mine. I might rush things so as to get more tanning time—or invent some really nauseous idiosyncrasies."

"Not you," May said shrewdly. "You're too conscientious."

"Ain't that true." Jan gave into the inevitable with, if not good grace, a resigned acceptance. "Okay, I give in…sort of. I'll do the month. When do I leave?"

"End of next month, and be prepared for two months."

"Nope. One or no can go." Why was she being so ornery? Jan had no idea except for one of those something-weird-is-up itches she sometimes got. Usually when whatever she had to do and didn't want to went pear-shaped. Or she cocked up.

"Hard woman. I'll pass that on. What if they say you have to give them the option of another month?"

Jan high-fived herself. "Then I stay here and go on holiday. Remember, there's nothing in my contract that says this sort of stuff is compulsory. I might be a facilitator or an arbitrator or just an administrator, whichever hat you need, but that's for this company here. It's a favour, no more no less." She thought for a moment. "And for goodness' sake tell me exactly what they are going to call me. I need to get the right hat on."

"Eh?" For a moment May appeared flummoxed by Jan's reference to hats, then her face cleared.

"Hmm. Right." May sounded almost resigned. "What role you're needed for. I get you. How we've got it so far gives you almost seven weeks to sort stuff out here, and hand over anything that can't wait. I'll check what they're going to call you in Scotland and get a detailed description of what's to be done there. Right. Now that's sorted, head off early and have a great weekend."

Jan looked at the clock. "Not exactly early," she pointed out. "It's five to." What was she heading off to anyway? A great weekend with a lot to think about? However, Jan smiled at May. It wasn't the other woman's fault that Jan had to use one of her granny's favourite expressions, 'got her knickers in a twist'. "Yeah, you too."

One thing, it was a relief to know that she'd got that length of time at home before she headed overseas. Still grumpy at the way May had convinced her she'd have to do the job *and* wondering what she'd got herself involved in—and with who—Jan logged off and closed her computer. Tidied her desk and got her bag before she headed to the bank of lifts and waited for one to arrive and deposit her on the ground floor of the office block where she worked. The lift was prompt, and before long she arrived in the foyer, headed for the main door and paused.

Taxi, bus or boat? She had a choice of transport to take to get home and swapped between them depending on her mood, the time of day and the weather. Whichever mode she chose it would take her a good hour to get to Sai Kung, the fishing village where she lived, but she reckoned it was worth it. Especially at weekends when she could wander down to the water's edge and choose what fish she fancied for lunch. Watch the seller pick it out of its tank and hand it up to her wrapped in paper and a plastic bag, via a long-handled hook. Co-workers and friends said they envied her, but never appeared to lose the opportunity to try to get her to move closer to the city centre. When she demurred, they extoled one of the other densely populated areas, where they said she would have lots of things to do and more people to socialise with. She didn't bother to point out she had plenty of friends and enough things to do where she lived. Just resisted their attempts at getting her to move. She enjoyed the contrast and didn't want hustle and bustle all the time. Plus, the journey to and from the central business district and her home was perfect for reading.

Just before she reached the door of the building, Martin, a colleague, hailed her. "Drink at the pier? Half a dozen of us going."

"Why not." It was Friday, she had nothing planned, and the convenient little red minibuses ran from Central to the end of her street until almost midnight. Taxis of course were twenty-four-seven, but most locals would shun them if there was any other way to travel.

The tiny bar was situated by the piers where the ferries to a couple of the islands that dotted the sea around Hong Kong docked. It was laid back, friendly and always busy. Jan thrust her arm through the crook of Martin's arm as they fought their way through the usual crowds in the CBD area of Central and made their way to the harbourside with their co-workers. May had declined with a 'got me my man and a hot date in front of the TV'. Her husband was something high up in a bank and frequently overseas.

As ever, the throng sounded like a flock of cheerful parrots. It seemed as if all languages were represented, and she found it amusing to see how many she could identify. With a wry grin, Jan realised she could understand quite a lot of cuss words as well as 'excuse me', 'please' and 'thank you' in most of them. It was said that as long as you knew those words and a few other essential phrases—could I have a wine or a beer or a soda', 'where are the restrooms please', and 'may I have the bill please, thank you', in several languages, you could get by anywhere. She hadn't tried every language she knew them in up until then, but it had been so far, so good with the ones she had.

An itch down her spine made her turn and look behind her, but she couldn't see any reason for it.

She mentally shrugged and put it down to Arietta's text and an errant hair that had decided to come loose and tickle her.

Jan sneezed.

Thomas Clare stared at the laughing, vibrant, woman who had strode out of the multi-storey office block arm in arm with a tall, suited and booted male and headed in the opposite direction to where he was standing.

Bugger. She's got a bloke. What am I doing here? Why didn't I at least make her aware of my presence? Say hi, do the fancy meeting you stuff? Not let on I'd deliberately tried to see her? Sod it all, why am I so dithery? It's just Jan. Except there was no 'just' about it.

So many random thoughts whirred in his mind as Jan and the unknown walked farther away. Why hadn't his sister warned him?

Probably thought it would do me good. Besides, if I did do the hi bit, Jan would probably ignore me, spit in my eye or laugh at my audacity and sense of self-importance that I'd think she'd want to speak to me. Or even remember who I am.

Which sadly he totally understood. With the hindsight of several years' growing up, he could understand what a self-centred arrogant idiot he'd been. As an only son, with a sister who would tell him he was an idiot when need be but sadly wasn't always around to do that, and elderly parents who were of a generation who accepted that what he thought best *was* best, his ideas were antiquated at times. The time he and Jan had been together had been one of those times.

Hopefully he was now wiser as well as older. He might be about to find out. Thom stared at the departing couple thoughtfully. Should he follow them? Would that be considered stalking? If he did walk their way and bump into them, what then? Say a casual, 'hello, fancy meeting you here'? Pretend he hadn't seen them? Admit he'd been hoping to speak to Jan? Ask her advice? Explain he was in Hong Kong for work as well?

Bloody hell, why is it all so flipping hard? Thom considered the options then shrugged. Sod it, he'd go for a drink and decide whether he could be bothered to cook—if shoving a ready meal in the microwave his forward-thinking apart-hotel provided could be called cooking—or grab something from one of the stalls dotted about the city and eat on the hoof.

Or splash out and eat in one of the bars or restaurants where I can people watch. An evening of relaxation wasn't going to be on the cards once he started work in earnest in a few days. He was only in Hong Kong for a month, and most of that time was accounted for. His role in the film wasn't the main one but, as he had been told on numerous occasions, pivotal to the plot. Pivotal or not, he considered it a fabulous role and was, in his own words, chuffed to bits to have been offered it. The time in Hong Kong was the best added perk ever. He loved the place, every last inch of it. From the blokes trying to sell him a suit, a watch or a handbag—all creative copies—to the flower sellers, high-end shops, trams, buses and boats. Everything pleased him. Even the sudden rainstorms. Like the one at that moment which made the covered walkway even more popular and the umbrella sellers ditto.

Thom sauntered along the busy thoroughfare, dodged several umbrellas held at a height which could take someone's eye out and those people talking rapidly into their phones and who were oblivious to their surroundings, and headed for the quayside down one of the many routes that could be taken.

As ever, the route was busy. It not only accessed the central business district but several shopping malls and streets and eventually the central escalator—the moving walkway that came down the peak first thing in the morning and went upwards for the rest of the day—and Lang Kwai Fong, the area where a lot of bars were situated.

Thom chuckled to himself as he remembered many a happy night there on past visits. Why had he left it so long to return to Hong Kong? It was one of his favourite places to visit.

Because Jan was here.

When she'd first moved there he'd sulked. He'd been offered a dream job in Australia and had thought Jan would jump at the chance to accompany him. Instead, she had told him she had been offered a fantastic job in Hong Kong and wasn't going to turn it down to spend six months in Australia whilst he spent his days—and probably a fair few nights—filming and she twiddled her thumbs and waited for him to find time to spend with her.

He'd sulked. Overreacted and, as his sister had kindly told him, spat his dummy out.

By the time he'd got over his snit, Jan had been in Hong Kong and he'd been on the other side of the world. When he'd flown home he'd gone via Hong Kong, spent a couple of nights there and wondered if he would see Jan. He didn't of course, and had been too proud to beg Arietta to give him Jan's address. He'd discovered her work address through a friend who had come across her by chance whilst looking for someone savvy enough to help out with a problem regarding his new hotel.

Zac Moncrieff had whistled when he'd seen her resume. *"This chick could be the one to smooth things over and be the answer to my prayers. What d'you think?"*

Thom had peered over Zac's shoulder. *Janetta Fraser.* His—or more correctly *not his*—Jan. A sharp, familiar prick of regret hit him. The one that he always experienced when he remembered what he could have had and threw away. He'd realised Zac was staring at him, expecting a reply.

"That she'd cut off your balls and fry them up for the dog's dinner if you called her 'this chick'. No woman wants to be thought of as 'this chick'. Honestly, Zac."

Zac had grinned, unrepentant. *"Only to you. Anyway, what do you reckon? Do I go for her to come?"*

Thom had shrugged. *"You could try, I guess. Why her, though? There must be lots of people who fit the bill."*

"I won't give you chapter and verse, but I just reckon she'd take no prisoners and get the job done."

"You could be right. Where is she working now?" Thom had hoped the question sounded an idle one, not one that mattered.

Zac had told him and Thom had looked the business up. So here he was, wandering through Hong Kong in a rainstorm having seen her from afar.

It had been fate, he decided, that not a week after that conversation with Zac, he'd been offered his present job and here he was.

For at least a month.

Surely that would be time enough to see if he could meet Jan and discover if that spark of awareness, that flare of arousal, was still there.

For goodness' sake, man, you might be an actor, but you're not rehearsing for a role in a hot romance. Enough. Thom chastised himself and noticed with relief it had stopped raining and the paths and lawns outside were steaming gently in the late evening sunshine.

"Beer, and a bite to eat," he said out loud, and earned a strange look from a passer-by. He smiled self-consciously and ran his hand through his unusually short hair. Cut and styled for his new role, it made him start every time he saw himself in a mirror. "Gotta get used to it." *Argh, enough.* He really had to stop his habit of talking to himself out loud, especially in public. Or, if he felt it necessary, at least pretend he was talking on his phone. He took some earbuds out of his pocket and plugged one into his ear. Hopefully that appeared better than nothing.

Of course, he reasoned, what would be even better would be to get out of the habit altogether.

Today's words of wisdom.

Thom veered to one side and headed down one of the covered walkways that led directly to the waterfront, turned left and went towards where he hoped a favourite bar still existed. Not one he would have dreamt of going to in the rain, but now? If the steps everyone used as a seating area were still wet, he'd stand. Or buy something and pay for a plastic bag to plonk his butt on.

The pavements were as near as dammit dry. Thom bought a beer from one stall, succumbed to a burger and chips from another and sat halfway up the concrete steps so he'd got one lower to put his feet on and one higher to lean against. He ate his burger in double quick time—he'd not realised how hungry he was until he'd scented the onions and his stomach had rumbled. Once he'd wiped his greasy hands on a napkin and put the rubbish in the appropriate receptacle, he took his tablet out of his bag, pulled up his script and began to read in between mouthfuls of beer.

People walked in all directions. As Thom watched, some sat nearby with drinks, others stood in groups chatting. He assumed they were waiting until their ferries arrived and they could be taken across the harbour to their destination. He had half his mind on his surroundings and the rest on the script as he relished the clever writing. It would be a hit, he was damn sure of it, and boy was he happy he was part of it. He got to a scene where his character had a big involvement and forgot everything except how he would play Sam Rolton, small-time crook and hopeless romantic who got tangled up with a private detective who thought Sam was more of a scoundrel than he really was. When they teamed up to solve a crime, things got interesting. Thom had been hooked the first time he'd read the story and now was even more so. He scrolled back to the beginning of the scene, oblivious to the hooting of the ferries as they came and went, the noise of the crowds and the engines of the vehicles on the nearby road.

It was only when he picked up his glass to find it was empty he realised how long he'd been sitting there.

Night had fallen, and the street—and quayside—lights were on. The crowds had thinned out, and the people that were around appeared less stressed and more chilled.

The Friday night feeling? Probably. Thom stared at his glass thoughtfully. One more?

Why not. He'd not got anyone or anything to head home to. Or in his case, head hotel to. The burger had taken the edge off his hunger, and if he was peckish later on, there were plenty of snack bars in the hotel's vicinity.

He'd have another pint.

He bought it and headed back to the steps only to see the place he'd been sitting was now occupied.

By someone he knew.

"Jan?"

Jan Fraser glanced up and froze. Her expression was wooden as she gave him the slightest of nods.

"Thomas? Fancy meeting you here." She didn't sound particularly enamoured at that.

"Fancy," he said and gestured to the step next to her. "May I?"

She shrugged. "I can't stop you, but please leave enough space for my companion. He's just gone to get our drinks."

As a mood depressor, she couldn't have done better. Thom inclined his head. "I wouldn't dream of usurping him."

Jan smiled. It didn't reach her eyes. "You couldn't."

It was enough for him to move to the other end of the steps and make sure he sat with his back to her.

Chapter Two

Bugger fu…flick and damnation. And why, oh why the sting of arousal now, for goodness' sake? Not needed, not wanted. Definitely not expected. The last thing she desired.

Or is it? Jan blocked that thought out.

"Now then, who was that?" Martin asked as he nodded towards the man now several yards away and well out of earshot. "Do I need to go all over masterful? Not easy according to Peggy." His wife. He sat next to Jan and handed her a glass of wine. "Peggy is on her way and she says to tell you she's remembered you wanted that knitting pattern or something and she's got it. The Sunny Bay ferry made a noise and I didn't catch exactly what she said."

"Great," Jan said absently, her mind buzzing. What on earth was Thom doing there so early, and at the quayside bar? Coincidence or on purpose?

"Right, I need to know, who was the bloke?"

"What? The…? Ah, an old acquaintance," Jan said. "Brother of a mate."

"He looked like he wanted to be more than that," Martin said shrewdly. "Seemed gobsmacked when you knocked him back. You did, didn't you?"

"Yup." Jan nodded. "He's not even an ember anymore." *I hope.*

"So he was a spark?" Martin queried as he sipped his beer. "I know, nosy is me, but Peg will want to know. I like to have the gen first for a change."

"Well now you have. A spark, well out."

"Have you told him that?"

"No need. If he didn't get it, that's not my fault. He went." *And it takes two to tango.* She ignored that thought. "Now let's change the subject. Did you try that recipe for chicken I gave you?"

"Fair enough." Martin stretched his legs out in front of him. "We did, it was great. Before I forget, and changing the subject totally and utterly, Peggy says, do you fancy a role as an extra in the film they're making?" Peggy worked for a small but up-and-coming film company. "She reckons it's going to be a big, big hit, and if it is, there's talk of a TV series. Couple of good stars from both movies and TV and a couple of the next hot ones. Her words, not mine."

"What are? Hi, Jan." Peggy sprinted up the steps towards them. "Martin, love of my life, where's mine?" She waved at their drinks. "Favouritism."

Martin stood up. "Just getting it, didn't want it to get warm."

"Fair enough." Peggy sat down on the step her husband had vacated. "Quick comeback. Okay, Jan, has he asked you?"

"Asked me what?" Jan procrastinated. Anything to do with TV series or movies with Thomas in the area sounded suspiciously like something she'd prefer to avoid.

"One, will you be an extra next weekend, and two, will you come to a wee afternoon barbie on Sunday. I'm being the good PA and sorting it out for the cast of this series we're doing. Not in our postage stamp, in Alex and Sasha Cheng's. Discovery Bay. Around two. Pretty please to all of it. Gives us a chance to be nosy."

Jan laughed. "Maybe."

Peggy gave an over-the-top pout and did her best upset whippet expression.

Jan waggled her finger at her friend. "Enough. Your face will stick like that if you're not careful."

"Ha, my mum used to say that as well." Peggy sniggered. "Seriously, though, will you? It would help me a lot. Get me brownie points."

"You told me you were never a brownie."

"PA points then. Will you? Pretty please."

"Oh, okay. Ditch the hangdog expression." Jan accepted she was beaten. Peggy was a good mate and mates helped each other out whenever possible. If Thomas was around, she'd deal with it somehow. "I'll come to the barbie and think about the extra. It's not really my sort of stuff. Don't like acting. Crap at it. What you see is what you get." *Though if Thomas is around for long, I better get used to putting on an expressionless face. No way am I letting him know I got the wee body tightening scenario when I saw him.* "Dish the gen a bit more. I need information. What exactly is it for and for whom?"

"Alex and Sasha of course. It's their new thing. Going to be a megahit, I reckon. Detective thingy, set here and in Scotland and with a couple of brits in it."

"Here and Scotland?" That made her 'something is going hit me hard' sense go on high alert, especially when she'd just seen Thomas and she was due to head to Scotland…

Jan spluttered the mouthful of wine she'd just taken. Here and Scotland? Brits? That sharp prick of suspicion hit her again. Was it a conspiracy?

Was it a TV series not a film near the hotel Peggy was talking about? She'd need to check. "Any idea where?"

Peggy smiled ruefully. "Can't say yet, sorry. But get this, evidently according to Lois, Sasha's sister, the supporting actor is hot stuff, and if he played his cards right he could have her any which way. Here or Scotland."

"Grief, Peggy, the pictures that conjures up," she said when she could speak without choking. "How old is she?" *And what's he like?*

Peggy rolled her eyes. "She's in her late twenties according to her. I'd add a few years onto that. Plus she's on husband or live-in lover number goodness knows how many. Or she might be over the last one, I lose count. According to one of the makeup girls, the bloke Lois has her eyes on is in his thirties, a really nice guy who metaphorically runs a mile when he sees Lois."

"Only metaphorically? She can't be that bad, surely?" It all sounded a bit over the top to Jan.

"Believe me, she is," Peggy said earnestly. "Maneater is an understatement. Even the guy who brings the mail makes sure she's not about when he comes in, and he's ninety if he's a day, with three teeth and halitosis."

Jan spluttered. "Bloody hell, that could give me nightmares. Put me off my food and whatever."

"Yes, well." Peggy shrugged. "You get my drift?"

Jan nodded. She'd be interested to see if this Lois person looked at all like Peggy painted her. "I get it, but why is it such a big deal? I mean, she's not got anything to do with the filming, has she?"

Peggy sighed. "Sadly, she's been taken on as a gofer. Not that she goes for much. Unless it's in trousers."

"*Miaow*. Or a kilt? You know? Scotland. Scotsmen. Tartan."

"Oh wow." Peggy sniggered. "Never thought of that, and a real, true Scotsman to boot. Gawd help him, he's got a couple of scenes in a kilt. Anyway, that's another story. When she said they need an extra to, er, be near him, we thought of you."

"Sacrificial lamb? Gee, thanks. Why? I'm not certified or whatever you call it," Jan said hurriedly. That suspicious sensation was getting stronger. The prickle was more of a pain. "So best not to count me in."

"It's only a nonspeaking extra, so it's okay. There will be a fair few of you. But you sort of look as if you'd be his type."

Whose type?

"So..." With a murmur of thanks, Jan took the fresh glass of wine Martin handed her and returned to the previous subject. "You want me to stand next to some bloke whose name you won't divulge, on my day off and what? Thump this Lois woman if she gets too close? Not my thing really. I don't do violence." *Well not all the time, though I do on occasion think I could make an exception for a certain bloke.* "Stare adoringly into his eyes? Not my scene either. Stand on his toes? I'd probably not make an impression in my size fives unless I borrowed May's Jimmy Choos, and they'd be too big for me." Much to Jan's sorrow. "Lust over the kilt? Been there, done that. Ignore him? That would defeat the objective I think. So what? Oh." She thought of something else. "Come to mention it, what sort of type is his? Do you mean the man or the role?"

Peggy appeared discomforted and Martin laughed as he gave Peggy her wine. "She has you there, my love. Time to tell the truth, the whole truth and so help you, miss nothing out?"

Jan nodded. "Succinctly put. So far you've told me bugger all, Peggy."

"Not true. I told you what we need," Peggy protested, but she didn't look Jan in the eye and twiddled with her earring.

"Liar, liar, pants on fire. You prevaricated."

Peggy stuck her tongue out.

"You'll catch flies like that. Come on, Peg, you know you've only shared part of the story and not enough. I need more than that to give one of my days off up, especially as—" Jan broke off. Was she supposed to keep her visit to the UK a secret? "As it'll soon be too hot to want to do much unless it involves the beach or air con," she added, somewhat lamely.

"Oh, okay." Peggy sighed gustily. "Put it like this, if you aren't there to do the stand next to him bit, Sasha is worried sick Lois will insist and who knows what will happen. The rumours of Lois' what should I call it, stalking the guy, have reached her ears. She insists it can't be true, that Lois would never make a fool of herself over any man, but…" She shrugged. "I reckon she's not prepared to take the risk. The guy is remarkably even-tempered, but even he will have a breaking point and in my opinion, Lois is it. I think Sasha and Alex are now having second thoughts about letting Lois be involved, but would never say so."

"Why did they?" Jan asked with interest. "From the way you've talked about her, it sounds as if it would be beneath her."

"Ah, but, it appears that husband number whatever is not as free spending as she'd like and she needs pin money. And a bloke to get her claws into, but they never thought about that until it was too late. Now she's determined to get said claws into this one."

"Who is?"

Peggy looked about them. Jan chuckled. The nearest couple were involved in tonsil tennis and oblivious to anyone except themselves. A few people were standing and chatting next to the bar and the only other person was a man with his back to them, scrolling through something on a tablet.

She recognised him.

Thomas. Dammit. Why is he popping up all over the place? I thought he'd gone. I couldn't see him last time I checked. Mind you, she reasoned, she'd only taken a cursory glance around. If he'd been at one of the stalls she could have easily missed seeing him. *He should have gone.* That was a bit unfair, but Jan was in no mood for fairness.

"Well?" she demanded a lot more harshly than she intended. "Fess up or I'll say no to everything." She tempered her words at Peggy's astonished look. "Please, Peg, I need info."

"Rotter. Okay, but this is for your ears only. Well, and big lug's." Peggy nodded in Martin's direction. He grinned and waggled his ears.

"Unfair, they aren't that big."

"Peggy, facts and bumf," Jan demanded. When the couple started their bantering it could go on for ages. "Or I'm off home."

"Okay, okay, right then. An up-and-coming actor who deserves more than Lois, and according to Alex will soon be at the top. A guy called Thomas Clare."

Bugger. I thought so.

"Not a cat in hells chance then," Jan said emphatically. "*Nada, non, niet,* nae chance."

"Why on earth not?" Peggy demanded. "Explain."

Jan smiled. Judging by Peggy's startled expression it wasn't a pleasant smile.

Jan nodded in Thomas' direction.

"Go and ask him."

"Pardon," Peggy said in a bewildered voice. "Ask who?"

"Thomas Clare. That's him over there, back to us. Dark hair. Reading. Not in a kilt sadly, but you can't have everything."

Thom glanced up at the tall woman who cleared her throat as she stood next to him. As far as he knew he'd never seen her in his life, but he'd not turn down the chance to speak to anyone at that moment. He'd never felt so lonely or unwanted in his life and it hurt. The fact he'd brought it on himself didn't negate that.

He smiled. "Hi, can I help you?"

The woman bit her lip. "I hope so. I've been told you're Thomas Clare. Is that right?"

I wonder who told her that. Interesting. It intrigued him enough to stand up, pay attention and learn more. "Sure is. Thom to my friends. Pleased to meet you, Miss? Mrs…?" He held out his hand and hoped she'd answer him.

The lady shook hands. "Mrs. Peggy Crossland. I'm PA to Alex and Sasha Cheng, who are directing your TV series, though I've been off a couple of weeks. I'm trying to persuade a friend to be an extra who has to stand next to you in one of the crowd scenes. She says you won't want her."

"Who is that?" Suspicion filled his mind. He had a good idea.

"My mate, Jan."

Thom grinned again. This was going to be interesting "Jan Fraser?"

Peggy's eyes widened. "The very one. You do know her?"

"Oh, yes. I'd be delighted to have her there, next to me." Anyone rather than the piranha who had been eyeing him up like her next dinner when he'd been to the offices of the TV series directors. He reckoned the woman was a good ten or twelve years older than him—not that would have been a problem if he'd fancied her, but he didn't. However, her predatory glances had given him the heebie-jeebies. He'd been relieved to get out intact and admitted he'd headed for a little-known bar to hide out until he was reasonably sure he was safe. Ever since, he'd done his best to give her a wide berth whenever he'd seen her. Apart from the time he'd accidentally stood next to her in a coffee shop, and trying to be polite—and no more—had bought her a coffee. He'd rued the gesture ever since. She'd obviously thought it had meant he was interested in her, and hounded him. Jan could be a good foil.

If she was prepared to be.

"Fair warning. Jan might think otherwise, though."

"Want to come and tell her she's wrong?" Peggy asked. "She's over there next to my beloved. We've all been friends since Martin and I came out here a few months after Jan did. They work for the same company."

Thom stood up. The next few minutes could be interesting. "It will be my pleasure."

But not Jan's, he suspected. *Tough.* Thom stowed his tablet in his backpack and finished his beer. "After you. Can we go via the bar?" He'd a suspicion he'd need a pint whatever the outcome. "Happy to shout a round."

"We're okay, Martin's just done it. Just get one for yourself. You can shout us one next time."

Jan scowled as they walked up the steps to where she and Martin sat. Thom could almost see her mind working.

Along the lines of, 'Of course, Peggy would invite him over and he'd say yes. *Sod him.*'

Sod her then. No, not that, be kind and charming? Maybe just cool and collected. Thom nodded to Jan as he shook hands with Martin. "Hi, Thom Clare, over here to make a film which might become a TV series. Some of it anyway. I'm just a bit player. Happy to be back in Hong Kong. It's been way too long."

"You've been before?" Martin asked as Thom sat down. "Miss it?"

"Yeah, fair few times and yeah, miss it. Not here recently, though, been too busy back home. But when I was offered this part I jumped at it. Great script, great big stars—I don't include me in there—great location and dare I say it a great chance to catch up with old friends."

"Of which Jan is one?" Martin asked, curiosity in his tone.

"Better ask Jan," Thom said easily and waited to hear what she would say.

The silence stretched as she considered him. Just as he was about to say, 'okay, no worries', and make his farewells, she smiled—reluctantly he thought.

"The jury is out."

He raised his eyebrows and she laughed.

"Oh, sit down. Feinites."

"Eh?" Peggy asked. "That's a new one on me. Sounds a bit medieval."

"Might be. Or some obscure London slang. Suspend the battle. My mum used to use it when she played alley gobs. That's chuck stones or five stones to most people. Means a truce, I was told, but don't quote me on my explanation, please."

Thom wiped his forehead in a theatrical manner and did his best to ignore the way the other couple were taking an interest in his and Jan's byplay. He'd bet she'd be peppered with questions later. "Phew. Standing up with all my stuff *and* not spilling my beer is not easy." He perched on the step next to her and apologised to a couple trying to get by. Jan shuffled along a foot or so and he did likewise. "Thanks. Or I might end up getting trodden on. And don't say I'd deserve it."

"As if I would. Might think it, though."

"Stop bickering, you two," Peggy commanded. "We thought we might head for a meal when we've finished these drinks. What do you say?"

If Jan's expression was anything to go by, Thom thought she'd rather go for root canal treatment.

"Er, thanks, but I better head homewards," Jan said hurriedly. "Transport can be chaotic on a Friday evening."

"Not at this time, surely," Peggy said with a wicked grin that made Jan want to scowl. "Rush hour home happened already. Home from the pub time is not for hours. Most people will be heading into town, not out. You don't have a dog or cat to feed, not even a goldfish."

"Chicken..." Thom said softly so only she would hear.

How she'd like to retort, 'no, not even a roast one'. Jan knew he didn't mean a bird, but an attitude or lack of nerve.

He'd got a nerve saying it.

Bastard. Jan counted to ten under her breath. "If I can't get on one of the minibuses when I'm ready to head home, you lot can spring for a taxi for me. Last one I got was around two hundred Hong Kong Dollars, and that wasn't at a premium time." She turned to Thom. "Around twenty quid."

He grinned as he put his hand into his pocket and pulled out some notes. "Seems fair, I'll cough up. Out of interest, where am I paying for you to go to?"

Jan tapped her nose. "That is on a need-to-know basis. You don't need to know."

He looked like someone had stabbed him in the gut. Jan felt awful. Why was she being so arsy? There was no need, They weren't a couple, not even a speck in the distance. "I live in Sai Kung," she said. "Long way out."

"Nice walks and fresh fish? I know it. Or I did, and I doubt the harbour front has changed that much."

He would. "Not that much, no. But after public transport stops, not a lot of taxi drivers want to go that far, as they would be more than likely not get a fare back. I've seen me having to change cab colours more than once." She referred to the fact that different parts of Hong Kong had different coloured taxis. "I'd prefer to go earlier rather than later."

Thom nodded. "Makes sense. Then how about lunch tomorrow instead? You choose where."

That put her on the spot. Martin and Peggy glanced from her to Thom with curious interest. No doubt Peggy was storing up questions for one of them to ask her later.

Damn and blast. If she said no she'd appear ornery. If she agreed, would it intimate she was ready to let bygones be bygones? That could be tricky, because she wasn't sure if she was.

"Well?" Thom said with a wry smile. "If it's that hard I guess it's a no. Shall I walk you to the bus stop? Or is that a no as well?"

Jan made her mind up. "No, it's not a no, and yes, please. Then Martin and Peggy can go their way and not worry about me. What time and how about in Sai Kung? Seafood of course."

"Sounds good." Thom turned to Martin. "One-ish? You two up for it?"

Martin nodded and appeared to ignore the dig in the ribs his wife gave him. "Yup, we love it out there. Opposite the ferry to town?"

Jan bit back a grin at the chagrin on Peggy's face. She'd obviously been up for a bit of matchmaking and Thom, with a little bit of unwitting help from Martin, had thwarted her. Did that mean Thom wasn't interested or that he was trying to slow things down or…

Argh, enough of the second-guessing. Just take it day by day. Jan winked at Peggy, who ignored her.

"Sounds great," Jan said with a grin. "After all, it *is* your turn to come over my way. We ate near yours last time, remember? Shall we walk along the front first? Get up an appetite?"

"Deffo. Then I can have a pint and not feel guilty," Martin replied. He patted his stomach. "Got to watch the waistline."

Peggy sighed. "You two always want me to exercise." As she said it she made quotation marks in the air. "I refuse to watch mine, it would depress me. Hey, I've had an idea. I could sit on a bench and read a book while I waited for you lot to have your walk?"

"Nope." Martin and Jan spoke at the same time.

Thom laughed. "Outvoted?"

"As ever." Peggy scowled. "Okay, if no meal together tonight, see you both tomorrow." Peggy hugged Thom and Jan." I will now endeavour to persuade my ever-loving to take me somewhere for posh nosh."

"The place that does burger, chips and shakes and is full of teens?" Jan knew Martin's Friday night preferences. He'd head for that chain nine times out of ten after the three of them had met up for their weekly winddown. "And a queue for the loo."

Peggy groaned. "No doubt."

Martin laughed. "Of course. I stand in line for food while Peg crosses her legs and takes her turn to go for a wee. See you tomorrow."

"Oh, the romantic picture that conjures up," Jan said and grinned. "Enjoy."

"So where to?" Thom asked as they left the other couple. "What's the best way?"

"MTR then minibus. Take me half hour or so." Jan gestured to the sign for the MTR, the train station. "I have a choice of ways, but this one works best at this time. After rush hour and before lousing-out time."

"Haven't heard that expression for last orders for years," Thom observed as they headed to the nearest station. "Do they have last orders here?"

"Good question. No idea, I'm usually home before midnight." They reached the entrance to the station. Jan stopped and turned to Thom. "I'll be fine from here. Thank you for walking with me." She didn't add there had been no need, even though they both knew it to be true. "I'll see you tomorrow. Will you find your way all right?"

Thom nodded solemnly then laughed. "Yes, miss. MTR and minibus. Or a taxi." He kissed her cheek lightly. "Thank you for agreeing. Er, in case you wondered, I asked Martin and Peggy because I'd thought you'd prefer it rather than just being with me. If I'm wrong, let me know and I'll invite just you somewhere next time."

There was going to be a next time? Jan decided she'd need to think about that.

"Thank you."

He sketched a wave. "I'll wait till you go through."

It wasn't until she was sitting on the train that Jan realised she'd neither asked him where he was stopping or for how long.

* * * *

Pleased the previous evening had gone better than he'd hoped, Thom leant on the rails next to the ferry dock in Sai Kung and idly surveyed the area. He was several minutes early for the meetup, due to a zealous taxi driver who'd known all the shortcuts and taken them. The speed and the overuse of only two of the four wheels on the car—or so it had felt like—had raised Thom's heartbeat by more than he was comfortable with. Thom consoled himself with the thought that he'd probably never need to get in that same taxi again. If he noticed the driver was next in line, he'd go around the block until someone else could drive him.

He grinned to himself as he remembered the time he'd gone to Beijing and had a taxi driver who thought he was an F1 driver and raised his, Thom's, heart rate way too high on the journey, only to find himself in the same taxi the following night on the other side of the city. He'd been relieved when the ride to the airport the following day had been by minibus!

As he stood and drank in the view, a boat moored below him and people streamed off and up the walkway before the next crowd got on. Mainly golfers heading out to the prestigious golf course on a nearby island. No player of the game himself—he'd gone once and only once with his brother-in-law, and had almost brained a fisherman nowhere near where he'd meant his ball to end up. Thom admired those who could hit the ball accurately.

Today, the various states of dress deemed suitable for the game amused him. One very natty gentleman appeared to believe he needed plus fours and a cravat, another tartan shorts with socks to match. The several people dressed more conservatively looked drab in comparison.

Tartan reminded him of where he would be after his stint in Hong Kong.

Scotland. And wearing a kilt for work, not pleasure. *Well, if that bloody Lois is around, sod it, I will* definitely *not be a true Scotsman. Some things are just not on.* He grinned to himself. Some things might not be on, but his boxers would be!

Although Scotland was his birthplace and still nominally his home, he spent as much time away from the tiny cottage he was slowly renovating as he did there. In recent times Thom had spent more time 'down south', as his parents would have put it. Lucky for him, Moss, his brother-in-law, owned a house just outside London, near to where a lot of Thom's work happened, and was pleased for it to be inhabited as often as possible. Moss and Arietta spent as much time as they could at their other home near Romansa Castle—coincidentally where a lot of the proposed TV series was to be filmed. The house, whimsically known as Moss End, was rarely used except by Thom or Moss when working. As Moss was one of the stars of the film *and* the new series, it looked like Moss End wasn't going to be used much in the near future.

Now Thom wondered idly what his living arrangements were going to be like during those coming hectic weeks in the highlands. He'd been told he could stop with Arietta and Moss, but as for once excellent accommodation—the company's words not his—had been secured for him, he was interested to see where he'd end up. If their idea of excellent didn't coincide with his, then he'd throw himself on his sister's mercy.

"Hey, sorry I'm late, I was detained by a phone call."

Thom turned to see a windswept Jan standing next to him and panting a little. Her blonde hair was all over the place, her long gypsy skirt and multicoloured top swaying as she grinned up at him. One glance at her and he accepted what his sister had told him years before. Your mouth could go dry when you looked at someone. Until then he would have scorned his sister's comment and her explanation that it went into the romance books she wrote because it *was* something some people experienced.

"I ran," Jan said. "And I'm out of condition. Martin rang just as I was coming out and I couldn't juggle the phone, my bag and my keys to lock up all at the same time." She handed Thom a bottle of water, which he took automatically.

"Martin?" Thom had an inkling what Jan was about to say next. "Martin of Martin and Peggy?"

"The very ones. It appears Peggy has a migraine so they send their apologies." Her tone told Thom what she thought of that. "That's never been mentioned before. Usually a tummy upset."

"Didn't she want to come?" Thom was intrigued by the way Jan had imparted the news. "I thought she liked it, coming out."

"She'd want to be here to be nosy, but I bet she's staying away—and told Martin so was he—so we have to communicate or something. Then she'll demand Martin grill me at work on Monday. Maybe *I'll* have a convenient migraine."

Thom laughed as Jan wrinkled her nose and rolled her eyes. "She'll be as mad as a pickled hen not to get the gen first-hand, though."

"A pickled… Where do you get these expressions?" That was a new one to Thom. He opened the bottle of water in an absent manner and raised it to his lips.

"It was one of my gran's. She was deaf and made up a lot of her own sayings rather than use one she might not have heard properly. Another favourite was 'choose your juice and don't spit it'."

Thom almost spat out the mouthful of water he'd just taken. He choked and suffered Jan thumping him on the back. "Okay now," he said eventually as his eyes stopped streaming. "Give a guy a warning before you come out with things like that. Out of interest, what on earth does it mean?"

Jan giggled, a lovely carefree sound that Thom relished. "Not a scooby. She never explained either and as she used it willy-nilly no one ever got a definitive answer. But it's a good one, eh?"

"Definitely. I'll save it up for a time I think appropriate." Thom recapped his water bottle. "Right, where to? I'm in your hands." *Boy, I wish.*

If you're up to a walk, we could head along the prom and round the bay, then when we get back here the grub rush will be over and we should be able to get a decent table at my favourite restaurant. It doesn't take reservations so it's pick your time and cross your fingers. And legs if you need the loo. How's that?"

"Apart from the loo bit it sounds great." Thom fell in next to Jan as they walked at a leisurely pace away from the town and along the prom towards the next bay.

Several dragon boats moored just off shore bobbed on the gentle swell. Farther out a few dinghies tacked from one side of the bay to the other. The farther they got from the hustle and bustle of the fishing boats the more peaceful it became.

And he was about to shatter that peace. He couldn't help it.

"I'm sorry to be about to add a downer to the atmosphere," he began, and cleared his throat as Jan stared at him quizzically. "But I have to know. Why did you go silent on me all those years ago?" Thom hoped he spoke slowly, as if he talked in a non-committal way, as if it was an idle question, not *the* burning one. He was afraid he still sounded petulant.

They rounded the corner and a new vista appeared in front of them before he spoke again. "Not answer my texts or emails. Total silence, cut from your life."

What?

They walked on for several yards whilst Jan counted to ten. It was that or punch him for the sheer gall to ask her that in such a 'woe is me' voice. She took a deep breath and spoke in a fierce undertone.

"You need to ask? Mr 'if you loved me you'd give up your chance of a fantastic job and follow me and hang around while I do what I've dreamt of always doing' Clare? Sheesh." She made a noise like a boiling kettle and slashed the air with one hand as she swirled around to face Thom so fast her skirt hit his legs. *Wish it was something harder.* "Listen to yourself, Thomas. It was only for six months. Six short bloody months. During which you would be working all hours of the day or night and with barely time off to eat or sleep. So what would I be doing, eh?" She glared at him, arms akimbo. "I'll tell you what. B all. Twiddling my thumbs."

"You'd've been having a lovely holiday in Australia and New Zealand," Thom said in a defensive way. "All expenses paid and all that."

"No, I'd be having a lonely holiday in Australia and New Zealand. That's not what I wanted. And, *and,* I'd've missed my chance of the job I really desired. The one I went through hoops for." She forced her shoulders down—a sure way, she'd been told, to make yourself relax. Jan wasn't sure it worked, but anything was worth a try at that moment.

Hell's bells, what a cow I am. What's happened to the cool, calm and vaguely disinterested me I thought I'd be? Gone out of the window the minutes Thom asked such a combatable question. *Count to ten again.*

"Okay, no need to be arsy. I just asked."

"Thom." Jan tried for a less confrontational tone and thought she succeeded—just. "It was the way you asked. How would you have responded if almost the first thing I said, once we were alone was, why did you take that job'? Or why couldn't you understand how important my job was to me? Hey, Thom, why didn't you turn your job down and come out to Hong Kong and have a lovely holiday there?"

Jan was on a roll. She realised she'd been storing the hurt up for a long while and now she could share it, oh boy, she intended to. "We'd both worked hard and deserved our success. Why couldn't we be happy for each other, work out some give and take and—" All of a sudden she ran out of words and steam. "Oh, forget it. Water under the bridge and all that. I thought we'd both be over it now. Older, if not wiser. Seems I was wrong."

Thom grimaced, took her hand and squeezed it.

"Definitely not wiser, it seems," he said wryly. "Right, cards on the table time. It's niggled me for years. I know I spat the dummy out, but I was hurt. You put your fledging career before me, and I was devastated. I thought I was the love of your life."

You were.

"Works both ways," Jan said. "So did you. Oh, enough already. We could go on and on and round and round and not change what we did or how we felt. Either we forget about it, accept it was then and this is now and talk about something else or we say right, that's it, goodbye and have a good life. Your choice." She waved one hand towards the fishing boats. "The bus stop and taxi rank are that way."

"Who do you think will win the Ashes?" Thom said without hesitation.

She'd forgotten his penchant for cricket and especially the match between England and Australia. The match, called the Ashes as years ago someone had sent a box to the English cricket team saying it was the ashes of English cricket. It was a must-not-miss to Thom, which had annoyed her when it had taken precedence over everything during their relationship.

Jan rolled her eyes and stuck her tongue out at him.

"What's that?" she said without batting an eyelid.

He laughed.

Chapter Three

"It won't work." Jan stood in front of May's desk and planted her hands firmly on the wooden top. "Will. Not. Work."

May looked up from a document she was reading. "What won't?" she asked mildly. "Want a coffee?"

"Wh... Yeah, please."

Jan plonked herself down on one of the two comfy chairs set next to the window and wondered idly if the sampan she could see was the same one as the other day. Did they have shifts, or was it first come, first served? Where did the rubbish they collected go? She made a mental note to find out. Her ignorance in a lot of things shocked her.

"Here." May passed a steaming mug of liquid over along with what suspiciously appeared to be a big cream cake. "Get stuck in."

"Are you trying to make me eat and drink so I can't talk?" Jan asked as she considered which bit of cake to tackle first.

"Maybe." May took a tiny bit of cake and sighed. "Oh, so good. Is it working?"

"Mrnn…" Jan swallowed a mouthful of soft sponge and washed it down with a swig of coffee. "Maybe not, but much appreciated. I will, however, not hit you with all I need to say until we've finished this gooey goodness."

May smiled. "Fair enough."

They sat in companionable silence for several minutes then Jan cleared her throat. "Right, time to talk. Like I said, it won't work."

"You said 'it', but not what *it* was." May put her mug down. "Okay, spoil my day. Even though I can hazard a guess about what it is. Spit it out."

"I can't go and work in Scotland if it's at Romansa Castle and there's going to be a film crew and the cast in the area," Jan gabbled. "It's just not on, why on earth did anyone think it would work I have not a scooby and I'd be crap and people would moan and complain and it's when…*oompt*." May had stopped her mid-spiel by the simple method of putting her hand over Jan's mouth. Jan waggled her fingers. She accepted her voice had risen and she had been well on the way to a full-blown panic attack. And for what? A problem that could surely be solved in a calm and rational manner.

"Rant over?" May asked in such a reasonable tone Jan had to fight not to scowl at her. "Take a deep breath and think cuddly lambs or chocolate or whatever you think of as nice things. Chill."

Jan nodded. "Though it wasn't a rant, more of a panic mode," she replied once her mouth was free and she could speak clearly again. "I really can't go, though, May. You'll have to make my excuses. Send someone else. Please." The last word was, she decided, whiny.

"I can't do that, hon. You've agreed, we've told them you'll go, and I have literally just got your itinerary through. Dates, flights, accommodation, expenses, you name it, the whole package, and boy it is good. Jan Fraser, facilitator. Wish it was for me."

"Feel free to take my place," Jan said without hesitation. "Use my name. I don't mind."

"The client might," May said deadpan. "So how about explaining?"

Jan bit her lip. "It's gonna sound daft, but it isn't."

"Tell me and then I'll tell you if it sounds daft or not."

* * * *

"So you see," Jan said half an hour later, "we spent lunch talking—stiltedly— about nothing, said goodbye and no mention of meeting up. I made up an excuse not to go to the barbeque Peggy had arranged for Sunday, though it transpires he got there late so I missed out on Peg's spicy chicken wings for no reason. I could have just popped in for a bit and then headed off while the going was good. I couldn't have faced going and it being as uncomfortable as the lunch, though. At one point it was a wonder the soup didn't freeze, we were so frosty. It was awful, really awful." The thought of it made her shudder. May patted her shoulder. Emboldened, Jan went on with her narrative.

"I had hoped we could at least be civil, but grief, May, it was horrible. Generalities ruled. It was pathetic. We were a right pair, but I hadn't got a clue how to change it. Even now, thinking back, the only answer I've got is we shouldn't have bothered. One thing, though—I did get to find out he's definitely in a TV series or a film or something that's going to be shot around Romansa Castle and there's been a bit of bother with locals and homeowners on the estate. They need a peacemaker. Or is it a troubleshooter? Not sure if its either or both." She didn't mention she'd checked with Arietta what was happening and was almost certain that was to be her remit. "It would create an awful atmosphere if it was where I'm off."

"But if it is, and until you sign your confidentiality agreement I can't confirm or deny that, you'd be working for the establishment not for the…well, whatever."

"Hmm. That's easy to say," Jan said gloomily. "But if this hypothetical wherever is where I think it is he'd be around. A lot."

"You got this from someone you said you only conversed with in the most general terms?" May asked. "Wow."

"Nah, I rang his sister and demanded all the info she had, both that for general publication and that what isn't. Not that I got much of the second. But anyway… I can't go."

May got up and went silently to a fridge in the corner of her room. Took out a bottle of wine and filled two glasses. She returned to Jan and passed one glass over before she went to her desk, extracted a folder out of the drawer then sat down again, folder on her lap, before she crossed her legs and held her glass up in the air. "Gone five, no longer at work. Cheers."

"Cheers." Not that Jan knew what there was to be cheery about. She glanced at May over the top of her glass to see the other woman was looking at her with speculation. "What?" she said suspiciously. "You've got one of your weird expressions on. The one that usually means something I'm not gonna like."

May sipped some wine and set her glass down. "You do know you've got no option, don't you." It wasn't a question. "You're all signed up, so to speak, and they are expecting you. Unless you develop a life-threatening illness, before now and three weeks on Friday, you'll be on the plane. Oh, and expect to be away for up to eight weeks or so. I've got all the details here." She passed the folder to Jan.

Jan stared at it. She had been correct. May was reiterating something she, Jan, didn't like. "You know all the stuff and didn't share?" she asked. "Why?"

"Yup," May said. She didn't sound at all repentant. "I wanted to see what you'd do and say."

Jan blinked. "Bi…big of you," she said as she bit back the epithet that immediately sprang to mind. "Why?"

"Because, my love, whatever you said or did you know and I know you can never turn down a challenge, and this is one in spades."

She had her there, Jan thought. *Damn it.* She sighed. *Doing a lot of that lately, moany Minnie.* It was true, she thrived on a challenge. Usually. However, she was apprehensive. Was this one challenge too far? "Okay, give me the gen," she said, resigned to the fact she'd soon be on her way to the country of her birth. "Who have I committed two months of my life to?"

"A guy named Zac Moncrieff. He heads up the consortium that has just bought Romansa Castle in Scotland. Been lots of problems. Owners of homes in the grounds not happy about what they call outsiders taking over and asking for said owners not to be allowed to use the facilities they pay a lot of money to use. Complaints left, right and centre."

"And what does this Zac Moncrieff think I'm going to do about it?" Jan demanded. "Wave a magic wand

and they'll all agree over everything? About as likely as a chocolate fireguard not melting in front of a roaring log fire." Something, even in the height of summer, she might be using if her accommodation wasn't windproof. A Scottish summer could be full-on sun and hot—or full-on rain and cold. Knowing her luck, it would be the latter.

"He thinks your kind of diplomacy might work," May said smoothly. "He'd heard of it over that antisocial bloke who thought he deserved the moon and his employers didn't. Plus of course, your kick-ass attitude if needed." She raised her glass in a 'well done, you' sort of toast. "Seriously, though, Jan, the poor man is turning himself inside out trying to suit everyone, and of course nothing is working. No one is prepared to compromise. What he needs is a fresh eye, the ideas of someone not connected to either side."

Do I say I am sort of connected? After all, my best mate is married to one of the people who live nearby and her husband is in the film. A thought struck her.

"I did tell you that my ex is in the film, didn't I? That might count as bias."

"Nope." May sounded firm about that. "He's an ex, exes don't count. Nor does the fact that you said you have friends in the area." She hesitated. "Mind you, perhaps don't broadcast it, eh?"

"If you think I'm going to be deceitful— " Jan began and stopped as May mimed a zipping motion. "What?"

"I didn't mean that, you moron. Zac Moncrieff said you'd been recommended to him by someone in the series or film or whatever. I'm like you, not exactly sure which it is. Does it matter?"

Jan sighed and shook her head. "All much of a muchness."

"I'd guess it's probably your ex who gave him the heads up. All you need to do is get on the plane, go and see what's going on, say your bit, do your stuff and then head off on holiday."

"Some all. Okay, enough already." Jan nodded, resigned, and headed back to her own office—via the coffee machine. She'd got a lot to do before she boarded that plane and had a feeling caffeine was going to help. Another hour at work would help, even if it was, as May had said, no longer work hours.

Martin caught up with her just as she added her milk to her cup.

"Still at it? I'm off in a sec. Peg says she'll pick you up at six a.m. to be ready for seven on Saturday. Wear jeans and a comfy top and be prepared for long minutes of nothing and boredom and multiple short bursts of craziness."

Jan groaned. She'd conveniently forgotten about that promise. "Ah..." She searched her brain for an excuse and came up blank. "With the proviso Thom might tell her to tell me to bugger off. We didn't exactly part on the friendliest of terms."

"Believe me, if you keep the unlovely Lois at bay, those terms will be friendly again. An octopus has got nothing on the bloody woman. Dammit, Jan, she even tried to grope me, and Peggy was no more than three feet away." Martin shuddered. "Hellish."

"What did you do?" Jan asked, fascinated. "Or should I say, what did Peggy do?"

"I spilled hot tea on her and moved so it missed me and Peg trod on her foot with her Doc Martens. Then Peggy said 'oops, so awful when you accidentally touch someone inappropriately isn't it, and thank goodness there would be no repercussions as long as it didn't happen again' and I nodded solemnly in agreement. She got the message from us. Apologised and said it was accidental."

"Was it?"

"Well, it could have been, I guess. But she is, in Peg's words, haunting Thom. He's hiding, Peg's scowling, and I'd hazard a guess Lois wouldn't rush to rescue either Peggy *or* me from a burning house in a hurry. Hence we need you."

In an awful way it made sense. Jan resigned herself to being an extra in a TV series over the weekend. "I'll bring my eReader," she said. "A few snacks and a bottle of water. Or maybe gin and tonic in a water bottle."

"Bring all of that," Martin advised. "And a bag full of patience."

* * * *

Peggy wasn't exactly a ray of sunshine when she arrived to pick Jan up the following Saturday. The weather forecast was rotten, she said, as she headed cityward, and several people had gone down with suspected food poisoning.

"Bloody nightmare. Yesterday's shoot was over on one of the islands, and people kept disappearing to be ill. Alex went spare, Sasha threw up, and we found out it was someone's great-granny who had come over from the UK and made an uncooked prawn soup or something like. Not only that, it was rumoured she hadn't refrigerated the prawns before she didn't cook them. That sounds a bit convoluted, but you get the gist."

"Memo to self, do not eat anything unless verified by you."

Peggy grinned. "Or Thom. I must admit, I wondered if Lois had done something just so she would have to cosy up to him, but nope…she was one of those throwing up."

"Does that mean she won't be around today and I won't be needed?" Jan asked hopefully. "You can just drop me off at the nearest bus stop."

"Not a chance. Anyway, you owe me after crying off from my barbecue. Thom did ask where you were…as he was metaphorically holding on to my arm and holding Lois off. She, by the way, hadn't been invited. Heard about it and turned up without batting an eyelid. Mind you, her eyelashes are so covered in gunk, I'm not sure if she *could* bat them."

"*Miaow.*"

"Yup. Anyhow, I covered for you, so you owe me."

"What did you say?" Jan asked.

"Migraine." Peggy changed lanes and weaved between a bicycle and what looked like a lawnmower. "I was tempted to say haemodementia, but guessed he'd know that anyway."

"It was not bloody-mindedness," Jan said indignantly, then laughed. "It was self-preservation and the protection of your star actor." She paused for a second. "From me, not cop-a-feel Lois."

"Okay, gotcha, but be nice to him today, pretty please. I got the impression he's not generally easy to rile, but oh boy he was ready to lose it last night. I had to get someone to haul Lois off—almost literally—to do something at the other side of the island, and she was still waiting for us when we got back. I'm pulling my hair out."

It sounded like it.

"Ready, not exactly willing, but able," Jan said, resigned to the fact she'd need to have her wits about her. "Um, what exactly will I be doing, apart from dropping a book on her foot, or elbowing her in the ribs?"

"You're going to be the innocent bystander who shares his table in the bar when he's chatting to the informer. It's crowded so he has to sit next to you. He'll ask you if you speak English and you just shrug and shake your head." Peggy shot her a quick look as she pulled into a parking space between two large lorries. "You could pass for French, or Icelandic or…well or not English."

"That's because I'm not," Jan said complacently, and sniggered at Peggy's jolt of surprise. "English. Dad is from Shetland with Viking ancestors, Mum from South Africa, and I was born at home in the Trossachs. So Scottish, as far as I am concerned."

"Fair enough. Right, let's get on with it."

"Hold on." Jan had a sudden thought. "If it's in a bar, why am I here at silly o'clock in the park?"

Jan switched off the car's engine and grabbed a tote bag the size of a small cupboard off the back seat. "Because you're going to run interference, aren't you? I mentioned you and Thom said you or no one."

I bet he did.

"Really? You told him I was coming?"

"Well, of course," Peggy said. "That was before he told me you'd not been on the best of terms on Saturday. And he did have a rather Machiavellian expression when he said that. What did you do? Kick him where it hurts?"

"Probably hit his sensitive emotions or something, not his you-know-wheres," Jan said. "Nah, I wouldn't agree to what he'd said and done, and he spat the dummy out. Mind you," she added reflectively, "I did my fair amount of spitting. We're a right pair. So he's okay with it?"

"He said he promised to behave himself as long as you did *and* kept him out of cop-a-feel's clutches."

Great. I don't think.

"Lovely." It sounded anything but. "What a fun-filled day I'm about to have. Not. I *should* have brought a gin and tonic in a water bottle."

Peggy laughed. "It won't be all that bad, and the grub is good. All verified. By the way, I discovered you do have an equity card—not that it's a requirement anymore. You wee fibber, you never mention that."

Jan cussed under her breath. How on earth had Peggy discovered that? "No need, I don't have a use for it anymore. It was a very short-lived profession. More of a dipped my toe in and decided it wasn't for me. I like what I do so much better." She'd discovered very quickly she didn't like having to do what someone else said when she didn't agree with it, unless she could at least argue her reasons and have them listened to. Even though in her current profession people didn't have to take her advice, she had her say.

"Well anyway, you're on the payroll, and once we get you all signed up and all the necessary forms filled in you'll be set to go. Or rather, set to stay."

Jan resigned herself to a day doing what was needed. "Boy, Peggy, do you now owe me one or what?"

"Several," Peggy said cheerfully. "Tit for tat. Come on, gird your loins or what the saying is that's appropriate. Let's get going. Oh, and whatever he says or does, please play along. You can kill me, him and whoever afterwards."

That sounded ominous. Jan chose not to reply.

* * * *

From inside the tiny caravan that he laughingly—although with more than a tad of truth—called his sanctuary, Thom watched the two women whom he hoped would help him get a bit of peace and give him the opportunity to concentrate on his role walk across the car park to where the vans and tents for the cast and crew were situated. He'd locked his van door half an hour earlier and ignored the knocks—on all the five occasions they happened—and watched from behind thick nets as Lois stalked away each time. What did she think she would achieve from harassing him, Thom wondered. He'd told her ad nauseam he wasn't interested in her and had a partner 'back home'. She'd either not believed him or chosen to ignore the information.

Now, as he watched Jan and Peggy head to the van that was used as an administration base, another idea sprang to mind. It would probably mean Jan would never speak to him again, *and* never forgive him, but Thom reasoned drastic action was needed. A foil Lois scenario. Something to really make her back off. He settled back in his chair and began to plot. Nothing too obvious, nothing too over the top, but something very definite.

He chuckled to himself. *Yeah, Jan will not be best pleased.*

* * * *

He was still refining his idea when he was called to makeup where, to his dismay, Lois was standing next to the makeup artist who he used. She waited in the one position that would make it impossible for him to sit down without brushing past her.

Bugger. Why didn't he call her out for sexual harassment? Stalking or something?

Because he knew every scenario could be—almost—plausibly explained.

Thom counted to three under his breath. "Morning, Cindy. Lois. Nice day, eh?" He waited until he was a foot or so away, stepped to one side and addressed Lois. "Sorry to be the one who tells you the bad news and all that, but you're being shouted for by the tea waggon. No idea why, but someone sounds irate. What have you forgotten to do?"

She glared at him for one brief second then the expression Thom called 'stalker coated with sugar' appeared. "Nothing. I was here to say hello and ask if you want anything." She emphasised 'anything'.

"Nope, but someone over there does." Thom turned so his back was facing her. *If* he was going to be touched, he decided, it was preferable to receive an 'accidental' bush of her hand on his butt than anywhere else. "Better go and see."

Lois muttered something and headed off. The hand brush almost missed. *Boy, I'm getting better at this manoeuvring.* Cindy, the makeup artist, grimaced.

"That woman is getting worse." She put a cape around Thom. "And so blooming arrogant. Was she really wanted?"

Thom smiled noncommittally as he settled in the chair. He had no intention of adding any fuel to any fires. "I thought she was," he prevaricated, and smiled at Cindy's snigger. "If she wasn't, oh dear and all that. Just ignore her as best you can. Be thankful for small mercies, at least you don't have to make her up."

Cindy nodded. "That's a bonus. Though I did hear she was angling to get a bit part. Someone, no names, said *she* said she was the one who should stand next to you in the bar scene."

Thom would have sworn he'd gone pale. He better get his ten pennorth in about that as soon as possible. "Nah," he said as nonchalantly as he could. "Someone else is doing that. Someone – " He broke off and tapped the side of his nose. "Someone different."

"Ohh, do tell?" Cindy consulted a page of notes and began to put his base makeup on. "Anyone important?"

Thom grinned. He got on well with Cindy. "I value my life. No can do. You'll no doubt see or hear later." He'd make sure of that.

"Spoilsport. How can I keep my crown as gossip queen without some gossip?" She began to do his minimal makeup with swift, deft strokes. "I mean, kill my street cred, why don't you?"

He laughed. "That will never do. Let's just say someone *very* special is going to be my rear guard. In every sense of the word." He saw Cindy had noticed the way he said 'very', and no doubt stored it up to be used later. Which was what he'd had in mind.

"Plus front, side and every-which-way guard?"

"I do hope so." He shut his eyes and wondered what he'd let himself in for. Jan might well kill him.

Cindy patted his shoulder. "I aim to watch. And get any other bits of goss from you ASAP. All done. Not a lot needed this time. Go slay 'em, or whatever it is today."

"Well, it was going to be ride the ferry, but for some reason it's all swapped about. Something to do with the tides which whoever was supposed to check didn't. Glad I'm not in their shoes. The upshot of which means now it's stand at a bar, drink cold tea and pretend it's a good single malt and look moody. Dream of the good single malt I'm going to indulge in when it's over. And wonder why there's a bar recreated in a tent and made to appear dark when it's high noon and blazing sun and lots of bars around that I bet would have jumped at the chance of being used."

Cindy laughed. "And yours not to reason why, eh?"

"You got it. Thanks, Cindy, you've made me look good. See you later." He sketched a wave as he headed to the door.

To almost bump into the two people waiting to enter. Thom glanced at them, about to utter a ready apology.

Then he saw who it was. And who stood a scant foot behind them, ready to pounce.

Perfect timing.

"Well, hi, honey," he said smoothly to one of the women nearest him and ignored the irate gasp from the woman behind her. The more he could get her to back off the better. "Thank goodness you made it." He pulled Jan tight into a bear hug and ignore how she went immediately rigid and tried to pull away. "I've missed you." He lowered his voice and spoke directly into her ear, hoping it would look like a romantic gesture to anyone—especially one specific person close by. "Please play along. If Peggy hasn't explained I will, but I need protection of the romantic kind."

What the? Jan listened to Thom's breathy voice and wondered when she would wake up. After their last more-than-frosty parting, there was no way he'd greet her so fondly.

And did she even want him to?

She'd be honest—the jury was out on that one. Then it hit her.

Did he emphasise the her? *Oh dear. This* is *the maneater, then. Hope Thom knows what he's doing. Duh, of course he does. Bastard.*

Behind them, hidden from her view by the way Thom held her, she heard someone angrily questioning Peggy.

"Who is this? *What* is this?"

And Peggy's reply. "Why? What's it to you?"

"What is he *doing with that…that…opmpt."*

Jan didn't hear the answer as Thom moved back a scant few inches without letting her go and turned the pair of them so they faced Peggy and a furious-looking other woman who at that moment had her mouth covered by Peggy, who had placed her hand firmly over said orifice.

Thom draped one arm over Jan's shoulder and the other round her waist. Jan gazed up at him and hoped only he could see the retribution promised in her expression.

"Lois meet, Jan," Thom said in a voice that Jan decided was so syrupy she might go into sugar overload—or throw up. "Jan, love, meet Lois, who is Sasha's sister and invaluable to her."

If looks could kill, Jan decided, she'd be pushing up daisies and her mum choosing hymns and preparing an eulogy. A nip on her waist reminded her of what Thom had asked of her. Now she had an inkling why.

Okay, it might be years ago but you used to act. Try to try again. Jan smiled at the woman and away from Peggy, who was trying to contain her mirth. That was all Jan needed. If Peggy giggled, without a doubt it would start Jan off.

"Hello, nice to meet you." She could almost hear the 'liar, liar, pants on fire' she had no doubt Thom and Peggy were thinking. "I bet you're kept busy."

Lois' eyes flashed. "Of course. People like Thomas need a lot of help. In all manner of things. I am here to cater to his every need."

Oh dear.

"Well, now my beloved is around, she can take some of that work off your hands and give you a bit more time to yourself," Thom said cheerfully. "Excuse us, won't you. I think we need to be somewhere else."

"Oh, you do," Peggy said with a hint of laughter. "That's what Jan and I were on our way to say. Ten minutes in the tent that's a bar. She's all done and dusted and ready for action. Will you take her over for me? Ta." She turned to Lois, who had taken a step forward towards Thom and Jan.

"Lois, can you go and hunt up the stuff Sasha asked you to get for her? She was shouting for it just before I left her over in admin. Sounded pretty steamed about it."

Jan decided the expression on Lois' face was priceless. It seemed she couldn't say no to Peggy's reasonable request, but would have loved to. Plus, Jan guessed, the woman wasn't best pleased about seeing Thom with someone else.

Ah well. Tough. Now it was she, Jan, who had to decide, continue to play along or… Or what?

Play along.

"Darling." She returned the nip. "Don't forget you promised me you'd make sure I didn't feel out of place. Maybe that means getting me to wherever I have to be as soon as you can." *Like get me out of here, buster, and do some explaining.*

"Good idea, because once we finish I've got something special to show you." He winked. "You thought you'd mislaid it years ago and I've found it."

"Can't be her virginity," Lois muttered under her breath. "Bet that's long gone."

Jan heard, as she was sure Lois had intended, and burst out laughing. "Well long gone. Innocent I ain't." *What is up with the woman? Surely she must know Thom does* not *fancy her and dislikes her attention?* Jan glanced up at him and watched as he stared at Lois and quickly masked an expression of distaste.

"That is nothing to do with you, Lois," Thom said in a hard voice Jan had never heard him use before. "I trust you will remember that. If you know what's good for you" He nodded to Peggy. "Thanks for bringing Jan to me. We'll see you later."

"As long as it's only Peggy," Jan muttered as they walked past Peggy and Lois—who still managed to brush up against Thom so hard he fell into Jan, who almost stumbled. "I sort of see what Peggy meant. Is Lois always so in your face?"

"Always," Thom confirmed. "It's more than unnerving, it's downright scary. I've started hiding behind the curtains. Now I can hide behind you."

"Ha, only for today. Remember, I have a full-time job and tomorrow I have chores. Peggy asked for today."

"And that's it?" Thom said in a mock—or she hoped it was mock—incredulous voice. "You'd throw me to that piranha?"

"I thought she was an octopus?" Jan said as Thom ushered her into a large, dark tent set out like a bar.

"Octopus, piranha, leech, whatever. I always feel threatened."

Jan could understand that. "Let's hope she's got the message then."

Thom nodded gloomily. "Somehow I doubt it, but hey ho, even one day of peace is a good day. Let me introduce you to who you need to know. And get ready to be bored. Or knackered. Or both."

"Oh, joy. When I could be sitting at home with a good book."

Chapter Four

All he could say was thank goodness for Jan. Thom let himself into his accommodation, then shut and locked the door behind him.

Was it weird to think 'safe at last'? He pondered the strange day he'd had—and wondered...what next?

He reckoned nothing would faze him. Men in green suits, dancing pigs or Jan being nice, not snippy. As long as they kept Lois at bay, he'd take them.

Especially the Jan one.

Not that she had been snippy, he concluded as he scanned the contents of his fridge. Just...polite and distant unless Lois appeared. Then with a decided glint of 'you owe me' she'd changed into a loving companion.

She definitely should have carried on with an acting career. Although, with hindsight, maybe not. He'd seen her metaphorically hold her retorts to some of the asinine things people said or asked him—and others—to do. When she'd been told to move to block his way out from behind the table they shared, the eye rolling he'd seen had been enough to force him to keep a straight face. He'd managed—just.

Thom dumped his backpack on the floor, flexed his aching shoulders and sighed with relief as the knots began to loosen. At least the day was over and to his surprise—and pleasure—he had a late call the following day to, of all places, Sai Kung.

That could be fun. He and Jan appeared to have suspended hostilities, and she'd even smiled before she'd headed off. To Thom's relief Lois had been nowhere to be seen, and he'd headed home alone.

Where he was now staring into the fridge as if it had the answer to all his problems.

It did solve one of them, though. There was a chicken and veg ready meal on one shelf, next to a bottle of a rather nice New Zealand sauvignon blanc and a fruit salad.

That'd do him nicely.

Pleased it hadn't been too late a finish, Thom poured himself a modest glass of wine and after putting his dinner in the oven headed for his minuscule balcony to enjoy the night time view.

There was something magical about the scene, Thom thought. Across the harbour, lights from traffic showed, some almost searchlights as the vehicle in question climbed the peak. Lower down, on the water, ferries and pleasure boats, merchant vessels and even a cruise ship showed their lights as they went about their business. Sirens sounded, car horns tooted and the general hustle and bustle of a busy city floated up to him. He could sit and watch for hours.

Except his oven buzzer sounded, just as his doorbell rang.

Thom frowned. He wasn't expecting anyone, and highly doubted Jan would have gone to the trouble of finding out where he temporarily lived *and* pay him a visit at—he checked his watch—past nine o'clock at night. Which begged the question, who was it? More to the point, that was the actual door buzzer, not the one outside the building which allowed residents to see who wanted to come inside and decide whether they would allow them to.

He stood in the middle of the kitchen and pondered his options. A nasty itch down his spine gave him food for thought. The sort of itch that shouted 'beware' or some such thing.

It was almost Pavlovian to answer, Thom thought. The 'someone wants me, find out who' reaction. However, that damn 'beware' itch was louder, more insistent.

Answer... Not answer... The buzzer sounded again. With an almost audible sigh of relief, Thom remembered the spy hole in the door. There was no way for anyone outside to see if there was anyone *inside,* but he could peep through and see who was there. He switched the oven off—just in case that buzzer went again—and headed into the hallway.

Walked to the door, put his eye to the spy hole and...

And couldn't see a thing. Someone had covered it.

On purpose or not?

That was the million-dollar question. Surely if you were visiting you would want the person you were about to greet to know it was you?

Unless of course, you'd got into the building under false pretences, and you *didn't* want your identity known.

Until it was too late?

Thom considered for a few seconds, shrugged and went back into the kitchen. He took his dinner out of the oven and stared at it. Put it back in to keep warm, picked up his half-full glass of wine and headed to the main doorbell app and the grainy image of the front doors of the building.

He leant on the wall and waited. Not the most comfortable of places to sip wine but it could be worse. At least he wasn't in the cold or rain or had nothing to prop himself against. He had to see if his suspicions were correct.

Five minutes later, his patience was rewarded. Lois stormed out and marched down the street.

Thank goodness for that warning itch.

He'd have to mention the fact she got into the building to management the next day. What was the point of a security system if it didn't work?

Curiosity satisfied, Thom finished his glass of wine and headed back to his probably dried-up dinner. It was worth it to be sure of his facts.

* * * *

Jan headed out towards the harbour on what was fast becoming a weekly ritual. Her part in the day of filming had been cancelled and she'd been thanked and asked if needs be she'd be available on another occasion. She'd replied with a cautious 'maybe'. Before long she'd be halfway across the world but as she wasn't supposed to broadcast that to all and sundry, she couldn't have been any more specific. However, she'd tempered her reply by adding that she did have a full-time job, and so couldn't promise anything. She'd left by taxi before the rest of filming had finished and suffered Lois glowering, *and* Thom kissing her long and deeply and telling her he'd not be late!

Then he'd whispered, *"Don't worry, I'm not invading your privacy, just setting up a Lois screen."*

Jan hadn't been sure whether to be happy or disappointed by that.

Now, though, with her presence not required as a smokescreen, she was about to indulge in one of her favourite pastimes. Sunday stroll, buy some fish, have a drink and read her book in her favourite café before heading home for a lazy afternoon and evening. If anyone said she was turning into an old maid she'd deny it. But okay, she admitted she did like routine. Her rhythm of life, her know what's going to happen when and where. If that made her an old maid, so be it.

Old at my age. Argh, go figure. Don't they say you're only as old as you feel? Which, come to think of it, screws me good and proper because I'm not feeling anyone. Maybe I better think as old as I want *to feel. Then in that case I'm still screwed… I have no bloody idea.*

Jan mentally rolled her eyes at the moronic thoughts she was having and debated where to go to have a drink. She'd got the newspaper, her eReader and phone and even a notepad and pencil in case she wanted to jot anything down. May laughed at her obsession with writing implements—there were never less than half a dozen assorted pens and pencils in each of her bags, and at least two notebooks—and told her ad nauseam that they were obsolete. What did she think the notes section on her phone was for? When Jan had admitted she always forgot she'd put anything in there and pulled it up to show the last entry was three years earlier, May had believed her.

Today she hadn't got anything she needed to remember. Or she didn't think so.

And that is as stupid a thought as the only old as one. Enough already. Wine, here I come. Sunday was the day she broke her self-imposed no wine alone especially at lunchtime and enjoyed a glass by the harbour.

The idea that she'd not have the joys of the treat for a couple of months was a sobering one. Why on earth had she let May coerce her into going to Scotland? Why hadn't she put her foot down and said no thanks, or even no can do? There was nothing in her contract to say she *had* to do such a thing, even if she had been specifically requested by the client.

She sat down outside her favourite bar and ordered her usual glass of wine and some dim sum before she pulled out her eReader.

Three minutes later she closed it again and admitted she really had no interest in her current book. Which was a pity, as it was the last book in a series she'd really enjoyed. Jan found the paper and turned to the crossword page instead.

She ate her dim sum and sipped her wine. Probably not the best combination, but she enjoyed it, especially as she watched the world go by and struggled with the crossword. Her brain had gone to mush.

A cough broke into her reverie and she glanced up to see Thomas standing next to her.

"Three down, fleet," he said with a grin. "Fast of foot or the ships together. Would you mind if I share with you? It's busy and I just want to sit." He bit his lip. "Not exactly true, I'd like to sit with you." He hesitated again and for once appeared uncertain.

So not like him, Jan thought as she scribbled the answer down

"If it's not what you want I'll go," he went on before she had a chance to wave him to the chair next to her. "I didn't come here to hassle you. I've had enough of that to know how bloody awful it is."

"I bet. Plant yourself," she said, and grinned as he rolled his eyes at the awful expression. "I didn't say plonk or bum, so I wasn't totally uncouth."

"Just as well, words change their meanings a lot. And thank you. I'm hoping that a certain someone doesn't think of trying here to find me. I feel like a wanted man, and I don't want to be wanted by she who wants me, if you get me." He groaned. "Argh, what a sentence."

"Lois? And what do you fancy to drink, the server is coming over."

"The very one. I'll have a pint, if you'll join me?"

Jan laughed. "Don't drink pints anymore, but I'll break my habit of one glass only and have another sav blanc please."

Thom gave the waitron the order and sat back to stretch his legs out in front of him. "Thanks," he said briefly. "Both for letting me enjoy your company and for helping out. After you'd gone, Peggy hauled Lois off somewhere and I made my escape. I'm not needed until later today and around here of all places, so I thought I'd come early and find somewhere to hide out. Seeing you was a very lucky bonus."

Jan laughed as their drinks were delivered and Thom paid for them. "A just-in-time one. I spy with my little eye…" She nodded towards the direction of the taxi rank.

"No?" Thom said in an incredulous voice. "Really?"

"Really," Jan confirmed with a chuckle. "Though she's with Alex and Sasha, so you may be spared."

"I hope so. Are they coming this way?"

Jan glanced around. "Nope, you're safe for now, they've gone towards the dragon boats."

"How far can they go?"

"Not far enough to give you a long breathing space. Never mind, drink your beer, and then once they're round the corner and out of sight we'll make our getaway."

"We will?" He downed his pint so fast it was a wonder he didn't splutter. "Ready when you are."

Jan laughed and resigned herself to not finishing her wine. She couldn't knock it back and still be coherent. She packed her paper away and slung her tote bag over her shoulder.

"Come on then. We'll sneak away like whatever it is that does that."

"Ships in the night. Er, where are we sneaking to?"

"My home. But a roundabout way to make sure we're not seen." Jan considered her half-full glass of wine and threw caution to the wind. It was damn good wine and she hated waste. She drank it in three gulps, coughed and giggled. "If I'm bosky it's your fault. I usually stop at one, and I sip it."

"I'll hold your head and wipe your brow," Thom said as they moved away from the harbour and Jan began to lead him down side streets. "Wow this is all new to me, I've never explored around here." He glanced around with interest. "I like it."

Even though it wasn't far from the busy waterfront, it was much quieter there, the buildings giving some well-wanted shade. Several open windows had bird cages in them, and the tweets of their occupants could be heard as they walked by. One or two cafes had every door and window open, and the sound of whirring fans could be heard.

Impulsively Jan tucked her arm through Thomas'. "I love this," she said, and gesticulated with her free hand. "All of it. Even the smog, heat, cold, rain, storms. Typhoons. You name it. It's great."

"Never want to leave?" Thom asked with a queer note in his tone.

Jan peered up at him. "I never say never. In fact" – *Sod it, I'll have to tell him something* – "the reason I said I'm not sure if I'll be available later is because I'm headed away for…a holiday in a few weeks or so."

"A holiday you don't know the dates of?" Thom asked sceptically.

Damn it. Of course he'd pick up on that. Jan turned into a courtyard and smiled at the security man by the gate.

"Hi, Peter. This is Thom. He's with me."

"Okay, Miss Fraser." He waved them by.

Jan waited until they were out of earshot and almost at the first of the five houses set around three sides of the courtyard. "This one's mine. I rent it, of course. And my holiday is dependent on work. They'll sort out flights if I have to change the dates."

"And accommodation?"

"Of course. If it's not my fault, they pick up the tab."

"Good company to work for."

"The best." Jan didn't mention why the dates might be changed. First she needed some information. She led Thom into the cool foyer of her house. Small compared to her parents' Scottish home but large for local ones, downstairs had the kitchen-diner and lounge that overlooked a small but precious garden. Upstairs were two bedrooms and a tiny bathroom. Perfect for one or two, Jan thought, but how more people coped easily she had no idea. She accepted she was spoilt and appreciated it.

"A very good company," she said as she ushered him into the lounge. "Let me open the doors into the garden and then I'll..." She'd what? Her mind went blank. Thom had stretched and revealed just a tiny bit of taut abdomen as the hem of his T-shirt lifted. Sadly, she bemoaned, it hadn't gone any higher. "Er, get us a drink."

"Coffee please," Thom said before she had a chance to list what liquid refreshment she could offer. "Or sparkling water. I might be running around later on. Coffee will give me strength, the water will refresh me."

"If you say so. What about food?" Jan wasn't hungry after her dim sum and her fish was earmarked for dinner. That reminded her, she needed to take it out of the coolbag she'd carried it home in and put it into the fridge. "I've not got a lot but could manage a sandwich." She was running down her food stock on purpose before she headed to Scotland.

"Sounds perfect. Any filling you have will be fine. I never look a gift horse—or a home-made sandwich—in the mouth." He made a funny face. "I just say thank you and wolf it down."

"Cheese and ham?" Jan remembered his penchant for that. "That do?"

"With tomato ketchup?"

Jan almost shuddered. Not her taste, but each to their own "Of course."

"Then you're on, thank you."

She nodded and headed into the kitchen. It was hard when they were chatting like old friends to remember all the angst and explosive arguments they'd had which had destroyed their relationship. Forever? At that moment, Jan had no idea. What she did know was that she was going to take things slowly if they ever did appear to be coming closer. She could see work-related problems on both sides and no way was she going to do all the giving and no taking. It had to work both ways. Jan grinned to herself. Wasn't she getting a bit ahead of things? A drink, a meal and a bit part in a movie did not a relationship make.

Thom followed her into the kitchen and looked around with interest.

"Nice gaff."

Jan laughed at his over-the-top cockney accent.

"Gee, thanks, gov. Ain't bad, is it?" She put the fish safely into the coolth of her fridge, switched the house aircon on and got out the makings of his sandwich. It was just as well she'd nipped into a well-known UK store and replenished her bread stock a couple of days earlier. Bread for toast—and, it seemed, sandwiches for unexpected visitors—was a necessity. "Do you use that voice often?"

Thom shook his head. "Only when asked, but I couldn't resist. This house is lovely. I saw it and wow. It was a true admiration moment. How did you find out about this?"

Jan nodded...she agreed with him.

"Word of mouth and a good company to work for. I love it." When she'd been told the house was hers if she wanted it, she'd jumped at the chance. To live in Sai Kung had been a long-held dream, and after a couple of years in a tiny flat in Kennedy Town, she had been ready to move. She'd never regretted it, not even when she'd had to stand like a squashed sardine on the MTR or wait for a bus in the rain. To get home to her own little haven was worth any inconvenience.

She looked around the kitchen, trying to see the room through a stranger's eyes. Tiny, not much more room than for the sink and drainer, her fridge-freezer, cooker, a couple of storage cupboards and a table big enough for two that was hinged to the wall, and two folding chairs. The washing machine and dishwasher were in what was described in the house details as the utility and she called a cupboard, albeit a quite large one. Painted in a soft greige, with a couple of good quality prints of her homeland on the walls it was, Jan had decided, perfect.

It appeared Thomas was of a like mind. "It suits you. I admire your taste in pictures."

Jan laughed. "The Swilken Bridge in St Andrews and Ben Lomond." She named the two places in her prints. "Saw them last time I was home and I couldn't resist. A bit of a contrast to here, eh?"

"You were home?" For some obscure reason, that hurt. How come no one had told him? *Probably thought it was none of my business.* "When?"

"When what?" Jan put a plate of sandwiches next to him, added a bag of crisps and a bottle of sparkling water and indicated the garden. "Outside, or in the so-called lounge?"

"Outside please, and when were you home?" Gah, he sounded like a disgruntled and stroppy teen. "Hope you enjoyed yourself."

"I did, thank you."

Jan appeared a lot more composed than he did, he was sure. Was she going to mention when she was in Scotland or leave him wondering?

"Last time was for Christmas. I go at least once a year. Stock up on midge repellent—though not always Christmas obviously—along with enough tablet to bring home back and eat sparingly and stuff myself with haggis."

Your mum's home-made tablet? I loved the way she made that sweet. Soft, sugary and creamy. Yum." The thought made his mouth water. "You go every year?"

"Of course I pack my HK stormproof rain jacket and go and be cosseted."

At least he knew now, but Thom wasn't sure he liked the sound of the cosseted bit. "Dare I ask by whom?" Try as he might, the whine in his tone was obvious.

"Well you obviously dare," Jan snapped. "Whether I answer you depends on if you stop spitting the dummy out and grow a pair. Build a bridge and get over it and all that."

Thom smiled, reluctantly, at all the old phrases for 'stop being a pain'. She was correct, he was behaving like an idiot. "Bridge built, big-boy boxers pulled up, ass no longer has a pain associated with it. Attitude adjusted. Sorry."

Jan peered at him so closely he felt like an insect under a microscope. "Really? Or are you just trying to placate me?"

"I mean it. I'll be honest, though. Seeing you again brought back a lot of memories, good and bad."

She wrinkled her nose, a gesture Thom remembered so well. He waited as patiently as he could and fought not to tap his fingers on the table or his foot on the floor. It rankled, but he understood why she was so cautious. He would have been the same in her place.

Eventually, just as he was about to tell her to forget it, she sighed and held her hand out. "Okay. Truce."

Thom shook it more fervently than he'd thought possible. The sick and shaky sensation he'd experience disappeared, to be replaced by a sense of relief.

"Thank you." He glanced at his watch. "Shit, I need to be back by the pier soon. Not for long hopefully, but no way can I be late."

"Going Lois dodging?"

Thom groaned. "God, I hope not. It's bloody wearing. What with her getting into the block of flats I live in and appearing like a lost penny everywhere I go, I'd love a few days' respite. I pray she doesn't come when we go..." he hesitated then guessed she knew anyway, "to Scotland next."

"Is that when Moss joins in?"

So she did know more than she let on.

"He's the star, so yeah. This bit is minor, and when we've finished won't be much of the film, and he's not in it here. Mind you, if it becomes the success everyone says and the series does materialise, there are hopes there may be more for both of us in Hong Kong. I'm keeping my fingers crossed. My beloved sister would love to come and annoy you."

Jan laughed. "I know she would, she tells me at every opportunity. I'd have to take some holiday time. Not that that would be a problem except May would want to go about with us and work might be a bit off about us both being out of the office for a long while. Last time she and Arietta got on like a house on fire. Listening to the two of them belting Rod Stewart's *Maggie May* out in karaoke and then doing the locomotion was a night to remember. Moss had to carry

Ari to their accommodation and May's husband booked himself and her into a hotel."

"What about you?" Thom was amused by this small insight into his sister's lifestyle. *And Jan's.*

"I stopped early and watered the pot plants dotted about the place with gin and tonic and the finest Australian wine. I had a horrible feeling next time we went to that particular bar they'd all be dead, but it seems they thrive on alcohol. I had a few glasses of sparkling water and got a taxi home."

Thom roared with laughter. "Probably their usual watery diet, plus the odd rum and Coke and martini." He finished his sandwich. "I'd better think about moving." He considered the woman in front of him. "Thank you for all this." He touched her cheek briefly with his lips. *Slowly, slowly.* "I hope we can catch up again before I head off. I've a couple of weeks left. Sooner than I thought, as everything has gone so well so far." He touched the wooden door frame. "Touch wood, and whatever is a good omen charm. Well, for the all-going-well good omen. Not for the heading off. Mind you, it might mean a few days' holiday in Hong Kong if the early finish meant the next bit couldn't happen straight away. I'd need someone to show me around."

"You know your way around," Jan pointed out.

Thom grinned. She'd followed his somewhat jumbled sentence with ease. It was a relief they had soon found their way back to easy conversation.

"Don't over-egg it."

Thom shrugged. "You got me there. Let me say it's so much nicer with a willing and lovely companion." He held his breath.

Jan did a pseudo-simper. "You mean Lois?"

"Rotter. Not at all." Thom shuddered. "She might be bloody willing, but no way is she lovely. And I'd be damned unwilling. How about it, if I can swing it? Could you manage a few days off to sightsee?"

Jan bit her lip, a habit she'd told him she'd got from him all those years ago. "If I'm here."

"What do you mean?"

She stared at the floor then over his shoulder until, finally, she brought her gaze back to him. "I can't give you a proper answer, but I will if I can. I might not be in HK. I told you before, I've got a job to do elsewhere."

Had she actually said that? Thom couldn't remember.

"You have?" *Where, why?*

She nodded. "And sorry, can't tell you where."

"Fair enough." *No, it isn't, but there's nothing I can do or say without sounding a pain in the bum.* "I understand about confidentiality. Just like all I can say is 'we're off to Scotland'. That bit is known already. Where exactly in Scotland isn't."

Did she appear sceptical?

"If you say so."

Thom narrowed his eyes. "Do you know something more?"

Jan shook her head. "Why on earth should I."

Which didn't answer his question.

"Oh," she added casually, "plus, I'm off to Portugal on holiday as well. But like I said, if I'm here I will."

And with that he accepted he'd need to be content.

And make haste to the piers.

"Don't suppose you'd like to accompany me? Stretch your legs?" he asked, more in hope than anything.

Jan tilted her head to one side and gave him a searching look. "Do you really want my company," she said at last. "Or am I a Lois-foiler?"

Thom laughed. "Sussed it. A bit of both to be honest. It's now known you live here, as I heard Peg telling Alex, so it's ten to one Lois knows as well. If we strolled up together, or ran if I don't get a move on, it would be good, because let's face it, if we were an item, where else would I be except with you? Especially as you live here."

Jan grinned. "Sweet talker. Okay, but I need to go to the loo first. I promise we'll run if we have to."

"And can I come back here after? Even if it's just until the coast is clear."

"You're pushing your luck." She didn't sound too upset about it. "Always have to take that extra yard."

"But can I?" He mentally crossed his fingers. *Please say yes.*

"Hmm."

He did his best woe is me, hangdog expression. "Pretty please. With bells on and a bar of your favourite chocolate? A big one. Two big bars?"

Jan laughed. "It's the chocolate that's swayed it. Now give me three minutes."

She was five, but he wasn't going to mention that. She'd changed her skirt and sandals for thin floaty trousers and trainers and grabbed a denim jacket. Thom stared at her and raised one eyebrow.

"Season's changed?" It was still hot and humid and there was very little breeze.

"The wind off the water is chilly later," Jan replied defensively as she turned the aircon off then slung a bag over her shoulder. "I'm sure you don't want a blue girlfriend, pretend or not."

"That's for sure. Not unless I'm in a sci-fi film. Er, were you thinking of stopping and watching for a while?" That would make life a lot easier if Lois happened to be around, and knowing her as Thom did, he'd not bet against it.

"Would you prefer it if I didn't?"

"I'd love you to hang around," Thom said honestly. "I didn't want to push my luck any more. I'm conscious how much I owe you." He didn't dare think she was helping him out for any other reason than to do her friend a favour. "At the risk of sounding soppy or getting a slap round the face, I like being with you. And you are helping."

"First time ever then," Jan said. "That you've not tried to push it, I mean."

He put on his best 'who, me?' face and she laughed.

"I'll stop for a while. Can't be too late, I've got work tomorrow. But I'll happily elbow Lois if need be." By the look on her face, she would relish doing that.

"Hard?" Thom asked.

Jan sniggered. "Definitely hard. By accident of course." She gestured to her overlarge tote. "Big heavy bags come in handy for more than carrying books and shopping."

Tom laughed and decided not to ask her to clarify her statement. She might show him. Bodily. "Great, so let's run."

"But then we'll arrive all hot and sweaty."

"You'll be that in your jacket anyway."

"Not if I put it in my bag." Jan scowled. "And, if you move your tush, let me set the alarm and lock up, I'll take you the short-cut way. Five, ten minutes tops."

She was as good as her word. Hand in hand they went down alleys and across a tiny park where three women and what looked like a dozen kids under the age of five sat gossiping or riding trikes and playing ball, depending on their ages. One of the ladies shouted something to Jan and she giggled before shouting her reply. Thom's understanding of Cantonese was limited and he had no idea what the conversation had been about, except it had seemed to amuse Jan. As they crossed a busy road and turned down a lane, he saw the glint of water ahead. He waved towards it.

"The piers?"

"Yup, and only been five minutes so far. Would have been four if Mrs Chen hadn't given me her opinion of you."

So that was what the conversation had been about. Him.

"Gonna tell me what she said?"

Jan grinned. "Might make your head swell. She was rather complimentary about your, shall we say, *attributes*."

Thom stopped walking and rocked on his heels, and didn't notice the bloke with his dog trying to get past them. The dog barked and Thom moved to one side of the path.

"Sorry," he said to the man, who did the no-worries shrug and let the dog drag him away. "My attributes?"

"Amongst other things. She's one of my neighbours, and someone who has really helped me improve my Cantonese. I use it and Mandarin now."

It reminded him how well Jan learnt other languages. He could just about get by in French and Spanish, apart from saying please and thank you and ask for a beer, the bill and the bathroom in a few others. She spoke all of them fluently.

"I hope you told her my attributes were perfect."

"Ah" —Jan waggled her finger at him—"that would be telling. Right, which way?" They'd arrived at the end of the lane and were somewhere along the harbourside.

Thom glanced about to get his bearings. "Golf pier, so, right?"

"Spot on. Less than a minute's walk."

Thom scanned the area and noticed the usual hustle and bustle he associated with outdoor filming, albeit without as much equipment as there sometimes was.

"No sign of you-know-who yet," he muttered as they headed in that direction. To the west, the sun was beginning to set, and the shadows were lengthening, casting strange shapes on the ground. It would be perfect for the scenes they needed to film, as the promenade got dark and with help from the authorities, some of the streetlights didn't turn on. Thom prayed he'd get away at the end of the evening unscathed. Both from Lois and tripping over anything. His character wasn't supposed to have spatial limitations. Cool, calm, collected, a ready temper when riled and a cat-like dexterity were mentioned in the character's profile.

They walked towards the large arc lights and Thom sighed. He'd enjoyed his day so far and the crawl of worry that slithered up and down his spine gave him the uneasy sensation that the status quo was about to change. For the umpteenth time, he wondered why Lois had latched on to him and wouldn't take a hint and let go. He wasn't famous, wasn't rich and had no clout. He accepted he didn't look like the back end of a bus, but as his mum had said once when he'd been moaning about someone's good looks and the girls who had fancied the bloke, 'with your eyes closed, how can you tell'? She'd added he might not be the most handsome, but he wasn't half bad. Plus, she'd proclaimed that at least he'd know he was fancied for himself, not for any fleeting other thing. He hadn't totally understood what she meant, but now, a couple of decades later, he did. With the exception of Lois.

Bloody woman. Turning what should have been a pleasure into something less. Making me cautious wherever I go.

Jan stared at him. "What's wrong?" She squeezed his hand. "Sucked a lemon?"

"If only. I could cope with that. You know, go have a beer or a coffee to wash my mouth out if need be. No, it's the damned sodding Lois itch. Why the hell can't she take a hint? I mean, God, Jan. You, Peggy et al. know I've not given her any encouragement. Anything but. It's shit. I keep expecting her to jump out from my wardrobe, or around the nearest bush, and latch on to me. She gives leeches a bad name."

"Yuk." Jan firmed her lips. "That takes some doing. I reckon, though do not quote me, she is too self-aware and self-important? Up herself," Jan suggested. "Thinks she has the right to ignore anything that isn't what she wants."

Thom thought about it. "Could be, but, oh boy is she wrong."

"Yes, I'm with you on that, but she won't ever agree there. However, never fear, Jan is here." She made a silly face. "With a heavy bag, sharp elbow and even sharper tongue. Can I tell her to take a hike?"

"Be my guest. With bells on."

Jan sniggered. "Oh, how I'm gonna look forward to that... Hold on...space invader at nine o'clock. Shall I start?"

Thom glanced to the left and shuddered. “Go for it.”

Chapter Five

"There you have it." Jan sat on the edge of her desk and twirled a pencil between her fingers. May had appropriated Jan's chair as usual and was swivelling it from side to side.

"A good weekend spoilt"

Jan touched her cheek, where a slight bruise showed. "It could have been worse. I could have ended up on top of one of the boats that sold fish if her aim had been better. Or one eye less. Instead, I've got a sore face where it seems a pebble hit me aimed from whom we do not know. Allegedly. Luckily, I'd turned my head to show Thom something and he'd moved, which moved me. God knows what she was trying to do. I think killing me is a bit OTT even for her. Thom was after someone's blood and it took a hell of a lot of, 'I'm fine', from me, and 'it could have come from anywhere' from Sasha, to even halfway calm him down. Lois of course was nowhere to be seen."

"She deserves to be had up," May said in a furious voice. "

Jan shrugged. She'd been over and over it in her mind, and in conversation with Alex, Sasha, Thom and Peggy. "There was no proof it was her. No one saw her throw it, or even where she was. It was only later when Thom said he'd have to leave the shoot because he was taking me to have the injury checked out that we got the suspicion she had something to do with it. She just about jumped on Thom and told him he couldn't leave, and I was pathetic and trying to grab his attention." She huffed a laugh. "He told her I'd no need to do anything. I'd got it already. Then before anything else could happen, Alex showed up with a first aider, who confirmed what I'd thought. I'd been bloody lucky. Then the bloke picked up the stone with a smear of blood on it. Lois grabbed it and sort of did one of those scornful huffs and puffs and dropped it again. Said some people just couldn't accept when they weren't wanted. I swear I heard Thom mutter under his breath, that was so true and it took one to know one. Which wouldn't have registered with her."

"Ah ha," May said. "Fingerprints. Where's the analysis or forensics or whatever?"

Jan laughed and turned her attention from the harbour view, shrouded with mist and rain, back to May. "You've been watching too many crime dramas. The pebble landed in a puddle, and of course after she picked it up it had her fingerprints on it."

"Clever."

"Oh yes. Anyhow, it's over and done with. Nothing broken on me and Thom has a respite as she's on set at a different location to him, for this week at least. Martin's Peggy saw to that. I believe there was a conversation along the lines of either Lois was sent away or Peggy was handing her notice in. Sasha was adamant she couldn't sack Lois, and Peggy was adamant she couldn't have her around. Thom meanwhile muttered words about stalking. Trouble is, a lot of it would be his word against hers. So the upshot for him is a week Lois-less." She rolled her eyes. "Better than nothing I guess."

"Means you've got a clear route or whatever the saying is?"

"No idea and no idea, and no idea if I want whatever it's called. Now," Jan said briskly, "not many ideas at all, except I believe I should be told when and where exactly I'm due to work. It can't be that far ahead. Or do I hazard a guess?" She slid off the desk. "After all, I need to make arrangements for the cat. And the budgie."

May got up and walked towards the door. "You don't have a cat," she said, bewildered. "Or a budgie… Do you?"

"Nope, but I do have a need to know. If nothing else, I want a few days to pack and sort out what I think I should take with me for work in Scotland and relaxation in Portugal."

"That's sensible." Peggy nodded. "I'll go and get the file. It's what I came in to say, actually, and then you sidetracked me. The info is all ready for you."

"Thank goodness for that." The more she thought about it, Jan was convinced the assignment was with regards to the TV series Thom and Moss were in. How she was to be involved she wasn't sure, and why her skills were needed ditto, but at least now she could hopefully find out a bit more. It would mean she'd hopefully get to see Arietta more often. She was certain she'd be in the vicinity of Moss. As an author, Ari always said give her a laptop and she could write anywhere.

May returned and handed a large brown envelope to Jan with a smirk. "This is where I say for your eyes only, and you say, why not a pdf or an email. And I say, ours is not..."

"To reason why," they chorused and high-fived.

Jan rummaged in her desk drawer until she found an infrequently used letter opener, slit the envelope and pulled out several sheets of A4 paper covered in typing. "Very old school," she commented. "I wonder why?"

"I was told that the person who wants help thought you could read it, make your own cryptic notes and then shred it or something. Sounds a bit convoluted but he said he wasn't happy about putting details in an email that could be hacked. He had more faith in the mail."

"To a business address?" Jan raised her eyebrows.

May blushed. "Well, er, no. I got it sent to my house, and it had a sort of sexy-sounding sender's address on it. Didn't think that would make anyone think it was notes on the situation. I did tell my beloved so he knew I wasn't doing the dirty on him, or indulging in whatever."

Jan laughed and shook her head in amusement. "Sent to an address in HK? A bit far-fetched when you think of the markets and shops you could go to for anything sex wise." It all appeared a bit cloak and dagger-ish. "Do I report to whoever in a trench coat and a fedora?"

May glowered then sniggered. "At dead of night holding a red rose and a furled newspaper? I doubt it.

Anyway, read and see and be ready to head off a week on Friday. That gives you several days' respite once you're there to get over jet lag and acclimatise yourself."

"Gee, thanks." Jan wasn't sure if the short notice was a good thing or not. "I'll need a couple of days off before I go. A day of shopping is on the agenda. I've a lot of bits and bobs to buy. To prepare for jet lag!" *Amongst other things.*

* * * *

Just over a week later, it was a real joy for Thom to be told he had the following day off. Long hours of hard filming had been happily Lois-less and resulted in a much more harmonious set. Lois, after her stint in the New Territories with a different set of actors—who reported she was the proverbial pain in the ass—went down with some lurgy or other and took time off. Whether she was really ill or not Thom had no idea and couldn't care less. It gave him time to concentrate on the job in hand, and not have to keep one eye out to enable him to Lois dodge if and when necessary. He'd been busy and not had a chance to see Jan since the pebble debacle, and any communication had been via text and a couple of phone calls. He still couldn't make his mind up what their status quo was. Jan gave him no clues how she felt about him, *or* their lack of communication. As he had no definite ideas there it was no help, and a not particularly comfortable mind set to be in.

Suck it up. Think about it, and… And he didn't have a clue.

Thom shook himself. *Concentrate on the next couple of days instead. Free time. No Lois around.* He did a mental finger cross there. *I hope.*

Not needed until Tuesday. *Bliss*. Then only a few more days before they wrapped up in Hong Kong and he headed to Scotland. After a few days as a tourist. With or without Jan, he had no idea.

None of which solved how he was going to spend the next couple of hours or so. Thom stood by his window and frowned at the haze he could see. He'd fancied going up the peak, but if the view was obscured there was no point. Which also applied to his other plan—to go to Lantau and see the largest sitting Buddha in the world, a statue that had filled him with awe the last time he went there. But again, part of the joy of the visit was the views. Thom sighed and gave himself a mental shake. *Just get out and shoo the cobwebs away. Wherever.*

Mind made up, he grabbed his jacket and phone and headed out. First stop the ferry, then a tram. He'd be a real tourist and just wander.

The road to the ferry terminal was as busy as ever, and he dodged the suit makers, watch sellers and handbag dealers with a smile and a few words of Cantonese he'd learnt years before that indicated he was not a person who wanted to buy anything—fake or not. It was a vibrant, busy and chaotic scene and Thom loved it. Every last inch.

He stood at the back of a crowd of people waiting to cross the road as traffic sped by a few scant inches away. Horns tooted and brakes screeched. Buses trundled past, and bikes were everywhere. The riders were braver than he was. The thought of riding a bike in the melee was enough to bring him out in hives.

The lights changed and the crowd surged forward. About to join them, something made Thom glance across the road towards the ferry pier.

A recognisable figure stood there. Luckily for him dressed in red, her favourite colour, and so as noticeable as a traffic light or a British post van. Right where he would need to pass to get on the ferry.

Lois.

Scanning everyone who headed in that direction.

What on earth was she doing there? *Shit, is she waiting for me? Wondering if I'm going to get on the ferry? Thank goodness she's dressed like that. I might not have spotted her otherwise.* Thom edged backwards and stood by the side of a building where he thought he wouldn't be noticed. Was he paranoid?

Maybe, maybe not, but he'd err on the maybe-not side. Too many accidental unexpected occasions added up to a non-accidental result. In a thoughtful mood, Thom went back the way he'd come and walked to the bus terminal instead. As he waited for a bus that would take him to Stanley—surely that would be far enough out of Lois' orbit—he scanned his contacts and speed dialled Peggy, who he knew would be at work. The crew were filming scenes where he wasn't needed and Peggy had intimated she'd be chained to her laptop. In her words catching up with all the crap.

Peggy answered promptly. "Hi, what's up?"

"Not sure to be honest. This might sound daft, but does Lois have a doppelganger or could she be hanging around the ferry terminal in TST? Outside the pier to Central."

"What? The bitch." Peggy sounded thoroughly fed up. "Bloody Norah. She came in this morning, asked where you were, and when she heard you weren't needed so had time off, said she had period pains and would have to go home. Now I think of it, she used that excuse for a day off two weeks ago. Last time you had a few hours to yourself. Why on earth Sasha doesn't accept she's a liability and send her on her way I do not know. Well, I do of course. Family loyalty and all that, but seriously, she is the outside of enough. Have you managed to avoid her?"

"Yeah. I mean, I don't know if she's hanging around there in case I go by or not. She could be waiting for anyone, I guess, except there's no flying pigs about. Or just loitering. Or should that be Lois-tering?"

Peggy sniggered. "I like that."

"You wouldn't like any of it after she managed to get into the building where my flat is and ring my internal doorbell a few weeks ago. And surprise, surprise, the peep hole was covered. No wonder I tend to be suspicious."

"Shit, so would I be. You should have said. What do you want me to do?" Peggy asked. "Legally, of course."

"Not sure there's anything you *can* do, except keep her out of my way as much as possible."

"Do my best."

"Cheers. Now I'm off on a bus ride." He ended the call as Peggy laughed and the bus he wanted drew up. First in the queue, like an excited child, he headed upstairs to sit at the front and get the best view out of the window.

He'd forgotten the route did a loop around TST and went past the ferry terminal before heading through the tunnel to Central and on to Stanley across Hong Kong Island. A journey he'd done many times in years past but still enjoyed. Okay, he'd missed the ferry ride, but with luck he could make sure he got off whatever mode of transport he chose for the return journey in Central and do that on the way back.

As the bus drew level with the terminal, Thom sat back from the window, not so far he couldn't scan the area but far enough, he hoped, not to be seen. At first he couldn't see Lois and wondered if she'd given up, or horror of horrors was about to get on the bus. Then he saw her, about to cross the road and head up the road that led to his accommodation.

Of course, it led to a lot of other places as well, including the MTR, a large number of multinational shops and the park, but…

Thom gave up a mental word of thanks he'd woken up early, got up and out sharply that morning and been alert. Because otherwise he could have easily bumped into Lois either by accident on his side or design on hers.

Stress central. The last thing he needed or wanted. Today neither would be on the agenda. Thom sat back in his seat as the bus moved away and prepared to enjoy his ride.

Looking out of the window and people watching was fun, easy and time consuming. The hour and a bit journey passed swiftly, and Thom was content to see what he remembered and what was new. Quite a lot of both, it appeared. It never ceased to amaze him how the old and the new merged so well together. By the time he got off the bus, he was in a great mood and looking forward to being a tourist around the market. He thought he might even pick up a couple of presents for Arietta. Something tasteful and something naff. He chuckled to himself as he waited for another bus to stop so he could cross the road and head down to the waterfront and the famous Stanley Market. Tasteful was easy. Nice earrings, silk scarf, new cashmere pashmina. What would she call naff?

It didn't matter, he had plenty of time to browse, have a coffee and a glass of wine or two as he watched the comings and goings on the water. With no set time to get back, the day was his.

Stanley, here I come. It wasn't as busy or commercial as Sai Kung, but equally as pleasurable.

The crowd waiting to cross the road grew and someone nudged him until he almost fell off the kerb and under a bus.

Thom rocked on his heels and hissed in a breath as someone grabbed his elbow and helped him steady himself. A female voice spoke.

"Grief, I'm sorry."

I recognise that voice.

He swung round to see Jan, who appeared as stunned as he was at them seeing each other there.

The crowd rushed across the road and without thinking Thom took Jan's arm and walked brisky across the tarmac as several buses, taxis and other vehicles waited none too patiently for their turn to clog the road.

"We must stop meeting like this," he quipped as they reached the pavement and everyone began to head off in every direction. "People will talk."

She chuckled. "They are anyway. What are you doing here?"

"Day off," Thom said succinctly. "Lois dodging and present buying. You?"

"Day off and ditto. Well, the present buying, anyway. I have no idea about Lois, but I'd happily dodge her. What's she up to now?"

"Stalking me, I think," Thom said dourly. "As in hanging about the ferry piers in TST today, and other odd places at other times. I swear I bolt my dressing area door *and* look under the toilet seat and behind that door at least three times before I lock myself in to go to the loo." He rolled his eyes and Jan grinned.

"To be hoped you're never in a hurry then."

"True. Still, at least I've hopefully dodged her and if not please, miss, can I hide behind your…" He looked at her legs and grinned. "Er, shorts?"

Jan followed his glance—to her denim, knee-length cut-offs—and stuck her tongue out. "Cheeky."

Thom winked, his mood having lifted with the unexpected meeting and the way they seemed to have resorted to their old chatting ways. "Nah they're not that short."

Jan spluttered and wagged her finger at him before punching him on the arm. "You. You have a good answer for everything."

"Wish I had." Thom crossed his eyes and made a face. "Can't find a good enough one to tell Lois to go for a hike it seems."

"True. Ah well, can't win everything." She tilted her head to one side. "Wanna be alone or want a companion?"

"If it's you, yes please," Thom said promptly. "Anyone else, I'll plead the right to remain silent. Where do you intend to go? The market?"

"Well, duh. I promised Audie a naff present. Her words not mine. Any idea what counts as naff for a teenager these days?" Audie was Thom's step-niece.

"For Audie, who knows. How about a plastic something-or-other, or some chopsticks in a silk bag?"

"Hmm. Not sure. Unless I got her the child's learner chopsticks with the plastic bit that hold them together. You know, as a real joke. I'll look about and see if anything catches my eye. I want to go to that shop that sells linen dresses and stuff as well. Oh, and the pictures painted on silk and..."

"And everywhere?'

"Just about. Be a tourist."

Thom nodded. "Fair enough. That's me today as well. Lead on, McDuff."

He waited until they reached the first market stall Jan stopped at. "So," he said casually. "Are you likely to see Audie soon?"

His oh-so-casual tone put Jan's sense of 'beware' on high alert. Was he fishing? If so, what exactly for? She searched her mind for the best way to answer him and not give anything away.

"Hope so. I'm off to Europe, remember?" she said with an insouciance she didn't feel. "Really chuffed that I'll have a chance to catch up with her. School and camp and fishing, riding, swimming, out or texting or whatever is the in thing these days with her friends, etcetera, permitting. She's a busy young lady." Jan laughed. "Which is as it should be."

That didn't answer his question but it was all he was getting. Jan was almost certain she'd see him in Scotland before long. All she could hope was that if he was involved with the filming at the hotel, they wouldn't be at loggerheads.

Jan gestured towards some silk scarves. "If I remember correctly, Ari loved these last time she was here and bemoaned the fact she'd snagged hers and it had a run in it." She grinned. "Said it reminded her of laddered school tights sewn up to make them last longer, but there was no way she could darn the scarf. She's into blues and greens mixed together if that's any help."

"Brilliant, ta."

Jan waited until Thom was chatting to the stallholder, a tall lady in a vivid red- and saffron-coloured floaty dress that made Jan want to shade her eyes. As she wandered over to some sarongs, one in bright pink and orange made her blink and think she would need sunglasses if she had to stare at it for long. Then she laughed. Audie would love it.

Thom was still flicking through the more conservative silks as Jan purchased the psychedelic one and a gauzy overblouse destined for Arietta. She nudged Thom. "I'm going across the passage to the leather goods stall. I need a new tote for the plane."

He nodded and held up two scarves. "Which one?"

Jan studied them both. "I like the purply-blue, but the blue green is more Arietta, I think."

"Fair enough, I trust your judgement." Thom smiled. "See you in a bit."

Jan nodded. He trusted her judgement? That was a first.

Miaow. She turned away from him and the beaming stallholder, who obviously smelled another sale or two.

Three steps took her to the bag stall. She'd got her eye on several of them in various designs and wanted to check them out. Jan accepted she was the first person to admit she thought you could never have too many hand and shoulder bags. After all, there were so many types for so many different things and you never knew what would be needed and in what colour or size.

That could be a spurious argument if there ever was one. Who was it who stated one of each size in beige does the trick? Well, whoever it was, I beg to differ. She picked up a pale grey leather tote of a soft-as-butter leather and checked the inside. Three pockets of various sizes *and* an inner bag that could be zipped up. Perfect. She held it up and asked—in Cantonese—how much it was and grinned at the stallholder's surprise and obvious delight.

They began to bargain.

Ten minutes later, Jan was the proud owner of the tote, a backpack for Audie with lots of cartoons on it as well as a neat shoulder bag and a baby rucksack for May's niece, who was about to give birth. All at considerably less cost than originally stated.

"Good bargains?" Thom asked as he reached her side.

"The best," Jan assured him and laughed as the shopkeeper spoke to them. "He says I will bankrupt him." Jan informed Thom. "But if my friend—that's you, want to buy—"

"For a friend of my friend here, I give you a good price," the man assured Thom. "What do you want?"

Thom wrinkled his nose. "A belt maybe?"

"Which," he said to Jan a short while later as they settled outside one of the small bars that overlooked the water, "I neither want nor need, but felt I'd better buy something. As he's a friend of yours."

Jan smirked and waited until their order had been taken. "I've never met him before in my life."

Thom stared at her and as realisation obviously hit, he began to laugh. "I've been had."

"True, but you did get a good deal," Jan pointed out. "And now you have a spare belt."

"That makes five then," Thom said with a chuckle. "It's evidently a fail-safe present if someone had no idea what to buy. Ah well, at least we made the bloke happy, and now we can sit and chill. Unless," he added with an expression of mock horror—at least Jan hoped it was mock—"you have more on your list?"

"We…ll," she began, then winked. "An ice cream maybe, but apart from that? Nothing really, unless I nip to the clothing shop along near Stanley Plaza while you sit and read or whatever. But not till after we've both sat and relaxed. I tell you, bargaining is thirsty work." Jan waited until their drinks were on the table then waved her hand towards the sea. "Plus, this view is stunning. Not dramatically stunning but…" She raised her shoulders and dropped them again as she took in the short pier, the people on it and Murray House, the old administrative buildings. "Not sure how to describe it really, except it gives a sort of comfort to my soul."

"That's as good a description as any," Thom said soberly. "When I walk past Pat Kan Uk, you know those eight houses where some of the elders of the place live, somehow I discover a sense of how the place evolved." He shrugged. "I'm a history geek. And it gives me goosebumps. So much has happened over the centuries." He laughed self-consciously. "I know it'll continue to do so, but it's how that fascinates me. And when."

Jan nodded. "I get that. Like, I suppose, our family histories as well." She sipped her wine. "Argh, enough. Let's just enjoy our wine and people watch. See the guy in the red shorts?" She waved towards a tall dark-haired man with a child on his shoulders. "Dad taking son out. Monday to Fridays he's a banker. Not quite a striped suit and all that for work, but definitely not jeans and a T-shirt. The Powers That Be would be horrified so he only goes casual at the weekend."

"Dad or son?"

"Ha, ha. Funny." She tapped Thom's nose. "Always the comedian."

"You know that about him? How come?" Thom asked with curiosity uppermost in his voice. "He works near you? Been for an interview at your place? Come on, spill."

"None of them. It's one of my fun things to do. Give people an identity and background. Your turn now." Jan wondered if Thom would play or think her stupid. She waited for what seemed like minutes but was probably no more than a few seconds.

A child whined somewhere behind them, and a soft sibilant voice answered him—her? Overhead a bird flew and called to another. A car tooted its horn and another one echoed it.

"Hmm. Okay now, let me see. The girl in the green cut-offs with her hair in a bun? Over by the shoe shop. A ballet dancer on a break between rehearsals. She's got to hurry back soon and practice. She's on tonight and needs to perfect her plies and hammer her toe shoes."

"You know a lot about ballet dancers," Jan said as a streak of jealousy hit her hard. The girl in question stretched and touched her toes before walking off in a jaunty, bouncy manner.

"The important bits," Thom said. "See? A ballet dancer's walk." He grinned at Jan. "I dated one once. Didn't last, as she could eat liquorice faster than me and thought rugby was for hooligans."

"Eat li—" Jan said bewildered. She glanced at his smug expression. "How old were you?"

"Eleven. She was twelve. Went to Miss Tweddle's School of Drama and Dance. I'd just got into the school rugby under fourteens so I wasn't impressed with her thoughts. We split up and she went out with a gymnast. Last I heard she was married with three budding ballerinas and he was a professional football player for one of the major teams. We all went through high school together, and if I remember rightly her husband and I played both ends of the donkey in one nativity play, and she was the prompter and kept calling us silly asses. Which as a teenage bloke caused us great hilarity. And got us all a detention."

Jan laughed at his description of the incident. "Did you have to write an essay or something?"

"I honestly can't remember except it meant I missed a match. Detention was on Saturdays and timed so it didn't finish before any match started. That was more of a punishment than the putting on uniform and trekking into the school hall on a weekend. But weirdly it got me interested in acting because the drama club met on Saturday afternoons, and I used to watch before I left. Then one day they asked if I'd help out and read a part for them and that was it. I was hooked."

"Did you give up rugby?"

Thom shook his head. "Not until I realised a broken nose might not be to my advantage. Then I did."

All the little facets of himself Thom she discovered were interesting to Jan. She'd never really learnt a lot about his teens. They had, she thought now, been too involved in the there and then to talk about their past when they had been a couple.

"I was a good girl," she said primly, and ruined it by sniggering. "I never got detention."

"Never did anything wrong? I'm impressed."

She crossed her eyes—the one trick she could do successfully—and pulled a funny face. "Nah, I didn't say that. I just never got caught."

Thom roared. "Go you."

"I did my best. Right, if you want to wait here, I'm nipping to the plaza. Ten, fifteen minutes max."

"I'm happy sitting here. Got my eReader in my backpack and I reckon we could manage another glass, don't you?"

What the hell, why not. "Small one please." Jan grabbed her tote bag and stood up. She only wanted a quick look at the T-shirts. The shop she was headed to tended to get stock before the UK shops and it usually gave her an idea what might be useful both for work and not.

She'd not got halfway across the square in front of the shop before a glimpse of someone heading down the outside stairs of the small mall made her blink. It couldn't be!

She squinted.

It was.

Hell on wheels. Had Lois followed them somehow, or was it by chance she'd arrived?

Jan had no idea and didn't particularly want to find out. What she did need to know was what Thom's plan would be.

She turned on her heels and walked swiftly back to the bar where Thom sat, probably oblivious to what was more than likely about to befall them.

Because if Lois walked along the front, it would be impossible for her to miss them.

Chapter Six

"Lois alert."

Deep into his book, where the hero was about to dive into the North Sea and drag out a lobster pot with contraband in it, Thom didn't register Jan's words at first. Then they penetrated his brain.

Sick dread filled him, along with, he realised, a raging anger. If it lost him his job so be it. Enough was really and truly enough. The woman was an out and out pest. A stalker.

"Damn it. Where?" He craned his neck to look around but couldn't see anyone Lois-shaped in the vicinity. "I can't see her."

"She's to your right. She was coming down from the bus stop above the plaza. No idea if she's here because you are or if it's just an unlucky fluke."

"Whatever, it's an unwelcome one. I'm putting up with her and her antics no more." Thom flipped the cover over his eReader and put it inside his rucksack. "Let proper battle commence."

Jan stood next to the table. "Want me to go? Let you get on with it without any distractions?"

"What?" Thom said. "Hell no. I said I might need your shorts to hide behind and I meant it. that woman is vindictive. I need a witness to anything said or done. On either side. You might not be impartial, well, I hope you're not, but if nothing else you can shout for help. Record it on your phone?"

"You've got a point." Jan got her phone out of her pocket. "It's ready to go, I'm not. I've almost a full glass of wine to drink and it's too good to waste."

It had been left in an unusual cooler perfect for her wine glass. The moment he'd seen it, Thom had decided he'd have to try to find out where you could buy something similar. He hated watering his wine down with an ice cube, and the 'stones' that you froze and put into your drink never seemed to keep it cool for long.

"I agree, you can't waste good wine. Can you see her?" Thom spoke in an undertone. "Where is she? What's she doing?"

Jan sat down and, with an imp of mischief in her expression, planted a kiss on the top of Thom's head as she did so.

He jumped. "On my head? I can think of better places."

"So can I," Jan purred.

Purring? He saw her expression—pure devilment—and hid his grin. "Then why my head?"

"No PDAs here, please. I need to keep my wits about me. So do you."

"Point taken. Where is she?" He was ready to bring things to a head there and then. How he'd like to stand up and scan the area. Be more prepared. This not knowing played havoc with his nerves. How on earth people in really tense situations coped he had no idea. His skin itched.

Gah, I'm a wuss.

"Hold on." Jan did a very elegant sideways swivel in her seat and leant over his shoulder. "About twenty-thirty yards away and…" She began to laugh, albeit weakly. "Danger over. It's not her. Someone very similar, though. Look towards the pier. She's heading down it."

Thom let out his breath in one long sigh of relief. He felt limp. Such a strange reaction. He picked up his wine, took a mouthful and wondered why it tasted of…water. He'd grabbed his water glass instead. Which was probably more suitable to a big gulp, so he took another mouthful. Less liquid this time.

"Which person?" The pier was far enough away not to see features clearly. He squinted, realised he'd taken his sunglasses off and shoved them firmly on his nose. "Ah, red dress?"

"The very one. Sorry, a scare over nothing."

Thom narrowed his eyes and stared at the woman who had turned to look out over the water and given them a good sideways-on view of her. "Almost a doppelganger for the not-so-lovely Lois," he commented. "I can see why you thought it was her. Especially at a distance. I reckon the only major difference is the height and that Lois has, how shall I put it, more generous assets."

"Busty and shows it," Jan replied. "Dare I be catty and says flaunts it…them."

"You can and I'll agree. Now, after all that furore I'm getting hungry. It's been a long time since breakfast and we still haven't had an ice cream. Fancy eating around here somewhere, or should we get a taxi back closer to town and eat there?" He suddenly realised how much he was taking for granted. "Er, that's if you'd like to share a meal, of course."

"Of course," Jan said gravely. "Actually, I'd love to eat here but it's a helluva long way home for me. I've as far again once we reach central or TST. So I guess it better be one of those."

"Or," Thom said slowly, wondering if he was about to make the biggest faux pas of his life, "we could eat here and you could spend the night at mine."

If silence could be called deafening, it was.

The expression on Jan's face was nigh-on enough to have him covering his balls. How he managed not to was, in his mind, one of life's mysteries. She stared at him without blinking.

Then slowly picked up her glass and began to twirl it.

"Elucidate."

What exactly did Thom mean by 'spend the night' at his? Was he offering her a bed? In a room? Alone? Or expecting her to share his room, his bed and…? She shut off any more thought along the bedroom line. Heaven knew *she – and Thom –* knew a bedroom and bed were not a prerequisite for anything amorous. Jan bit her lip so as not to show where her thoughts had headed.

"Please," she added to her demand, then waved her hand at an inquisitive bird who thought there might be easy pickings for his lunch near their table. "Darned birds. Sorry, not even a crumb here for you."

Thom chuckled. "Heard us talking about food. Right." She watched him take a deep breath. "The choice would be yours as to where and how you spent the night. I've two bedrooms, two bathrooms, both furnished. Spare toothbrush and paste and of course towels and so on. Up to you. If you want to go home, I'll put you in a taxi after we eat. Or before if you prefer. I'll be honest, I'd prefer we eat and sleep together, but that's bloody cheeky and I know it. Pushing my luck is an understatement. So, it's all up to you, and yes, I'll accept what you say, and no, I won't spit the dummy out. I'm hoping I'm past that sort of behaviour."

"The jury's out," Jan said sombrely then tapped his nose as he scowled. "Sucker. I'm sure you are or I'd not be here. If, *if* I stop, I'll need some clothes. No way am I putting sweaty clothes back on."

I could go naked…or not. "There's the shop you were headed to," Thom pointed out. "I assume you didn't get there? Or, of course, I do have a washer and dryer. Never mind the 'my house is your house' bit, that's a given, but my washer and dryer are yours etcetera, etcetera. And you can choose your bed and where we go for food."

Jan studied him for a few seconds. She hoped the expression on her face made him sweat. That he'd bet she was going to turn him down. All of his offers. *Taxi for one then. Sai Kung please.* Then no doubt he'd eat and get the bus home. *I wouldn't. Not now. Scrub the eat, not fun alone after a day spent with someone…hell, someone special. Bugger it.* That would take a while to get her head round.

Damn it. She knew what she would like so for once she'd throw caution to the wind and go for it.

"If you book us a table at that noodle place, I'll nip to the clothes shop and get some basics. Maybe we could go for a walk to the shrine before we eat? Or, if you prefer, we could eat by the harbourside in central. I'll leave it to you."

Did that mean she would stop the night?

"And," Jan added, "I'll let you know what bedroom later. Now I'll head back to the shop and hope I get there this time." She stood up and thought she was being akin to a jack-in-the-box. "By the way, do you need to get up at silly o'clock? That might be a decision maker."

"Nope, I've got tomorrow off."

Jan smiled. "How nice. So have I." She headed away from the table and back towards the plaza, leaving an open-mouthed Thom behind her.

As she reached the edge of the pavement she heard him whistle. When she turned round, he gave her a thumbs-up. She waved and turned into the shop.

* * * *

Half an hour later, her credit card used more than she'd thought it would be, and her person laden with several bags, Jan headed back to where she'd left Thom.

He was still sitting there with a bottle of water and an empty coffee cup on the table next to him.

"Done?"

"I hope so. My credit card is muttering dire warnings if I haven't." She'd nipped into a posh lingerie shop and succumbed to a sexy lingerie set and a demure at first glance, sexy at the second nightie. Not that she was certain she'd wear it. She had bought a T-shirt nightie from the other shop as well as a pack of knickers, and taken advantage of a two-for-one bra sale. To say nothing of two T-shirts, a denim skirt in the sale and a pair of thin, floaty trousers. That should keep her going until the next day.

I could change three times at least.

"Want coffee before we walk? Do you still want to go for a walk with all those bags?" Thom asked doubtfully. "I can get a couple in my rucksack but it's a lot to carry on a 'just because' walk."

Jan had to agree. "Anywhere I can stash them?"

Thom appeared dubious. "Not sure, but as I couldn't get a table at the noodle place I'd say it's unlikely. I hope it's okay with you, but I've made a reservation at the bar above the piers back in central. I just hope the food is as good as it used to be."

"Better," Jan assured him. She looked at the number of bags she'd collected and grimaced. Even if she doubled some up, she still didn't fancy an extra couple of miles carrying them. "I think we should forego the walk here."

"Put it on hold until another time?" Thom asked. "A time when we're bagless."

That was the problem. "If I'm here. I go abroad in a week-ish."

Damn. Thom knew she was due to leave but had hoped for a bit more time together, there in Hong Kong on neutral territory.

"That when you go to Scotland?" he asked casually.

"Yeah and then… Shit, shoot and bugger. Bastard." Jan sounded disgusted with herself. "To, er, visit friends."

"Yeah, and if you think I'll believe that, you've got another think coming. Try again." Thom rolled his eyes then crossed them. "'Fess up, buttercup."

Jan scowled. "I hate that you can do that with your eyes without thinking about it. I have to concentrate."

Thom laughed. "Practice."

"Yeah, okay. Look, I can't say anything about where exactly I'm going or why," Jan said earnestly. "It's part of my contract. So please don't ask or try to get me flustered so I tell you. I love most of my job and don't want to lose it."

The flustered bit made him wonder. So did the most. What was wrong with part of it?

"What exactly is your job? Or is that top secret as well?" He'd often wondered but hadn't ever asked Arietta or Moss. He didn't want them to know how often he wondered 'what if'. "Tell me to naff off if you want."

"My official job title is administrative manager," Jan said carefully. "I make sure things happen as and when they should. May sometimes says arbitrator, facilitator, or any other 'ator' she can think of."

Which didn't tell him a lot and which he was certain was all he was going to get.

"Enjoy it?" *Stupid, she's already said* most *of it.*

"Mostly," Jan said with caution. "Like I said. Except when I have to deal with idiots who think whatever is supposed to happen shouldn't involve them if they don't want to do it. There's plenty of them around."

"How do you sort that out?" Thom asked with genuine interest. "You didn't do any law exams did you?"

"Nope, not interested, even if I did do a law degree. I leave that bit to others. I prefer solving problems. Like the eejits who assume if they keep saying no I will give in. I don't. I show them the error of their ways by whichever legal way I can. They either accept I'm right or find out very soon how wrong they are." She broke off for long enough to munch on a pretzel. "Not everything is an argument, though. Sometimes it's as simple as advising someone the place best suited for them to relocate to. Schools, transport, activities, office space. You name it. I love the variety."

"And something of your expertise is needed somewhere in Scotland. Good luck then."

"Thanks and…watch out. Oops, too late." Jan ducked.

Thom didn't have time to move. A football hit him hard on the shin and he forgot all about flustering and winced at the short, sharp and unexpected pain.

"Bugger, that hurt. What little sh—" He broke off as Jan glared at him and shook her head a fraction as she caught the ball as it flew over her shoulder. A small boy of around six years old was walking towards them with a worried expression. By his side a tall blond man walked with one hand on the lad's shoulder in reassurance.

It brought back so many memories for Thom of when he had been small and hit someone or something with a football—or a rugby ball—and his dad had told him he had to own up. Then gone with him for moral support.

The pair stopped next to the table and the man smiled at Thom and Jan and nudged the child. "What did you say you had to say?"

The child sighed deeply. The sort of sigh Thom would say came from his boots. He noticed Jan's lips twitch and forced himself to keep his expression blank and concentrate on the boy.

"I'm sorry I hit you. I didn't mean to. I'm just not that good at kicking. Dad says I'll get better with practice."

"Apology accepted," Thom said gravely, and shook the hand the child put out in his direction. "I wasn't much good at your age either."

The young lad tilted his head as if he was considering Tom's words. "Did you get better?"

Thom nodded. "I did. Then I hit what I aimed for."

The child grinned. "I was aiming at my big brother, who keeps telling me I'm rubbish. I'll show him one day when I hit him in the you-boolies. The you-know-whats."

"Archie," his dad said. "Remember what we said about politeness." He gave Thom and Jan an apologetic look. "Sorry."

Archie gave the man a pitying glance. "I never said the words, Dad. I did think them but didn't actually say the proper words.'"

The man nodded. "Point taken. We best head back to your mum and Eric." He turned to Thom. "Thanks from me as well."

"Nice pair," Thom commented as the man and boy headed back up towards the beach area, where they joined a woman and a toddler. "My dad used to do that with me. After he'd threatened to make me go and say sorry by myself. Never did, though—he always metaphorically held my hand, if not physically."

"Like I said, I was a good girl," Jan said primly before spoiling it by grinning. "At least, I was never found out. Then of course I met you and all the goodness left and ran away."

Thom roared. "Is it still away?"

She gave him a saucy smile. "You'll find out later. After I've been wined and dined."

Thom made a production of gathering up the shopping. "Ready to go?"

It was one thing to sound confident, another thing to actually be so. Jan was no innocent. She'd been with Thomas for several years and of course they'd had an intimate relationship. However, she would be the first to admit her lovers had been few and far between. As she'd once put it to a close male friend—one who had no ideas of being any more than that—living alone, and abroad, she was probably incredibly choosy. He'd told her that was sensible and proceeded to teach her self-defence. Luckily, she'd never needed to use what she'd learnt, but the knowledge she could give a good shot of defending herself gave her a lot of confidence when she was out and about. Not that she thought she'd need to defend herself from Thom, but her cautiousness was one reason she thought her romantic skills were more than a bit rusty. Her last partner had been almost two years previously. No one had interested her since then.

Except Thom of course. Which is weird. After their spectacular bust up, Jan had thought she'd never trust him as far as she could throw him. Years later she had discovered, via Arietta, that one of their more enterprising friends had set up a betting book over whether Jan would deck him with a textbook or pour his beer all over his head. As it had happened, they'd had taken their row home with them and it had culmilated with Thom very ostentatiously picking up his toothbrush and walking out. Now, when Jan thought about it, it had been a very 'actory' exit. She wondered if he remembered it, but in the interests of a harmonious evening decided not to mention the scenario.

This is now, not then. Time to do what I want. It would help if I knew what I want. Her tummy rumbled. *I want food.*

The place Thom had chosen for them to eat was an unassuming bar-restaurant with a reputation for excellent foods. Situated above one of the inner island ferry piers with a stunning view overlooking the harbour, it was a popular venue. The menu was simple but perfectly cooked and the wine—in the main Australian—all complemented the food.

As they left the taxi they had chosen to get back across the island faster than on the bus, Jan admitted to herself she had butterflies and wished she'd not been so open about how she felt. That was half an hour ago and those butterflies were out in force. One thing was certain, if, and it was a big if, she decided to stop at Thom's, it would be on her terms. If she didn't, she'd have to explain why.

She sighed.

"What's up?" Thom asked as they climbed the stairs to their destination. A ferry hooted in the harbour and one of the prettily lit harbour tour boats headed by on its sunset cruise. "That was one down-to-your-socks sigh."

Jan grimaced. "Me overthinking."

"Used to be one of your fatal flaws," Thom remarked as they waited to be seated. "Still got it then."

"Yeah." Jan tucked her bags under the table and stared at the outlines of the skyscrapers that made up the impressive skyline. "Sorry."

"Nothing to be sorry about," Thom answered briskly. "You do as you think right. If you decide not to stop over, there's a taxi rank here and one not far from my accommodation."

Jan stared at him. "How did you know what I was thinking?"

He smiled. "I know you."

The prosaic words, the tone and the matter-of-fact way Thom accepted she was swithering was the catalyst that made her mind up. Jan smiled back. "Where's the menu?"

Thom grinned wolfishly and Jan giggled.

"Idiot. Food. Here. Not whatever. Wherever."

A long, drawn-out boat's siren made them both jump and burst out laughing. It seemed like an apt answer.

The much calmer, no-stress atmosphere their joint laughter created set the tone for the evening. A couple of hours later, as they sat side by side on the upper deck of the Star Ferry and crossed the harbour, Jan counted to three.

"If I said I'd stop with you just as a friend, what would you say?"

I'd like to say shit and bawl my eyes out. "The spare bed is made up."

Jan nodded and clutched his arm as the ferry did its usual sideways, back and forth, roll and lurch manoeuvres before it docked.

"Do you have a hot water bottle?"

"In this heat?" Thom asked, puzzled. "Not a chance."

"Then do you have a fan?"

"Well, as you know, I have a stalker."

Jan spluttered as soon as Thom gave his deadpan response.

"True, but she won't cool the room down."

He was inordinately pleased when Jan responded to his admittedly weak sally in a light-hearted manner. As they crossed the harbour the atmosphere had become tense and that was the last thing he wanted. That stupid comeback had reduced the tension by several notches.

"I'll open the window," Jan said. "If nothing else, it would get rid of the smell of her overpowering perfume that appears to linger around you."

"You noticed that as well?" Lois favoured a highly perfumed scent that overwhelmed any other scent or aroma in a radius of what seemed like miles. "All my flat stinks of it."

Thom stood up and held onto Jan as the passengers on the ferry made the usual surge towards the gates that would lift once the ferry was safely docked. The tide was high and so the floating gangway wouldn't be as steep as it could be, but with the wind increasing, it was rocking around a fair bit.

"Can't really miss it, can you. I even claimed it set off my asthma, and as you are well aware I don't have asthma, but the bloody woman said I would soon get used to it. Thanks and no thanks."

Thom knew he sounded bitter and frustrated. Hell, he was bitter and frustrated. It was getting to the point where if he were offered another contract, he'd be inclined to say not if Lois were anywhere near.

"Can't you say something?"

He sighed and steered Jan round a moving newspaper stand and dodged the man pushing it. "If only. But it's been made clear that Sasha thinks she's responsible for Lois and needs to give her a job. Parents overbearing and insisting she settles down and works. As Sasha is the big sis she's been roped in to help. I guess this is a way of doing it. And it's not that she's annoying anyone else, I've asked. It appears she singled me and only me out and God knows why. Plus, she's clever. Never acts up in front of Sasha or Alex. Everything proper then. I wouldn't ask any of the makeup girls or camera men to put their jobs on the line by telling it how it is so I'll just have to continue with the diversion tactics and, if you agree, play 'the this is Jan, my partner,' card."

Jan scrunched up her nose.

"Only play?"

How he wished he could read her mind.

"I hope not, but I'll abide by what you agree to."

"Quick drink on the way back?"

He hoped it wasn't delaying tactics.

She didn't reply until they had left the dock and were at the entrance to the bar they had decided to stop at before heading home. "I hope not as well, but we'll see." She gave him a smile. "Lead me to the grub."

Halfway up the stairs she stopped and turned to stare at Thom. "Hold on a sec. I've had a thought."

"Really? You?" Thom feigned astonishment. "No…"

Jan scowled. "Be serious. Think what you've just said. That all your flat stinks of it."

"Yeah?" Thom nodded. "It does. Even after I've washed the clothes."

"Next question. Has she ever been there? Visited you?"

"She's been to the door. I didn't answer it."

"Therefore, why all the flat? Why not just where the clothes you've worn are when she's been around? And, let's add to that, around and close up for more than a few seconds so the smell lingers."

Thom rocked on his heels as alarm bells didn't just ring, they jangled violently.

"Why indeed?" he asked softly. "Well, well. I think, Ms Poirot, we need to investigate further." Red-hot rage filled him. If somehow Lois had entered his flat there would be hell to pay. Sasha and Alex's sensibilities and family loyalty be blowed. It was bad enough having her around at work, but breaking and entering or whatever entering without consent was called was not going to be ignored or forgotten about. "I think I need some cameras or something. Where can I get them?"

"Night Market."

"Fancy a wee trip?"

"Why not," Jan said. "After a drink."

"Definitely after a drink." They'd only had water with their meal. Thom laughed. "Tomorrow night will do. Or…" He paused as one of the servers looked at them in query.

"I wonder if this gentleman has any idea where we can get one now?" He smiled at the man as he asked the question.

The man did, and delivered it to their table half an hour later. Thom thanked him profusely, gave him a tip along with the cost of the cameras, and showed it proudly to Jan. "If we set it up to cover the door of the apartment it will be perfect. I hope."

"That's all well and good," Jan said. "But you need to know how she can get inside. You said she got to the door the other day, but no farther. We need to consider the fact that if she is getting inside, then how? Does she have a key? Well, let's face it, she would have to. So how did she get it? We need that info."

We? I love it.

Thom stared unseeing at the view. "No bloody idea."

"Then forget about it," Jan said calmly. "We can plot tomorrow."

"Why tomorrow?" Had he missed something?

Jan smiled. A feline sexy smile that made him hard in an instant.

"I'm hoping we'll be busy tonight."

Hell, so am I. Thom grinned. "I like your style. How long until we head out?"

Jan gave him another arousing glance. One he remembered so well. "As soon as you want."

Thom picked up his pint and downed it. "Let's go."

They were halfway back to his apartment before either of them spoke.

"Shit, I hope I remember what to do," he said in a rush, and grimaced. "It's been a while."

Jan glanced up at him. "Bet you it's not longer than me."

Thom stared at her as they reached the apartment block door. "*Shall* we bet on it? Or just go with the flow?"

Jan sniggered as they got into the lift. "Let's flow."

The lift was swift and gave no time for second thoughts—or the heebie-jeebies. Something Jan was relieved about. She wanted to be with Thom, make love with him, but not have time for the what ifs. They'd been done ad nauseam. Now she just wanted to say bugger it and go for what she wanted. Everything else, including recriminations, could wait.

And she wanted to see what his flat was like. One of the perks for the main actors, according to Peggy, was the standard of the places they lived in whilst on location. Alex refused to stint on that. He said that it was important his actors could be comfortable and relax when need be. Jan knew from May and general gossip that the building they were in was supposed to be of a very high standard and Jan was interested to see if it lived up to its hype.

They exited the lift at the twentieth floor. As the door swished softly closed behind them, Thom turned to one of the doors ahead of them.

"I must admit that the chance to live in a place like this is some incentive to work out here for a few weeks." He laughed as he punched in a key code and opened the door. "Mind you let's be honest, if they'd offered me a room in some one-star hotel I'd probably still have said yes. It's a great script, a fabulous part and time spent in Hong Kong. What's not to like?" He stood back and waved his hand to usher Jan in. "Yeah, I know, except for Lois the leech. Step into my parlour said the spider. Lounge straight ahead. What do you think?"

Jan moved past him and took the few steps forward to the entrance of the room Thom indicated. Three steps inside she stopped dead. "Wow."

"If you mean the view, it is, isn't it. If you mean the aroma of eau de Lois, it's wow in a negative way."

Jan sniffed as she stared out of the picture window and drank in the view. There ahead of her was Hong Kong Island, lamps glowing, lasers flickering and lights flashing. Beams went skywards. Some from buildings, some from cars ascending the peak.

"I meant the view but yeah, I agree with this pong. It's like a very overpowering air freshener. An old dodgy one." She turned reluctantly away from the view—she could have stood there for hours, just looking—and glanced towards Thom. "Do you know who lived here before you?"

He shook his head.

"I wonder if it was Lois?" Jan mused. "Or if she helped clean it."

"Clean?" Thom laughed. "Not her. It would be classed as work. Not in our Lois' vocabulary. Might mean she broke out in a sweat. Or broke a nail."

"*Miaow*." Jan sniggered. "And they call women the catty sex."

"Yes, well, we men have our moments. Anyway, now you know what I mean. It's everywhere."

Jan thought about it as Thom waved a bottle of wine at her, and she nodded. Why not break her one-glass rule good and proper for once? She'd only had two glasses all day, and a lot of water. "Yes please, and I have another thought on the subject. Scary how many of those I'm having on a non-workday. I try not to think at all then."

"Should be a workday, though," Thom pointed out. "Anyway, what is it? Your thought."

It seemed so ridiculous the more Jan pondered, however if she didn't share her musings with Thom they would niggle her and spoil their evening and night together.

"Don't laugh," she warned him. "Or I'll take a huff and storm out, throwing my dummy after me."

"I was under the impression you'd decided I was the dummy thrower," Thom said wryly. "Okay I promise. At this moment any daft or sensible ideas are welcome. At least it means we've thought about things, so we can cross off a what-if list, or highlight them."

He had a point. Jan took a deep breath. "Two things. One, I could ring Peggy and ask her about who lived here before you. And even who the cleaners are and were. Because I reckon there are people in to clean. Secondly, when we were talking about air fresheners… What if that's it?"

"What if what is it?" Thom said. "You've lost me."

"Air fresheners. But made with Lois' scent." Jan paused and marshalled her thoughts. "I have another idea as well. You know you can get those air freshener things that let out a puff of perfume if something goes by them. Motion sensors in them. Have you seen anything like them plugged in anywhere? Because I'd bet my last toffee that somewhere you can buy ones of whatever scent you want. You know, like fake perfumes. Especially in Hong Kong. You can get most things at one of the markets if you look hard enough."

"Wow, there's a thought. Hmm." Thom shook his head. "I haven't noticed anything like that. But then as there's no one here when I'm on set, why is the scent so strong?"

That was a puzzle. Jan wandered around the room. The air con buzzed on and the scent intensified until it was almost overpowering. She gasped. It was so simple when you thought about it.

"The air con. It's coming through that."

Thom stared at her in an uncomprehending manner. Jan managed not to tut.

"Like when you go into a supermarket you sometimes smell the scent of baking bread. Supposed to entice you in or whatever. But this just sends the scent everywhere. To remind you of her maybe?"

Thom shuddered. "I don't need reminding. She bloody haunts me."

"But when you can't get shot of her perfume, whatever you try to do, you can't help but be reminded of her."

"Reminded too much. I get you. So now what?" He looked as if she'd handed him the holy grail. "How do I go on next?"

"Easy. No air con, use a fan. I bet there's a battery-powered one somewhere in case of power cuts. Then ask Peggy about it on the QT."

Thom laughed and high-fived her.

"My genius. There's a fan in the bedroom."

Jan took a deep breath. "Then maybe we better go in there."

Chapter Seven

A few weeks later, Jan stared out of the window of the elegant and superbly well-furnished and equipped cottage that was to be her home for the next few weeks and sighed at what appeared to be a misty grey cloud not far from the window.

"Bloody midges," she muttered as the cloud danced and swayed. She could, if she squinted, see the insects moving around. "Could you not at least have let me have my first evening sitting out for a while?" She'd arrived in Scotland early that morning after a plane change in London, and been met at the airport and driven north. A car would be delivered the following day, but thankfully the person she was due to help—hopefully—had thought she'd prefer not to drive straight away. As she rarely drove in Hong Kong, and the traffic conditions to say nothing of the roads were somewhat different in Scotland, she'd agreed and said thank you with relief.

She'd been even more thankful when her driver had had to manoeuvre round a broken-down tractor and trailer on a narrow road a good hour into their journey, when she could cheerfully admit she was flagging.

The midges hadn't been obliging by taking a hike—or a holiday—and after a day where she'd fought jet lag and struggled to stay awake, she'd only got as far as looking around the private patio behind the cottage and walking to check the gate in the rear wall was locked—it was—before she headed to bed. Even before the sun went down and the midges came out in force.

Eventually the few midges that had appeared early had driven her inside. With a fair few muttered imprecations she had admitted defeat, fished out a bottle from her hand luggage and drained it of the slightly flat, not so fizzy water it had contained and stood by the large picture window to growl at them. *Bloody things.*

Nevertheless, if midges were the only thing she had to complain about, she'd be happy. Jan stared at the neat, flower-filled garden behind the cottage and smiled. If nothing else good came from this sojourn, the opportunity to stay somewhere like Romansa Castle was an opportunity in a million. The cottages were almost exclusively privately owned and rarely did anyone else get the chance to occupy one. Zac Moncrief, the relatively new owner of the castle, had explained the setup to her after she'd arrived and they'd met for the first time. He had also explained that two of the cottages still belonged to the hotel and were kept for special occasions and therefore she'd got the use of one of them. Who was in the other—if anyone—wasn't mentioned. Nor where it was. There were several dotted about the grounds, the nearest one to her just visible behind a high privet hedge.

She and Zac had talked about trivialities. For instance, where the sporting activities were. Jan wasn't sure if she'd need to find some of them. Real tennis and croquet weren't in her remit. The swimming pool, gym and spa were. There was an office for her in the hotel if she needed it and there was also one in the cottage—"more private". Zac had mentioned her everyday living necessities would be provided. She just needed to put a food request into the hotel and it would be brought to her there and then or the following day if it was something they didn't stock.

Zac had grinned cheerfully. "*We do a weekly online shop for people—but for you, we'll get it as and when you need. Let us know and we'll deal with it. Part of the package.*"

Jan had nodded. "*Thank you.*" She had no intention of putting *everything* she needed on a shopping list for the hotel. Some things she would purchase herself—online herself—which, now she thought of it, could be a bit like a slap in the face to Zac if he found out—or in person depending on the circumstances. There was no way her favourite deodorant, shower gel or sanitary products were going on the list. Even if it made whoever did the online shop think she was a dirty sod.

"*We've put some basics in your store cupboard, fridge and freezer, but I did wonder if you'd prefer to come to the hotel tonight to eat?*" Zac had asked. "*As we didn't know your specific likes and dislikes, feel free to ask for alternatives.*"

Jan had thanked him for the information, declined the offer of a meal politely, with the information she might fall asleep in her soup if she did, and asked if he would mind if she took a rain check until the following evening, when she hoped she'd be more alert. Zac had agreed straight away, admitting he well knew what jet lag was like, and taken her immediately to her new, temporary, home.

She yawned as the sun began to dip behind a row of trees a good distance away and remembered she hadn't checked what Zac considered to be staples. He might not think satsumas, Kenyan coffee and chocolate digestives came into that category. Jan was damn sure they did.

Reluctantly she turned from the view and headed into the kitchen to explore.

Five minutes later, she sat down on a chair next to the kitchen table with a thump. Zac and the castle's idea of necessities far exceeded her own. There weren't any satsumas, but there were other types of citrus fruit, plus grapes and soft fruits. Three packets of biscuits, two types of bread with butter, low-fat spread, jam and marmalade. She'd noticed bacon alongside sausages and eggs and some ready meals with a note they were made on site.

There was enough food to feed a family of four for a fortnight, as her mum would say. That reminded her, she needed to contact her parents. Typical that now she was in Scotland they were travelling on the continent in their motorhome, though her mum assured Jan not on purpose to miss her. The van—affectionately called Clara, no one had the foggiest idea why—was their pride and joy, and they went away in her as much as possible. Her mum had given Jan a rough itinerary of where they intended to go and when. They spent at least half of every year in her. It didn't appeal to Jan, but she was glad it did to her mum and dad.

Jan yawned. When she got the energy she'd get up, get her phone and find out where they might be. If they were somewhere remote, a connection could be dodgy. There was also the fact that the itinerary was, as her mum had indicated, rough, and could be changed at very short notice.

She better check in there and then before she dozed off. Jan found her phone after a scrabble through her oversized tote and a few seconds of panic. It had slipped out of the pouch she kept it in and was at the bottom of the bag along with several tissues—luckily clean ones—a notebook, pen and pencil and a few squashed toffees.

Something else to add to my to-do list. Tidy tote. She scrolled through her notes and grinned. Helpful as ever. The information from her mum for the week was simply, 'no idea, will let you know'. She sent a quick text saying she'd arrived and yawned again. It was no good, bed beckoned. Better to have a proper sleep, even if it was hours too early by Scottish time, and be semi alert the following day, than eat something she didn't really want, force herself to stay away and be a zombie.

Jan headed for the largest of the bedrooms and stared at her as yet unopened suitcases. Where the hell was her nightie?

Sod it. She knew where her toilet bag was. A quick wash and teeth brush would do. Jan noticed the luxurious robe hanging in the wardrobe. She'd sleep in her birthday suit and worry about unpacking when she woke up.

* * * *

Thom boarded the plane for Heathrow in a pensive mood and pondered about what he had heard Sasha discuss with Alex the day before and how things could go wrong in Scotland if the crap wasn't sorted. Not the best thing to hear when it involved his livelihood. They'd talked about people not being cooperative, arsy owners and why they were bothered about being unable to use things for a few hours. It was unfortunate they'd moved away before he had a chance to hear anything else he might find useful.

He'd missed Jan more than he was prepared to admit after she'd headed off to places supposedly unknown to him. The mystery of the apartment's smell had been easily solved. Peggy discovered the air fresheners were of a similar scent to Lois' perfume. That begged the question that who on earth would like to smell like an air freshener? There was no accounting for taste.

Lucky for him, Lois hadn't been around a lot, and he admitted how much happier the atmosphere at work had been. Peggy had told him the woman wasn't gone for good, but had made a brief visit to Singapore and wasn't due back until the day after Thom flew out. Great news. He hoped his plane wouldn't be delayed and they wouldn't bump into each other at the airport.

Luck was on his side. He settled down in his seat, accepted the drink offered to him and decided he could get used to travelling long haul if it was in business class. The leg room alone was enough to make him metaphorically weep with joy. No more knees around his armpits. He might not be *the* star of the series, but Alex and Sasha treated him well.

Actually, he reflected as he buckled his seatbelt, listened to the announcements and realised he understood a little of them in both languages, they treated all the cast and crew in a decent and thoughtful manner. It was only Lois who was the fly in the ointment.

The plane began to taxi towards the runway and Thom took his last look at Hong Kong—he hoped not for ever. He hadn't done half of what he would have liked to do. On the other hand, he *had* met up with Jan again and, fingers crossed, they seemed to be getting on well.

Very well.

After a night of reconnecting with each other, of long, slow lovemaking and sated sleep, she'd been apologetic when she told him she still wasn't able to say where exactly she was going for work and why. She'd promised to keep in touch, and arranged to see him somewhere as soon as possible. If she had thought about spending their day off together, she didn't say so, and after breakfast she'd left him with a kiss and a hug.

Thom had bit back all the negative things he would have liked to have said and merely nodded. It wouldn't have been fair to add pressure.

The seatbelt sign flashed off and he stretched, prepared to enjoy himself and not think about how, where and when they would meet. He had a job to do as well, and after a few days' break with Arietta and Moss, he'd be in the thick of things.

Fighting baddies and midges. The next segment of the film was to be filmed in Scotland. He'd also been told that they were going to be checking out somewhere they could possibly use in the series, if it materialised. Specifics weren't mentioned.

It could be near Jan, but then, contrary to what some people thought, there was a lot of Scotland north of the Central Belt—the area where Glasgow and Edinburgh were situated. Thom well remembered when he'd worked as a tour guide in his student days, a tourist had informed Thom that he was taking his family to John O'Groats, the most northerly point in the UK, then on to Skye, before returning to Edinburgh. All in one day. He'd assumed there would be motorways covering all the route. Thom had done his best to disabuse him, and explained both the distance and the conditions of the various roads. The tourist had appeared sceptical and Thom wondered if the man had thought that for some reason Thom was lying. He'd never found out.

Accepting the menu and choosing some food he fancied, Thom settled down to flick through the in-flight entertainment and sip on a gin and tonic. Once he'd eaten he'd get some sleep and pass the journey with his eyes closed.

He was looking forward to meeting up with his sister again. Arietta had promised she wouldn't be in the middle of writing her next book—she'd recently sent off a manuscript to her agent—and had said she wanted to pick his brains about an idea that was rolling around her brain. They had exchanged the usual friendly brother and sister sarcastic banter about he didn't know she had one and Arietta retorting that was because he didn't possess one.

He missed his sister. Not only because she nagged him about the state of his clothes, but also for her clear-headed thinking, unspoken sympathy and levelheadedness. Even so, there was always a fight over his old, faded and well-worn T-shirts. There was no way he was about to throw out a long loved, not quite ragged Rolling Stone's T-shirt from the 70s given to him by their dad. Arietta had taken one look at them and called them rags. Thom had declared that some could almost be considered heirlooms, although he accepted a good number had seen better days. However, there was no way he was throwing them away. They had compromised. Several did go into the rag bag, others back into the chest of drawers to live—or be worn—another day. Or, he acknowledged, saved just because!

A couple of them had accompanied him to Hong Kong, but there he had admitted they really weren't fit to be worn in public and he'd headed into town and replenished his stock.

His favourite, faded, AC/DC one had been washed and put away.

Until Jan had put it on before they'd eaten breakfast.

Enough. This is not the time or the place. Thom finished his meal and settled down to pass the next few hours fast asleep. Arietta had promised to meet him when they reached Heathrow. Then a few days' catch up and she was accompanying him to Scotland. Moss had already headed north.

Thom was looking forward to all of it, especially as Jan was already in the country. He wasn't even fazed by the drive they had decided to undertake. Not because of the distance—anything but. That was several hundred miles, and the last few dozen of those were on narrow roads. But because it then gave him a car that he knew would cope with the traffic and any foul weather that they met, or had to contend with. It might be summer, but that meant nothing. You could easily get all four seasons in an hour.

Thom put his seat into bed mode and settled to sleep.

* * * *

A good night's sleep worked wonders. Jan woke just after seven a.m., and for a brief second had no idea where she was. Then it came back to her. A cottage. Romansa Castle. A day off and the work she was about to undertake. Whatever it precisely was.

The words 'day off' amused her. She had a lot to do in those few hours. Unpack, sort out what essentials she needed, speak to Arietta and discover if her friend knew where she was. A mile or so away from Moss and Arietta's home in the area, but as far as she knew Arietta wasn't there. Send a note to Thom and let him know she had arrived at her destination, and discover what Zac really wanted her to do. 'Be prepared' wasn't solely reserved for Scouts.

She rolled out of bed and headed to the coffee pot. Coffee followed by a shower and she'd be raring to go. Almost raring, she corrected herself. At least one more cup of coffee after the shower would be needed before she started to go through her agenda.

* * * *

Showered, dressed and suitably refreshed, Jan headed to her new office in the cottage, admired how it was set up and opened her laptop. First to scroll through her messages, answer those that were urgent and ignore the rest to be dealt with later. Then, satisfied there was nothing left in her inbox that needed to be replied to there and then, she began to read the folder Zac had prepared for her once more.

Nothing had changed.

It was a mess. A load of rubbish combined with a lot of egos and people who thought rules didn't apply to them—or they could bend them.

Why she was required, Jan could not comprehend. To her it was obvious that certain things had to be adhered to and there could be no deviating from them. Why it was thought possible she had no idea. Surely Zac understood that?

Did he just want her to be the sacrificial offering to the owners? What did he think she was? She wasn't a lawyer or a miracle worker just, she guessed, what people called a troubleshooter. She preferred the title Administration Manager.

Jan shut the folder with a thump. She would ignore it until the following day and unpack instead. After all, she'd better find something to wear for the meal that night, as well as clothes more appropriate to business meetings than the leggings and loose shirt she wore at that moment.

The well-designed walk-in wardrobe swallowed up the clothes and accessories she'd brought with her, and Jan chuckled as she stowed her suitcase in one corner and put her few pairs of shoes in the racks provided. They all looked very lonely. Maybe she needed a trip to the city to give them some friends.

"That, my girl," she said out loud, "is a very lame excuse to go shopping." Not that she needed any excuse. Jan had promised herself a trip to the well-known department store where a large percentage of ladies purchased their underwear. She needed to do a stock-up of knickers and bras to say nothing of other staples like jeans and T-shirts. It was probably just as well she had been given a boost to her salary. Her credit card would be taking several hits.

That was for another day, though. First, she had to collect the car that would be arriving for her by lunchtime and, she decided, go for a short drive to reacquaint herself with the single-track Scottish roads she knew she'd have to drive on. Once upon a time she'd have navigated them without a second thought but these days... Jan grimaced at herself in a mirror. She was older, if not much wiser, and the way some people drove them—as if it was one way and there was no other vehicle in a ten-mile radius—gave her the heebie-jeebies. But get used to them she must. There was no way she intended to be dependent on other people to get around.

Not that she thought she'd have a lot of time to spare for galivanting. It was more for when she needed to go to the chemist or go to choose her own baked beans or ready meal. It was good to know she could head up to the hotel if she didn't fancy cooking, but Jan had an idea she'd be ready for some 'me time' after work each day. Be antisocial and not have to interact.

Maybe today she could go for a swim and head back to the cottage for a curry and a good book. Finish off with an hour of knitting or needlework. Both things relaxed her and she enjoyed them.

Typically, whilst she'd packed and decided what was necessary and what wasn't, she'd dithered over what leisure activities she might fancy indulging in as she contemplated her plans.

The list of those activities didn't fill her with joy. Once her cases were emptied, Jan realised she'd forgotten the tapestry hanging she was working on. She was halfway through it and it would have been a good hobby to do in the evenings. She groaned and made a mental note to look up online what she could get as a stand-in.

At least I have some knitting. At the request of Audie, Arietta's stepdaughter, she was knitting a big sloppy jumper in colours Jan thought clashed and Audie said was all the rage. Where exactly that rage was Jan had no idea, but she'd agreed, mentioned nothing about needing sunglasses when she knitted and now admitted that actually it didn't look half bad. A promise that she would try to finish it before winter looked as if it could be upheld.

The ring of the doorbell brought her out of her reverie and she headed to open it to a smiling man holding a set of car keys and some documents for her to sign.

Fifteen minutes later she was in possession of a smart—and new—four-by-four, had had a lesson on what was what—luckily with no mansplaining—and was debating whether to go out then or later.

Sod it, now.

Jan collected her jacket and handbag, checked she had her phone and purse, put the nearest town in the sat nav and headed off down the drive. It was funny how everything you'd ever known about driving somewhere came back to you. Before long she'd got back into the rhythm of driving on the left. Hong Kong was also a drive-on-the-left city, but as she rarely drove there, her driving tended to be on holiday and on the other side of the road.

Not that on the first few miles of road from the hotel there was a lot of difference between left and right. Checking for traffic around bends and keeping a good look out for any animal that might fancy a quick dash across the road in front of the car, hoping no itinerant tourist forgot where they were and that the passing places didn't have some idiot parked in them, she drove competently on, hummed along with whatever tune was on the radio, and listened to the sat nav.

It wasn't long before she reached the small town closest to the hotel complex. First thing was to find somewhere to park and hope at least one or two shops were open. Then a leisurely browse and maybe a coffee with an indulgent piece of shortbread or a yummy. The sugary bun was full of calories she didn't need, but it had been so long since she'd had the chance to try one. Mind made up, Jan manoeuvred the car into a parking space, got out and locked it and headed up the only street that appeared to have any shops—or many people on it.

It might not be busy and looked to have a limited shopping area, but Jan was happily impressed with the facilities. She wandered around the euphemistically called supermarket and bought a few things she'd need. Some tampons and deodorant and, to her delight, the type of hair shampoo and conditioner she preferred. With them tucked away in her bag, Jan headed towards a shop which had a café sign outside it, only to be diverted by another board with 'Cally's Crafts' written on it in a flowing script.

It was too much to resist. Jan changed directions and opened the door.

Talk about an Aladdin's cave.

The shop might be tiny but its range of crafts wasn't. Tables and shelves were crammed with every type of craft Jan could think of, plus several she'd never seen before. At one end of the room a myriad of colours spilled from silk, satin and cottons. Next to where she stood a set of shelves held every colour of wool imaginable. Alongside was a handwritten note. 'If we haven't got it, we'll get it.'

On one wall tapestry cottons and embroidery silks filled tiny cubby holes along with the tapestries and embroidery cloths, and beneath it a box of patterns for sewing, knitting and crochet sat with a label 'make me an offer' attached to its sides.

Jan loved it. A small dark-haired woman of about Jan's age popped up from behind a counter at the end of the room. Jan blinked. If colour was the theme of the shop, the woman carried it to extremes. Shades of blue, green, red and orange all vied with each other to stand out the most in her skirt. In contrast, her top was black.

The effect was startling *and* stunning.

"Hi, I'm Cally. Welcome to my… Jan?" Cally took a step forward and peered at Jan. "Jan Fraser?"

"Yes. I'm sorry, you've got the better of me. I don't recognise you." She didn't know the name either.

Cally laughed. "I do look a bit different from junior school. We both played in the junior netball team at Lochcraig High. You were centre and I was wing attack. I was Catherine Black then. Still am, now I come to think of it, but I prefer Cally."

A tiny memory began to form as Jan stared at the woman in front of her. "You had long plaits and couldn't half run fast. Lived up the hill near the library? Dog called Tosh or Tash?"

"That's me," Cally replied cheerfully. "Tash. Missed her dreadfully when we moved to Australia when I was fourteen. She stayed with my nana. I came back to go to textile college. Now here I am, living my dream." She winked. "Well, one of them. I wouldn't mind a hot, hunky man around. Even if was just to bring the coal in." She rolled her eyes and made kissing noises. "Have to love a man who can warm…your feet. The one I have my eyes on is dragging his. Feet."

Jan burst out laughing. "The pictures that conjures up. Do I know who you have in mind?"

"Well," Cally said with an impish grin that Jan immediately warmed to, "wouldn't mind a bit of Moss Kirby, but he's spoken for. Thom Clare maybe? But guess he'll never come into my orbit. Suppose I'd best settle for Dougie Hogg. He's been asking me out for ages but he's the polis, and every time we agree on a date something pops up."

Jan raised her eyebrows and grinned.

Cally howled. "Agh, lordy. Does sound a bit dodgy, doesn't it?"

"It does, but I know what you mean. "

"How about you?" Cally asked. "Any significant other?"

How to answer that? "Sort of maybe, early days. An old flame I've met up with. Taking it slowly," Jan said carefully. "Don't want to jump in and all that."

"Best way," Cally replied cheerfully. "Anyhows, what can I do for you? Anything takes your eye you cannae reach, give us a shout. Want a coffee while you look round?" The more she spoke the more pronounced her accent was. A lilting mix of Scottish and Australian.

"Love a coffee, just browsing."

"In the area for long?" Cally asked as she disappeared into what Jan presumed was a backroom or a kitchen of sorts.

How on earth should she reply? Jan hadn't had a chance to discuss what she should say her reason for being around was. "Not sure yet." She thought frantically. How she hated to have to prevaricate. "Will go with the flow."

"Well if the flow stays around here, I live above the shop and you're welcome to drop in," Cally said as she returned to the shop and handed Jan a mug of coffee. "Usually about."

The mug amused Jan. Inscribed on it were the words, 'crafty is as crafty does'.

"I'll remember." Jan took a sip of coffee and did her best not to grimace. Sludge was a better description. It was obvious coffee making didn't come under the heading of crafts and wasn't one of Cally's talents.

Cally must have noticed Jan's swiftly masked expression because she made a face. "Crap, isn't it. I can't make coffee to save myself and my all-singing, all-dancing, do-it-all-and-you-just-drink-it machine gave up and died on my last night. This was made in a cafetiere. I followed the instructions on the side of the coffee pack." She wrinkled her nose. "I think. Want tea instead?"

Jan shook her head. "I have had worse," she said diplomatically. "And I'll need to head back soon. I just saw your shop and realised I could do with a tapestry kit. I forgot mine."

"Big, small, in between?" Cally waved her hands at a stand covered in packets that held everything you'd need. "A kit or bits?"

"A kit, it's easier for now." Jan thought for a second. She usually designed her own, so a pack would be a novelty. "A cushion cover, I guess." That would keep her occupied, if she ever got any spare time. The more she thought about it, the more she reckoned the next few weeks were going to be full-on.

* * * *

Jan stared at the man sat across the table from her. They'd had a superb meal and chatted like old friends.

Until Zac had pushed his coffee cup to one side. "I don't want to talk business until tomorrow, not really, but just before we met I got an email from the damned people. This perhaps TV series is beginning to get on my nerves. They want to send their own communicator over, before the people in charge arrive. Someone for you to, ah, communicate with."

"That sounds feasible." Or it would when she knew exactly what might be expected of her. "When is he or she coming?"

"Week on Thursday. A Ms Nimmo. Lois Nimmo. Ring any bells? You look puzzled. Or is that alarmed."

Jan blinked. It couldn't be. Could it? But Lois wasn't a common name. If only she knew what Lois the Thom hunter's last name was. There had been no reason to find out.

Damn, blast and bugger it. That's all I need. I'll have to find out exactly how much authority I've got.

"Um, could be either. Or both. I hope I don't, I'm afraid I do. I'll have to say if I'm afraid, well, goodness help us all."

"Clear as mud," Zac commented. "Any chance of clarification?"

"Probably. When do Alex and Sasha get here?" Her notes had mentioned them, and she'd realised it must be to do with the film and series Thom and Moss were involved in.

Zac blinked. "A couple of days after. They want a week to look around, then do some shooting and to see if the area works. If it does, we negotiate for next year. If we can. A lot depends on you helping everyone to see the positives in it all."

Great, that was all she needed. Jan nodded. "We'll see what people's arguments for and against are, then—" She knew she didn't sound very positive. That was because she wasn't.

"But that's not for tonight," Zac said firmly. "Enough workspeak. There's time enough for that tomorrow. Want a liqueur?"

"No thanks." Jan shook her head. She suspected the following few days were going to be hectic. "That was superb but I'm flagging. I want to be bright and raring to go in the morning. I'll come over to the office here for nine, shall I?"

"Make it ten. I'll be through with our weekly staff meeting by then and all being well l can give you my full attention."

She nodded and stood up. "Um, could you find out if the Lois who is coming *is* related to Sasha? Because she is, there could be trouble, as I mentioned."

Zac raised an eyebrow in query as he also stood.

"Not with me per se," Jan reassured him. "However, if it *is* her, she's got her sights set on Thom Clare and anything he does to rebuff her is like water off a duck's back."

Zac whistled. "I wish I'd said no to this bloody idea straight out. Shit. It's getting more complicated every day. Do the crew know that?"

"The crew do, but I can't say, as in I have no idea, with regards to Alex and Sasha. As Lois is Sasha's sister I got the impression people were loath to say much. It's a flaming nightmare," Jan said forcefully. "I was roped in by a mate to run interference one weekend. Hell on wheels."

"Did it work?" Zac asked in a speculative way Jan mistrusted.

"Not really. She doesn't seem to know or care he's not interested. If she could glue herself to him she would. Even made sure the air freshener in his flat smelled like her perfume. And boy does it reek."

"Good grief." Zac sounded shocked. "Aah, and you know this how?" He gave her a speculative look.

Damn. She'd dropped herself in it well and truly. Jan decided that some truth was better than none.

"We were at uni together. Thom Clare and I. My mate is his sister. She's married to Moss Kirby, as I'm sure you know." Jan didn't wait for Zac to reply. "I hadn't seen Thom for years until recently when we met by accident in Hong Kong when I was out with friends. The wife of a bloke I work with works for the film company and was out with us then. Of course, when the Lois problem arose I was around and after she begged a bit I agreed to try and help. Not sure how much help I was." She considered for a second. "I did wonder if the fact we looked to all intents and purposes that we were interested in each other made her all the more determined."

The more she thought about it the more feasible it sounded.

"Hmm." Zac poured out two more cups of coffee in a preoccupied way. "Could be."

He slid one across the table to Jan, who wondered if she could pour it into a plant pot. Her nerves were jangling without any more caffeine needed.

"Now it seems she's on her way here. And you're here already," Zac commented as he stirred his coffee. "I wonder if she knows that?"

Jan had wondered that as well, but had no idea why she would. "She's got no reason to. Even Thom doesn't know."

"How come?"

If Zac didn't remember the clear rules laid down before she'd even got an inkling of what and where the job she was about to undertake was, there was something seriously wrong with this whole setup. Did that mean she could head off on holiday sooner rather than later? Jan hoped so.

"The contract I signed with you was on a need-to-know basis and had a non-disclosure clause," she pointed out. "Therefore, the only people who know I'm here are you, me and my boss. With a statement to my solicitors in case I go inexplicably missing."

Zac's head went back as if she'd hit him. "That, I never thought of. I was more concerned with keeping all the arguments quiet."

"They're quiet now but I'll have to let people know I'm here," Jan warned him. "My parents, Moss' wife will need to know. Can you imagine if I accidentally bumped into Arietta? That's not fair. All I need to say is I'm here to help out for a few weeks as, ah…as…" She had no idea how thy could phrase her role.

"We'll think of something," Zac assured her. "Go ahead and tell them where you are. Maybe just say a special project?"

"Okay, will do. Oh, and I met an old schoolfriend today. Though I just said I was in the area for a while and gave no specifics. I'll probably meet up with her, though. She owns the craft shop in town."

Zac nodded. "We'll worry about it tomorrow. I agree you'll need to keep people informed and we'll need to think up a suitably ambiguous title for you. Maybe a new information officer. Letting people know about what's in the area and so on. There's enough information around that you'll not need to do a lot with regards to that."

Jan stood up. "Sounds good." She wasn't sure it did, but they would see soon enough. She'd better mug up on what was where, just in case. "Then, if that's all right with you, I'm off to bed." She waved her hand at him. "No need to come with me. It's not far."

"It might not be far but it's late and it's dark," Zac said firmly. "My mum always said a lady should be looked after."

He accompanied her to her door and waited until she went inside.

Jan listened to his footsteps retreating on the gravel. A nice man, but not for her. She suspected he felt the same way about her as she did for him.

And he was, for now, her boss. She had a rule never to get tangled with a boss in any way.

She sighed as she thought of the one person she wouldn't mind getting tangled with. Tomorrow she would tell Zac that Thom had to be given the news of where she was and why. It was important to Jan, and now she thought even more important to forewarn him about Lois' presence. If it was the same person, but Jan was of the mind there couldn't be two Loises working for the same film company. Especially as the place she would be based in was where Thom would be filming.

There was nothing she could do about it then. Jan took off her makeup and headed to bed.

Chapter Eight

"It's all a bit song and dance and hell on wheels," Thom remarked as Arietta and he drove north from the airport in Glasgow towards Romansa Castle. He overtook a small red car that seemed to think the idea of the white line in the middle of the road was that it should be straddled and ignored the indignant toot on the horn its driver gave him. The guy was a menace. The minute Thom passed him, he moved back to the middle of the road.

"I wasn't due to come north yet and now it's get here ASAP from Moss and don't let anyone else but you know," Thom remarked as they left the red car far behind them. "Moss said we've only got a day or so filming there, but we need to get it done or something. Then what? He said something was up and didn't know the specifics. Have you heard any more?"

Arietta shook her head. "My beloved is about ready to spit nails. At least he's in our home and not in a hotel or something, but it is, in his words, a shit load of crap-fest. As Moss rarely swears properly, if you know what I mean, I reckon he's not a happy bunny. There's still a lot of argy-bargy over people who own property there, and Alex and Sasha are not happy about that. I think, though don't quote me, that if it wasn't for the fact he's damned sure the series could be a great success he'd just pull out and face the consequences. Don't worry, he's not going to, but I have a feeling the next few weeks are not going to be at all straightforward. Too many chiefs and all that."

Thom nodded as he passed a lorry then a minibus with 'do it the highland way' inscribed on the side. Idly he wondered what that meant. He wasn't curious enough to find out.

"I know how he feels. The concept is spot on, but sometimes they can't find their ar...ah, behind from their elbow. I wouldn't be surprised if they thought that owner would say oh, of course you can ban us from our own activities. And I discovered that from eavesdropping so it's for you and Moss' ears only." He'd inadvertently heard Alex moan to his wife. They had been standing outside the makeup area. "Crazy, I bet there was bugger all discussions. Gonna be interesting, and maybe a shorter visit than I thought. Ah well, time for a holiday. no stress."

He didn't mention Lois. Having had a few Lois-free weeks, he was a lot more sanguine about the next few. Surely she wouldn't be in Scotland. There was no need. As for Jan? All he'd had was a text, saying 'See you soon tell you all then. Take care.' She'd added a couple of xxx, but he didn't intend to set a lot of store by them. Most people did that these days.

"So," Arietta said in a casual way that immediately sent his 'oh ho, what next' sense on high alert. "Did you and Jan come to blows?"

"You know we didn't, so stop fishing. And don't nag or I'll make sure you don't get told anything at all." He knew his sister, she could nag like an aching tooth until you told her what she wanted to know out of sheer preservation of your senses.

"Why would I know?" Arietta asked in what Thom assumed she had decided was a hurt and hard-done-to voice. He would call it devious.

"You two are thick as thieves. If she hadn't chatted to you about what we did, where and when, I'll be surprised." *Though not everything, please. Some things need to be kept from nosy siblings.*

"We haven't. Well, not much. She just said you saw each other a few times and might get to see each other here."

"Where here?" It was his turn to try to sound casual.

"At Ro..." Arietta's voice trailed off and she sighed. "Bugger it, now you know more than I'm supposed to say. Moss said it's part of the crap-fest but nothing else."

That made sense. He'd chatted to Peggy a fair bit when he was waiting to go on set and had discovered that Jan's vague job description covered a lot more than basic administration. According to Peggy, Jan was a genius at defusing situations that could easily become nasty. That description sounded about right for whatever he was heading into.

"I won't klype," Thom said promptly, using the slang word for telling tales. "Shall we share what we know?" He waited for an anxious few seconds until Arietta laughed.

"I'd love to say yes, but you've had all I know. Moss is almost zipped-lipped about it, except for dire, unintelligible muttering and words like 'never again'. Oh, and if they don't do something about, and I quote, 'that bloody woman' he'll quit and not sign up for anything else, even if it would make us millions. Or is that lose millions? Either way, we'd lose out. I'm guessing that whoever the bloody woman is, she must be really rattling his cage, because he swears the film is a box-office winner, and so the series would be a hit."

Thom's stomach churned. "Did he say who the bloody woman is?"

Out of the corner of his eye he noticed Arietta grimace and shake her head.

"Just that if it came to him or her staying he'd not bet on who they chose."

It sounded as if Moss was referring to Lois. *Damn and bugger.* "Did he say if she were around?"

"Nope. Why? What aren't you telling me?" Suspicion laced Arietta's tone. "Something to do with Moss?"

Thom hastened to reassure his sister. "Nope, you numpty. Me, if it's Sasha's bloody sister Lois. She's akin to a stalker. They shipped Jan in to run interference and bless her, she did. She's one of Peggy, the PA's husband's, work colleagues and a friend of Peggy's as well. She didn't know it would be me she was going to help."

"Or she wouldn't have?"

He shrugged. Arietta was fishing and he wasn't going to bite. "Who knows."

Was the shit-fest Moss referred to why Jan could be at Romansa Castle? In her troubleshooting role? Or to help out again? Half of him hoped so, the other half would prefer the next few weeks to be Lois-less.

"I am not a numpty," Arietta told him in a frosty voice she spoilt by giggling. "Not all the time. And watch it or you'll be a baby in my next book." Her historical thrillers were getting ever more popular. "One who meets a very gruesome end."

Thom laughed. "Okay, promise no more nasties. But I've a nagging feeling that it's bloody Lois of the octopus arms who Moss means. And I'm about to say enough if she's sniffing around Romansa Castle. So now we both admit that after my few days' holiday with you I'll be working there, why do they need Jan? I'm sure it's not to protect me. No point in beating about the bush. We both know it's there and it's her and Moss is anxious to get what we have to do over and done with. Yes?"

"Yeah, but we don't say we've pooled our knowledge, eh?"

"I can go with that. Now why are owners up in arms?"

Arietta told him. Thom whistled.

"Blimey, am I glad it's not my problem. Poor Jan. How's she coping?"

"No idea. I'm not supposed to know she's there yet. I suspect we'll find out soon. Only another half hour to go."

Thom put his foot just a little bit harder on the accelerator.

* * * *

Jan hummed as she walked briskly the long way through the grounds of Romansa Castle on her way to the office Zac had allocated her. Over the few days she'd been around, she had somehow created a mini-routine to do the otherwise short journey. Take the path around the pristine lawns, through the orchard, and skirt the rose garden. Have a furtive scuffle through the few crisp leaves, which she thought shouldn't be there, and head into work having had a good dollop of fresh air, which made the coffee she would pour when she reached her destination all the more delicious.

She sniffed appreciatively. The weather had been gorgeous the last few days, the sort of conditions that made her wonder why she had ever left the country. However, Jan well knew that when the forecast changed and wet, windy and downright chilly for the time of year elements arrived—as they would—she'd wish she were elsewhere. With luck, that would be well after she'd left. Whatever anyone might think to the contrary, she had no intention of being around when autumn arrived. Even if local lore insisted it could start before the end of August if the weather gods so decreed. In fact, one story her dad had told her ad nauseum when she was younger had been that the last frost of the year could be in July, but the first frost of the next year be in June. It had taken her a long while to fathom that out. The vagaries of Scottish weather. Rain, sun, snow, hail all in one day. The sun playing peek-a-boo, and sudden mists or fogs dropping down with little notice. Midges whenever they felt like appearing, day or evening.

Midges! Even the word was enough to make her itch.

Jan turned up an avenue of native trees and headed towards what had once been the stables and had been re-configured and was now used for administrative purposes. Even though she had a room designated as an office in her bungalow, Zac had also offered the choice of a room off reception in the main building or an office in what the staff called the Dung Heap. Due, it was said, that on a hot day, with the wind in a certain direction, the now long-departed manure heap seemed to still be around.

Jan liked the idea of not always working in her accommodation and took advantage of the room in the Dung Heap. So far she hadn't scented any pungent aromas, but her base was on the opposite side of the building to where the late manure pile had been situated. Her view was of the nearby formal gardens, not the old stable yard. She'd fallen in love with the spacious room and the vista spread out in front of her the first time she had seen it. When she sat at her desk, Jan was not one of the 'face a wall to concentrate' brigade. She'd like to think and stare towards the horizon when needed.

She climbed the three steps to the side door of the old stables, now officially renamed Effie Barnet House after the wife of the first owner of the castle, and headed to the communal kitchen where the dozen or so people who worked in the building met up. There they chatted or moaned depending on how their day was going and drank their beverage of choice. Someone had instigated a 'go to the kitchens and bring the goodies' rota, so three times a day food would be available. Jan was amazed how well the staff—all of the staff—were treated. No wonder people didn't leave on a whim and most stayed for years.

One of the older ladies was already in the kitchen pouring water into a cup. She smiled at Jan.

"How's it going? Getting settled in? When does the bun fight start?" All the staff knew there was a meeting the following day between people from the filmmakers and the residents, to see what everybody's concerns were and how they could be allayed. Plus, Jan privately thought, see if there could be a resolution satisfactory to everyone. After reading over complaints, concerns and pure bloody-minded comments, Jan wasn't sure there ever would be.

Jan fixed a coffee from the top-of-the-range coffee maker and smiled back. Nettie was nearing retirement and said she was dreading it.

"Thon thought of ma man under ma feet al'o the day. He's gan tae get into fishin' or else bowls."

Jan laughed. "He said or you said?"

Nettie's eyes twinkled. "We'll say it's a mutual decision to ensure marital harmony." Her voice had lost its dialect and she spoke in a soft accent with no slang words. Jan marvelled at the way she could do that. Nettie had told her it came in useful at times. "*So as not to upset some people.*" Jan knew what she meant. If a local spoke too pan loaf – that was posh – they might be considered above themselves. Too much local accent and they might be said to be taking the mickey. Sometimes, Jan reckoned, you just couldn't win.

"I'll wish you luck for later," Nettie said as she finished her coffee. "Meant to say the boss will be over with our food in a bit. Wants to chat to you. Luck there as well."

A chat was the last thing Jan wanted. She had a busy day mapped out with little time for chatting. If, of course, he really only did want a chat.

She would soon find out. She came out of her reverie to see Nettie staring at her. How long had she been in a dream?

"Thanks, I reckon I'll need it," she said wryly. "Then think of me tomorrow at seven. I swear some people would complain and object to an RAF plane flying over at nine a.m., fifty miles away in case it disturbed them. On the outside. Some of the arguments given are so ludicrous I had to read them twice. One was that it might increase the midges, and another that it might mean the lines on the car parking spaces need redoing. Their private spaces, mind you. Outside their own cottages. Not by the hotel or golf course." She grimaced as she thought of the dratted meeting. One she'd suggested so at least there could be a concerted effort to find out what both sides wanted and were or were not prepared to compromise on. "I think I'll need a drink after, and I try not to drink weekdays."

Nettie patted her shoulder. "Rules must be bent if needs must. And I must dash and see what complaints came in overnight. Yesterday's best one was that the flowers in the outer gardens weren't in full bloom. Might it have something to do with the fact they're sun-blooming ones and the sun wasn't out? I swear I'm with you over the stupid things people complain about. Right, I'm off. See you later." She bustled out and Jan heard her footsteps as she climbed the stairs to her office.

Jan poured a second cup of coffee, snagged a chocolate wafer bar—it would do until the breakfast pastries and fruit juice arrived with Zac—and headed to her own domain along the corridor. As she didn't have a formal appointment with her boss, and had no idea when he would arrive, she'd start to clear whatever was waiting for her.

* * * *

Half an hour later a polite cough made her jump, swivel around to greet her visitor and blink. It wasn't Zac who stood inside the doorjamb holding a basket of what she assumed were the morning pastries. It was several seconds before she could gather her scattered wits together and speak.

"Well, well. Look who's here." Jan jumped out of her chair and hugged the man who stood in front of her. It wasn't a total surprise to discover who he was. "What have you done with my boss, and did you bring the pastries?"

Thom laughed as he returned the hug one-handed. "Pastries and lunch basket on the table in the room down the corridor, though I filched a couple for us." He waved the paper carrier bag in the air as Jan released him and took a hearty breath. "Zac will be here in a few minutes. He was fending off a very irate bloke off who seemed to think that if he just turned up and said he wanted a room he'd get one. The last I heard was him—the bloke, not Zac—asking if Zac knew he was and Zac answering very politely with the bloke's name and saying as he had no reservation and as the hotel was full he was unable to accommodate him."

"Who was the man?" Jan asked as she relieved Thom of the bag of food and noticed two Danish pastries nestled on top of a cool bag. "What else is in the basket?"

"No idea re the bloke, never seen him before in my life. Lunch just for us. A working lunch." He grinned. "Allegedly."

The aroma was making her tummy rumble. "Do you want coffee? There's my secret stash in the cupboard and my super-duper fast maker on the shelf. I just need to jot down a couple more reminders." She'd thought of something she could mention at the owners' meeting.

"Yes please, I'll make it, do you want one?"

"Eh? Oh, um, I've got one here." Jan waved to her desk as she sat down and typed rapidly.

Thom lifted the mug and waved it under her nose. "It's cold."

"Then please." Jan smiled her thanks and promptly ignored him until she'd added what she needed to do.

She saved her work and turned her chair in the direction of where Thom sat on a settee to one side of the long floor-to-ceiling window that opened onto the gardens.

"Sorry, I'm all yours now." Heat rushed into her cheeks as she registered her words and Thom smirked.

"Oh, I do hope so."

"Shut up." She threw a pencil at him. It missed.

"Sorry, couldn't resist. Anyway, how are you? Really?"

"Frazzled," Jan confessed. "Honestly, they're all a bunch of kids. Your film lot included. I wish I'd never let May persuade me to come."

"Even if it would have meant we only had a few weeks together in Hong Kong and then no idea when we'd meet up again?"

"We didn't know we were going to meet up so soon," Jan pointed out. "Even if both of us thought it on the cards."

"Point taken. I'd hoped anyway."

"So did I," Jan confessed. "If only it wasn't for this shit-fest."

"That sounds like Moss has given you a clue." Thom drank in the sight of his beloved and mulled over her words. She looked tired and dark shadows showed around her eyes. Temper sparked in those eyes and Thom wondered just who she was ready to go head-to-head with and hoped it wasn't him.

"They spitting the dummy out?"

"Oh yes, and more. I swear, if we gave all of them everything they wanted they'd still find something to argue over. Moss didn't say anything, but it's a perfect expression. As there is no way we, or rather, the hotel lot can get everything everyone wants, it's up to me to try and find something that everyone is sort-of okay with." She grinned with a swift change of attitude. "Look out for flying pigs."

Thom laughed. "Will do. Meanwhile, I forgot to say Zac will be here around eleven and until whoever the film lot send over for the meeting, Moss and I are the only two around, and he says hi, and not coming within two hundred yards of this place. He's at home with Ari, and we're both invited for dinner tonight."

"Great, so until then?"

"Zac and you have your chat or whatever, I'll sit in the corner and be quiet and we all then think sod the lot of it and go for a round of golf."

"I don't play," Jan pointed out. "And you say you're crap at it."

"It's a good place to talk. I can pretend and you can drive the buggy."

* * * *

In the end the so-called meeting was held as they made their way round the golf course. Thom hadn't played for several months, hadn't been any good then, and was no better now. It wasn't that he didn't take any exercise—he got plenty of that in his job—but it was a different set of muscles used when swinging a club. He was better off at squash, or tennis. The banter between the three of them was cheerful and inconsequential until, as they reached halfway round the course and munched on hot sausage roll in the halfway house, Zac led them to a table set to one side of the tiny room.

"Okay," he began as soon as he finished eating. "Who knows anything about a Lois Mc…McDonald?"

"McDonald?" Jan said with a dry throat and a faint sense of nausea. "Please tell me she's not a McDonald. You didn't call her that before. You said Nimmo. No wonder she puts my back up. I'm a Fraser."

Zac laughed as Thom spluttered the coffee he'd just taken a mouthful of.

"I was told Nimmo, now informed she wishes to be McDonald. Good old ancestral history?" Zac said and shook his head. "Tell me about it. Or rather, no need. Any true Scot knows who their ancestors fought with and against. I'm informed that Ms McDonald *is* to be one of the film liaison people, and definitely will be here today." He cleared his throat. "I was also told in a separate email that you, Thom and she are *very* good friends and should be housed together."

"What!"

Coffee went everywhere as Thom thumped his mug down on the table and stared at Zac.

"Say again? No way, not a cat in hell's chance. If I had my way she wouldn't be within a thousand miles and even that is too close. That woman is a menace, a troublemaking, full-on, pain-in-the-you-know-what menace. A pest. A stalker. No, more than a stalker. A…" He stood up and began to pace, much to the alarm of two golfers who had just entered. Jan tugged at his jacket to force him to stop.

"Thom, enough. You'll traumatise everyone else."

"What?" He looked around, then sat down with a thump as Jan saw realisation dawn on him.

"Oh damn, sorry. Yeah. Just because I'm traumatised, no need to make others the same way."

"Stop the dramatics." Jan waggled her finger at him as Zac stared from one to another. "Save them for work. Honestly, Thom, behave."

Thom rubbed his hand over his chin. "Yes, Miss." He glanced at Zac. "Sorry, but that mere name gives me hives. She's a bloody nightmare."

Zac sighed. "This whole bloody thing is a nightmare. I'm beginning to wish I'd never seen Romansa Castle. As for films, tenants and molehills on the tennis court? No wonder I'm losing weight."

Jan stared at him for a second. Thom could see what she was thinking. If he was indeed losing weight, she wondered where. He had to agree.

Zac rolled his eyes at them before he laughed.

"Well okay, but I'm definitely losing sleep. Any suggestions?"

"Over Lois or lack of sleep?" Jan asked.

"Either or both. Plus owners."

"Have the meeting, get every pro and con offered, be it stupid or not, and we'll try to come to a compromise. If not..."

Thom didn't want to think what the 'if not' would be. With regards to Lois, though, he had an idea. If Jan went for it remained to be seen.

"I have an errand to run. Want to come with me?" He held his breath as Jan checked her watch.

"Why not, nothing on for a while. Be good to get away and try not to think of—well, things that thinking about probably won't solve."

"You all ready for tonight's bun fast then?" Thom asked as, arm in arm, they headed towards his car. He was proud of the way he had commandeered her, with Zac's blessing. They'd finished their round of golf early. Or rather, as Zac remarked, he had played golf and Thom played the part of a golfer. A bad one.

They'd not reached his car before Jan's mobile rang.

She glanced at the screen. "May. I better answer it, she's ringing from home. Er, where shall I meet you?"

"I'll ring in an hour." Thom kissed her cheek and got into his car. "Got to run that quick errand." He didn't say for what. "Be good, and if you see Lois, hide."

"She's not due till around five." Jan pressed answer on her phone as Thom sketched a wave and drove away. "Hi, May, how's it going?"

* * * *

Fifteen or twenty minutes later, Jan ended the call and scowled. She could have gone with Thom on his mysterious errand after all. May had rung to say that she'd heard on the grapevine, i.e. via Peggy, that Lois was telling everyone she was headed to Scotland to be with Thom. She'd decided to forewarn Jan. Jan thanked her, informed her they already knew she was on her way—but not about the especially for Thom bit—and they'd had a quick chat.

"So," May had asked cheerily. *"How are you two getting on? Thumped each other yet? Done the deed? Any good goss?"*

If it had been anyone else but her friend, even Arietta, Jan would have been inclined to take umbrage at such a loaded question. Instead, she'd laughed. *"Done the deed? Good grief, May, what an old person way of asking if we have been to bed together."*

"That's no more modern, is it?" May had said. *"Have you then?"*

"We have both certainly been to bed," Jan had said. *"I can truthfully say years ago we did indeed go to bed together and do the deed, and what an awful sentence that is. Seriously, May, we've only just met up again and are being cautious and careful."* She'd crossed her fingers.

"I should hope so. When you eventually do whatever it's called these days, I hope you are both of those."

"What?" Jan had been confused. *"What are you on about?"*

"Getting together and having sex. Careful and cautious? But things are progressing? I worry about you."

"No need, my lovely, I'm a big girl now. And if I keep eating the pastries we get for mid-morning snacks, I'll be an even bigger girl." There had been no point in upsetting the applecart by saying getting nowhere fast. May was an incurable romantic, and certain there would be apple blossoms and wedding bells whenever any of her friends entered a relationship.

After a few more minutes of general chit-chat, they'd ended the call. Which meant Jan had an hour to kill. She might as well have lunch in her cottage and go over her notes and ideas for the meeting later.

Morose and out of sorts, for no apparent reason as far as she could think—unless being thwarted of a ride out somewhere counted—she stared at the contents of her fridge and saw nothing that appealed to her.

"Jan Fraser," she said out loud in a severe voice, "you are spoilt rotten. Now just because you missed out on a drive and not being the driver, you're sulking." She refused to admit she'd wished Thom had offered to wait for her, or at least said just where he was headed. Although if he had told her, and it was a treat she'd have enjoyed, then he'd still gone without her, wouldn't that have been worse? She shook her head at her arsy attitude. *Definitely acting like an entitled brat. Enough was enough.* She made a ham salad sandwich, ate it at the breakfast bar while she read the news on her tablet, and did her best to forget Thom, the forthcoming meeting, Lois and anything else designed to give her a headache.

The thump on her door made her jump. Why would anyone be bothering her at that time of the day? With a great deal of reluctance, she closed her tablet and headed towards the door as her phone rang. She glanced at the screen. Zac.

"Hey, I'm only in the cottage. Quick lunch and back to the grindstone."

"Do not answer the door," Zac said urgently. "Not yet, and don't let her see you. That bloody incompetent Linda. What does she go and do?"

"Zac, you're confusing me. Don't let her see me? Who?"

"That Lois person. She's headed for Thom's cottage even though Linda and everyone else has been told never to divulge who is staying or where. But to make it worse, she gave her your cottage address, not his. Or does that make it better? I'm not sure."

Nor was Jan. "Shit. Right, er, not sure what to do for the best. Why on earth did Linda tell her where Thom stays, even if she got it wrong?"

The sigh Zac gave echoed through the phone. "Because she never bloody listens properly. She—Linda that is—says the Lois person told her Thom was expecting her and surely he'd remembered to tell reception? Let her in and so on?"

"She hasn't got a key, has she?" Jan said tersely. What a guddle that would create.

"Thankfully not. Linda couldn't find one. Somehow there wasn't anyone to sort that out, or anyone to drive her down in a buggy, they were all out. Lois sort of stamped her feet and said she'd walk. Linda gave her directions. To you. Silly cow."

The thumping on the door started again.

"Is that her?" Zac asked.

"No idea but I'd guess so. I'm in the hallway and not near the window." *Thank goodness.* "Thanks for the warning. If she thinks this is Thom's cottage and I'm here it might help things." Or it might not, but if she didn't answer the door, she'd never know. "Look, I'll go and confront her and let you know how it goes."

"Okay if you think that's best. You know her. I'm on my way anyway. See you in a few minutes. I *have* a buggy." He rang off and Jan headed to the door. Took a deep breath and counted to three then opened it.

Lois swung round. "Thomas, why did you not tell them I was coming? You knew… You!" She nigh-on spat the word when she saw who faced her. "What are you doing here?"

"I live here," Jan said truthfully. "What are you?"

Chapter Nine

"Do you honestly think this will work?" Jan rolled her ring finger from side to side and watched the row of diamonds and platinum sparkle and gleam. "I mean, won't she be instantly suspicious that we've suddenly become engaged, no fanfare, just me sporting these rocks? I know we intimated we were close in Hong Kong, but…" She wrinkled her nose. It was hard to put her worries into words. "Oh, I'm just stressing over nothing I hope. But—well, the visit from her unnerved me. I honestly worried about my eyes for a moment. Those talons she calls nails were pointed in the direction of my face. Thank goodness Zac arrived and told her that her room was in the main hotel, and he'd take her there. He also said if she intimidated anyone like she appeared to be doing to me, she would be asked to leave. When she tried to protest you and her were close, Zac said how nice and he'd be sure to ask you what you wanted to happen. Apologised to me for her unwarranted intrusion and almost dragged the woman away. Her last words were I hadn't heard the last of it and didn't I know how pathetic I was, hounding you. I almost did the pot, kettle, black thing. But I resisted, not sure how. Mind you, Thom, I'm not sure anything short of seeing the marriage certificate would work and even then it would be doubtful, and no, that is not a proposal." *Though if you proposed to me, it would be a different matter.* "This ring, gorgeous as it is, might not do any good."

"Rocks?" Thom said in what Jan hoped was mock affront. "Rocks! Heavens, woman, that 'row of rocks', as you call them, are high-quality sparklers. I had to pledge my firstborn and my favourite signed rugby shirt to Roddy, the jeweller. Just as well he's a mate of mine. And of course to do a wee bitty name dropping wherever possible. Remember Roddy Kilsythe? He designs bespoke jewellery for the discerning. And rich, but don't mention that bit. And before you ask, no, it didn't bankrupt me. He's a mate and I got it cheap. You know me, I'm a cany Scot and my gran was from Yorkshire. Both people who are said to be careful with their money. Therefore that means it's all sorted. Oh, and worrying is daft. She can't prove we *aren't* engaged." He winked. "Who knows, we might make it real one day, and no, that is not a proposal."

"If you say so." *As you said it wasn't for you, I doubt it.* However, it wasn't worth arguing over. Jan knew once Thom had made his mind up, it would need a good, reasoned argument to make him change it. She couldn't think of one. I wish it were for real, or why engaged and not just loving together were not strong or plausible enough. Plus, if she were honest, she rather liked the idea of trying to put a spoke or three in Lois' wheels, and the ring was exactly what she would have chosen for herself. "It's gorgeous, and I love it."

Thom appeared relieved. His next words reiterated that. "I was worried you'd not like it, and I reckon that would have showed."

"I love it," Jan told him honestly. "Just what I would have chosen. It's simple, elegant and, well, perfect. Thank you." *Even if it isn't really mine.*

He smiled and the way his eyes crinkled up at the corners sent sexy goosepimples down Jan's spine. *Every time, it gets me. Every blooming time.* Why such a simple thing had such a great effect on her, Jan had no idea. After puzzling over it, she mentally shrugged her shoulders and accepted she had that reaction to Thom.

"I hope it's insured and I promise I'll put it in the safe whenever I don't need to wear it."

"You need to wear it all the time and yes, it is insured. Now on to more business. Zac and I think, if you are agreeable, we'll keep up the charade that we both live here. I'll add a few bits and bobs and just use the other cottage for storage?"

"Really sleep here?"

"If that's okay." For once, Thom sounded very unsure.

"Of course it's okay. Then if she comes knocking again you can sort her out and I can hide behind the door." Jan grinned as Thom hugged her.

"Or I can hide behind your skirts."

"I usually wear jeans," Jan pointed out and rolled her eyes. "Now what?"

Thom did a very dramatic grimace. "Sod it! That's buggered that idea. Tell you what, we'll take turns. At being the big brave kick-ass one, and the one to stand back and get ready to blast off if need be. And, er, Zac said a united front for an early dinner? Or a late one?"

Jan pondered that. "Early, I'll not be able to eat. Late I might not want to, but I vote for late. That way we can try to hurry the meeting on. You know, rumbling tums and all that."

Thom laughed. "Go for it. I'll tell Zac we need to be done before nine, shall I?"

Jan liked that idea and said so. "Spot on. Right sorry and all that, but bloody duty calls. You coming to be my rear guard? In case octopus Lois attacks with her tentacles. Or is that talons?"

Thom shrugged. "Either or. And of course, it works both ways." He sighed. "I am so sodding sorry to have got you embroiled in all this."

Jan considered him, and his statement. "You know? Actually, I'm not. It's got us on good terms again, and I hated the sensations that we both, well, not exactly regretted everything, but were so intransigent and then not prepared to try to make amends. Me especially."

Thom kissed her hard and swift. "It works both ways, hon. I was an up-myself arrogant B with no consideration for you or anyone else. Ari didn't speak to me for a month, and my parents threatened to cut me out of their will. As I was due to get a carving from China that my grandad brought back in nineteen whenever that hurt, I can tell you. I love that wee statue. Still do. But what really did it was when I tried to ring you and it said 'number not recognised' and I thought, 'shit, what have I done'." He bit his lip. "Can I say sorry now?"

Jan's anger and hurt melted away. She had always insisted she wasn't the sort of person to hold a grudge unnecessarily. Wasn't this the time to act on that?

"You've said it and let's be honest, I was no better. Wouldn't have listened to you whatever you said. So sorry from me as well and let's not mention it anymore. Over and done with. Not another word on the subject," she added in a firm, no-nonsense voice.

Thom nodded and cleared his throat. "Not even to say I've changed my mind about a marriage and a family?"

That hit her hard. *Sod him. No way was it going to be that easy*. "Really? Wow, so have I."

She watched him go white.

"What? You don't want marriage or kids?" His hand trembled. "That's ah—" He ran his hand through his hair. "Never?"

Jan waited for the count of ten. "Now then, did I say that? A marriage will be okay. Kids? Not quite. In those days I wanted five." She smiled slowly, sensually—she hoped—and purred the words. "Now I only want one or two with a lot of practising."

Thom rocked on his heels. The minx, she always knew how to get him going. His heart rate returned to normal and his clammy skin cleared.

"I do hope I can help you practice." He lowered his voice two octaves. "Just say the word."

"Help?" She patted his shoulder, dropped her hand and gave his groin a quick—and arousing stroke. "You're the teacher. But not till after this sodding meeting. Onwards, Thomas. Gird your loins and put your armour on."

"Always." Thom looked out of the window. It was drizzling. Just what they needed. A wet and fractious group of people all intent on being awkward. Or was that doing a disservice to people who were concerned about things that were theirs? "We need coats. Mine is next door." Typical Thom thought that he didn't have a jacket with him. "I'll nip and get it."

"And get wet?" Jan made a disgusted sound. "Look, there's one in the hall cupboard. Zac said there's always a couple of jackets and brollies left for guests. Stick it on for now, and then when we can we'll do a dash and grab from your place to stash whatever we think best at mine."

He nodded and headed for the cupboard. It seemed to make sense. The jacket was a little on the large size but not enough to make anyone notice or comment, he hoped. A dark navy, it was inconspicuous and could have easily been his. "Right then, got all you need?"

Jan waved a large briefcase at him. "Well, who knows, but I have this."

It appeared to be big and bulky enough to knock someone out. He hoped it wouldn't come to that.

In a companionable silence they headed out of the cottage and into the golf buggy Zac had assured them was theirs whilst they were at Romansa Castle. It might not be the fastest of vehicles, but it was admirably suited for nipping round the estate when it wasn't walking weather, as then. Or, as Jan remarked, when you might need to make a quick-ish getaway. Not that either of them was under any illusion that it was faster than a fit person could run.

Jan climbed into the passenger side. "Over to you, if that's okay."

Thom nodded. "Sure." He loved driving the buggy almost as much as he disliked golf. If only he had the chance to do the first a bit more often—and at least get to enjoy a round of golf, even if he was rubbish at it. It was good exercise if nothing else.

Not so much if you drive round the course. That made his lips twitch.

In a companionable silence, they headed up the rosebush-edged drive that led from their two cottages towards the castle. A five-minute walk by the paths that cut through the gardens, it didn't take a lot less by the buggy, but in the drizzle they both called 'dreich', it was a lot more convenient.

"I spy a Lois by the front porch," Jan said as they swung around the last corner and parked in one of the designated spots. "She pops up everywhere. She should be called Jack, as in jack-in-the-box."

Thom groaned as he got out and waited for Jan to join him. "Not everywhere I hope. I like privacy in the loo and when we're making love."

Jan reddened. "The images."

"Half great, half gruesome." He took her briefcase from her and winked. "Never say I'm not a gentleman."

"As if I would." She took the arm he proffered and together they walked up the three steps to where Lois in effect barred the way indoors.

"Thomas, we will sit together." She ignored Jan. "Sasha and Alex are late. We will represent the company."

"Hi, Lois, sorry, no can do," he said cheerfully. "That's not my job. I'm Jan's right-hand man tonight. But I'm sure there will be plenty of places for you to sit."

"We need to be together," Lois insisted in a harsh voice. "You will not sit with her. Your place is with me."

"Don't you tell me what I can and can't do," he replied in a voice as hard as hers. "I'm not at this meeting on behalf of the film, I believe you are. I'm here with my fiancée to support her if need be. I might be interested in the outcome, but that's it. I'm impartial. Unless anyone tries to impugn my fiancée's integrity and impartiality." *Good lord, I sound as if I've swallowed a dictionary.*

"Fia…" Lois looked at the hand Jan waggled in front of her and paled. "It is a lie."

"No, it's not." Arietta appeared next to them and kissed Jan and Thom soundly before she tugged them. "I'm so excited. My best friend and my brother together. It's taken them long enough, mind you, but at last they've done the deed and got engaged."

Lois gulped. Thom almost felt sorry for her until she spoke. "You must have forced him. Why would he want to d—"

"Enough." Thom stopped her mid-word. "Lois, enough. You're making a fool of yourself. Go and find a seat and leave us alone. Ari, do we save a seat for Moss?" He deliberately turned his back on Lois.

"Yeah, he won't be a sec."

"He's here now," Moss said as he caught up with them. "Hi, you two, lots of congrats. Audie says she's chuffed to bits and if you're having bridesmaids and want her as one—nothing like hinting, eh?—no soppy clothes please."

Thom laughed. "Duly noted." Out of the corner of his eye he watched as Lois hesitated for a second then moved slowly away and inside the castle.

Jan let her breath out in a long whoosh. "What is it with her? Why is she so insistent?"

Thom shrugged. "No idea. I certainly haven't given her any encouragement. I was introduced to her when I first went on set. Shook hands, said pleased to meet you, all the normal things you say. Then I bought her a coffee when we bumped into each other one day in town. She was a bit pushy and overfamiliar but I took that to be her way, you know? Thought no more about it. But then she acted like we'd had a date. She just latched on to me and did her best to be around at every opportunity possible. I asked one of the makeup team if she'd been like it with anyone else and they didn't think so. It's a mystery." One he'd prefer not to have, but then, as his mum would say, you can't always have everything you want. "It's a bummer."

"One we'll have to try and solve," Jan said. "After this bleeping meeting. I'm off to start encouraging people to sit down so we can start and get it over and done with."

"Getting ready for a bumpy ride?" Arietta asked as they all headed for the conference room that Zac had deemed the most appropriate place to hold the meeting. Not too large as to be intimidating, and not too comfortable for people to settle down. That, he had said, would encourage everyone to head off home and not loiter once the main business was over. He was, he'd insisted, in no mood for that. He'd want his dinner. A hungry Zac was not something anyone would relish. Thom knew that from past experience.

Jan grinned at Arietta. "I've got my armour on and my hero to rescue me if needed. Right, you lot, grab those chairs and I'll see what's what."

Thom winked. "Go slay 'em."

* * * *

It was easy to sound confident, not so easy to be so when you were faced with a lot of people glaring at you. It appeared that whatever side of the debate—

argument—you supported, Jan and Zac were the enemy.

"You look cool, calm and collected." Zac spoke softly and kept his back to the audience as he did so. "Ready for the fray?"

"As I'll ever be. Let's get started." Jan had no doubt the next hour or so wasn't going to be easy. But the sooner they got everyone's views the better. She sat outwardly composed as Zac called everyone to order.

"This," he said, "is a preliminary meeting to hear your views regarding your concerns about a film company stopping here and filming for a couple of weeks next year. There will be two or three days' activity up on the hills this coming week but that will not affect anyone here. It's—" He stopped speaking as the door opened and two people walked in with whispered apologies. Zac nodded his acknowledgement as the couple, Alex and Sasha, sat down next to Lois. That was a relief as Jan had been informed someone would answer questions on behalf of the film company. Thank goodness it appeared it wouldn't be Lois.

Lois whispered something to her sister and Sasha nodded and patted the other woman's arm.

What's that all about? Jan didn't have time to mull it over before Zac introduced her, and she stood up. Quietly, Nettie sat down to one side of the platform. Her role was to record everything said, both by a written—typed—transcript and by recording it. She nodded to Jan that she was ready.

Once Jan began to speak, her confidence grew. There was no need to be nervous. She knew her role and how to control the way the meeting progressed.

"Hello, I'm Jan Fraser," she began. "I'm here as an impartial chairperson. To discover what people's fears are. To outline what would happen if filming does take place. What wouldn't. How things would work and to get your views about anything and everything connected to those two weeks. First of all, I'm going to ask a representative from Salexco Films to join me and let them explain what from their point of view exactly would happen. You can then ask questions. After which, Zac—Mr Moncrieff—will offer his point of view and the reasons it would perhaps benefit the castle and the area, which includes your homes. Then it will be over to you once more for questions and opinions. I will say now," she went on in a no-nonsense way, "that if you choose not to be polite you will be asked to leave. This will not develop into a slanging match. Mr Cheng, over to you."

Alex stood up and headed towards Jan. The look in his eyes—he appeared furious about something—startled her, but she gave him a brief smile and held out her hand.

He shook it then immediately dropped it as if she'd scalded him.

Ah well. Jan was philosophical. You couldn't be liked by everyone.

"Ladies and gentleman, please give Mr Cheng your attention." She took a step back and sat down to get ready to listen and make any notes about questions she might need to answer.

It was a long hour. Alex spoke eloquently, and at length, and fielded all the questions put to him. However, Jan could tell people weren't satisfied by his answers. A tall gentleman dressed in tweeds stood up.

"Ernest Donaldson on behalf of the owners. Young man," he began in the sort of tone often used by someone of authority. Clear and confident. "You have told us what you want, but not at all how it will benefit the owners here. The hotel can have upgrades you say, but not what, when and how. As far as I can see, you want to take over the hotel for a month, and during that month, for at least two weeks, you want to bar us from using the facilities we pay for. All of them. You say there will be compensation, which is all well and good, but you also say no visitors will be allowed anywhere in the complex. Does that mean we are allowed no visitors? "

"I…" For the first time Alex appeared flustered. "We would need to discuss who could be allowed here."

"You cannot dictate who we can see or invite into our homes. That is not acceptable. Nor is your suggestion that we could move out," Mr Donaldson said stringently. "To where? Most of us live here, we do not merely nip in and out on the odd occasion. Are you expecting us to let you have our houses as well?"

"It would be a help if…" Alex started but the older man cut him off with a slash of his hand.

"I can tell you now, categorically, under no circumstances would I let strangers live in my home. Or move out so you can take over."

He made the sort of *pshaw* noise Jan admired. *If only I could do that.*

"I must say," Ernest Donaldson continued in his strong emphatic manner, "this is not what we expected when we were asked if we would mind you here for a week or so and I was told there would be very little disruption to our lives. Mr Moncrieff, were you aware of these draconian demands when this was first broached?"

Well done, Mr Donaldson. Now what?

"I was not," Zac said with the ring of truth in his voice. "Which is one reason I wanted this meeting. Ms Fraser here will compile a list of everything said and done, and then we can see what, if anything, would be a compromise both sides will accept. My understanding at first was little disruption, but I can see that peoples' ideas of little varies. When I was informed of more and more, I hesitate to say demands, let's say suggestions, I asked for Ms Fraser to come and work on behalf of all of us, both the film company, you the owners, and me on behalf of the hotel. She will now give you an idea of when we can hear more and what solutions we might have."

He was good, Jan allowed. Very good. He really didn't need her there. However, she stood up and carefully thanked him and Alex for their contributions and Mr Donaldson for putting forward the concerns of the owners. "I will have the notes ready in a day or so and then address each question in turn."

She smiled and looked round the room. Thom winked and gave a swift thumbs-up. Lois appeared bored and Sasha worried. Arietta looked amused and Moss had a poker face.

"Thank you all for coming. Any other questions?" There was silence.

Phew. "If you think of any, I'm available during working hours. Just ask at reception. Thank you." She sat down and counted to ten under her breath. She had to say she would be around to help, but oh boy, she hoped no one took her up on it.

"Well done." Zac grinned then wiped his smile off abruptly as Alex stood up and moved in front of him and Jan.

"That man is a menace. He cannot see what would be good for this place. I warn you now, I want a definite answer in two weeks or…" He left the rest of his sentence unsaid. "Goodnight."

"Or?" Jan queried. "They pull out? That would solve a lot of problems, wouldn't it?"

"And add a few more. Ah well, let's go and eat. I see your fiancé approaching."

"Well done." Thom kissed Jan's cheek and hefted her briefcase up. "This still weighs a ton. Arietta and Moss have headed home. She says she'll see you tomorrow. She'll bring lunch. Moss and I are supposed to be checking out where in them there hills would be a good place for us to hide in the series. If it ever gets made round here." He knew he sounded doubtful. He was. "Luckily the permission to do that was straight forward. Zac gave it to us, it's his land and not the cottage owners'. We had to sign stuff to make sure he's not liable for anything and that we know where we're going. We also had to state we are certain we won't fall into or off anything nasty." Even though Moss, as an ex-owner, probably knew the area better than anyone, he was, he said, not taking that responsibility on. "No idea how we can be sure of that but hey, we've signed. It's Moss, me, Alex and a cameraman. If we bump into any local, so be it."

"Probably be a poacher," Zac said gloomily. "Be just my luck. Or someone after the salmon."

"Cheerful, isn't he?" Thom said. "Any more doom and gloom to put me off my dinner?"

Zac laughed, reluctantly it seemed. "Not at the moment. As long as whoever is pinching the salmon has left enough for me to have a legal go at when I can."

"Fair enough." Thom's tummy rumbled and he put his hand over it and gave a comical grimace. "It must be dinnertime."

"It is. I've booked the small dining room for us. A bit of privacy and oh-ho, here comes your octopus."

"As long as we don't shorten it to puss, because soft and purring she ain't." Jan moved swiftly and stood as close to Thom as she could.

Zac did the same thing on his other side. Thom smiled inwardly as he put the briefcase in front of him, and like a row of warriors they moved forward together.

Lois stopped a few yards away and scowled. She did a good line in scowls, Thom had to admit that. It was a pity it changed her from what was a very pretty person with good bone structure to one who appeared disgruntled, frowning, angry and unhappy with life. What must it be like to feel so—so jaded and dissatisfied all the time? Thom couldn't imagine being someone who never even tried to see something positive in life. Unless her being positive showed as always expecting to get what she wanted and in her own way? He had no intention of finding out.

Thom, Jan and Zac stopped moving and Thom noticed all three of them, straight-faced, stared at her.

"Excuse us," Zac said politely. "We would like to get by."

Lois ignored him. "Thomas, I wish to dine with you. We have a lot to talk about."

He shook his head. "I don't think so. Anything you wish to say can be discussed at another time. With witnesses."

She stared, open-mouthed. "You wish to talk about our life in front of others?"

"Lois," Thom answered, as even-toned as he could manage. He was holding onto his temper. Just. "We – *we* – do not have a life. Not a Thomas-and-Lois life. You know that and so do I. This harassment has got to stop. My fiancée and I are getting mighty sick of your attitude. It verges on stalking and if it doesn't stop, I am not only going to explain to Alex and Sasha why I won't be taking up the option to another contract, however successful the film appears to be, and whatever I think of the chance to be in an award-winning series but I will also contact the appropriate authorities about your behaviour. Do you understand?"

She blinked, opened her mouth and closed it. Then, slowly, she nodded. "You are making a great mistake which you will soon discover. I love you."

"That sounds remarkably like a threat," Zac said in a steely voice. "Which I have taken a note of. That sort of attitude is not condoned around here. Not at all. I suggest you rethink your recent behaviour, stop acting like a spoilt brat and grow up."

Lois wheezed. A strange noise, Thom decided. One that was almost enough to make him feel sorry for her. Almost but not quite.

"I am *not* a spoilt brat," she said in a choked voice. "It is you who are horrible and – " She broke off and turned away, her backless clogs clacking on the parquet floor as she walked. "You will regret it."

"I wonder who that remark was directed at?" Thom said to no one in particular.

"All or any of us," Jan replied and sighed. "I almost felt sorry for her. She really didn't think that through, did she? I reckon she still thought she'd say jump, she loves you and you'd go how high and marry me." She shook her head. "I'm guessing she's never been told no before."

"She thought wrongly," Thom said, short and terse.

"Yeah. Wonder what next?" Zac drawled.

"We eat." Thom deliberately chose to misunderstand. "Lead on, Zac."

Zac inclined his head. "Our table awaits and we can even get there without going through the main restaurant. Comes in handy sometimes."

This was no doubt one of those times, Thom thought, now fed up and exhausted. Somehow he doubted it was all over, but he could live in hope.

Jan tucked her arm through his, a gesture he loved.

"Come on Mr Wanted By All. You'll feel better with some food in you."

"I hope so. Sod the wanted by all, wanted by you is enough." Thom flashed her a grateful smile as Jan chuckled.

"Always," she said solemnly as they followed Zac into a comfortable dining room. Furnished more like a sitting room that just happened to have a dining table in it, it was elegant and welcoming. The settee and chairs grouped around the fire invited you to sit, sprawl or curl up. The glowing coals of the fire reminded him of how he could enjoy just watching them, make up pictures in the flames and dream.

How good it would be to sit next to a fire like that one, with Jan next to him. Discussing their day, making plans? To come home after a long day's filming and be able to sit and relax with the one he loved.

The one I love. How do I persuade Jan I mean it? Truly mean it? Grow old together, share the highs and lows of life? He was afraid he might not be able to. Oh, she said she wanted him, but that wasn't enough. Want was good, need was better.

Zac coughed and brought him out of his reverie. "Earth to Thomas."

"Sorry, wool gathering," he apologised. "Admiring the room."

"You were in another world," Jan teased. "Not here with us."

"Not quite true," Thom argued then grinned. "Okay, almost true. I love looking at a coal fire. It's like a comfort blanket."

"I remember," Jan said. "But Zac wants to know if you'd like a drink before dinner or just one with our meal." Her tummy growled and she bit her lip. "Oops, sorry."

"I think that sort of answers the question," Thom said with a grin. "Let's eat."

* * * *

Several hours later, they wandered back to Jan's cottage, as Thom put it, stuffed to the gills. Their golf buggy was left to be picked up the following day on the grounds of too much alcohol—even though neither of them had had more than two small glasses—plus a need to walk some of the sticky toffee pudding and apple crumble cake off. As they reached the door, Jan slid the key from her pocket into Thom's palm. "You open it." She didn't say why.

In the glow of the porch light, she watched as realisation hit him, and he gave the slightest of nods.

"That food was fabulous," Jan remarked as Thom opened the door and stood back to let her precede him inside with an extravagant bow and a grin that made her giggle.

"My lady, our bed awaits."

"My hero."

Our bed? Once the door was shut, she turned to him and gave him a quizzical glance. "I didn't see anyone around, but you never know. Did you?"

"No, but like you said. In case there was anyone in the area, who might, shall we say, be wondering if indeed we are sharing this cottage now, I saw the sense. Not that you aren't capable of opening a door or anything but…"

"Yeah, but." Jan wandered into the kitchen, shut the blinds—she'd not done so before they went out—hung her bag over the back of a chair and picked up the kettle. "Cuppa?"

Thom shook his head. "I'm fine, thanks. I'll hang around a bit, though, if that's okay with you?"

"I'd hope you would," Jan said, and decided just to say what was on her mind. "Like a good twelve hours."

Chapter Ten

"This is shit on a stick," Thom said grimly to Moss as they clambered up the side of a hill, pushing their way through bushes and round trees of all shapes and sizes. "The not knowing what's going to be the outcome I mean. It would be perfect if not for all the problems us being here could bring."

Moss nodded grimly. "Yeah, and not just Lois-shaped ones. I'd not have been surprised to see her pop up disguised as a rowan tree or a clump of heather."

Thom laughed as Moss' droll comments and deadpan voice lightened the atmosphere. They'd been out in the extensive grounds of the castle, an area Moss knew like the back of his hand, for most of the day. He'd spent a lot of his youth playing there. The long day of walking, climbing and, if Thom were honest, swearing, was coming to an end. *Thank goodness.* He was certain his midge repellent was wearing off.

"That's just great. I'll examine every tree closely."

The cameraman with them was an outdoor enthusiast, which Thom decided was just as well. Anyone less fit would have given up hours before. At lunchtime, or even earlier.

Thom and Moss jumped over a narrow stream and Alex, who up until then had gamely struggled on, took one look at the rushing water and rocks a few feet below him and declined.

"I'll stay on this side," he said. Pale and a little bit green, he shook his head. "You two are the tough guys."

Thom nodded but didn't speak. He glanced at Moss and saw the moment his friend also decided not to comment about the tough guys comment. He thought himself reasonably fit and strong, but that sentence referred to their characters in the film, not them.

The cameraman shrugged. "No need to go over, boss," he said amiably. "They did it, that's all that matters. Where next?"

Alex glanced at Moss. "You know the area, where next? A cave, didn't you say?"

Moss nodded. "It's just over this rise." The rise was a good-sized hill. "Up and around that cluster of trees." He waved his hand towards the crest of the hill. "You don't need to jump here. Head up your side of the stream about a hundred yards or so and there's a wee bridge. Used to be used by shepherds. Cross there. Then after the cave we go down away back to the castle."

Thom waited for an argument. Alex had been determined to check out every place that could be used for filming—even when Moss told him there wasn't enough time to do it all in one day. Now the man appeared thoughtful.

"A bridge, you said?" he asked slowly. "Then how long back to the castle?"

"'Bout an hour, hour and a half. From the cave." Moss smiled evilly. "Take us ten, fifteen minutes to the cave."

Thom bit back a grin. He was damn sure Moss wasn't being honest there. Even he knew from his visits to Arietta and Moss you could get to the castle without climbing the hill first, and it would take thirty minutes, tops, from the cave, all downhill.

"Think we'll give the cave a miss for today then," Alex said. He turned to the cameraman. "I reckon once we've seen how hidden they are in that clump of stuff behind us we've got enough to see if this is feasible to use as well as the nearer areas."

The cameraman, a tall lanky guy called Shuggie, nodded. "Aye, I reckon so, boss. I'll sort it oot when we're back."

"Okay, that's settled," Alex said in a tone tinged with relief. "Nip into those bushes, both of you. Then lead the way back."

Moss glanced at Thom and winked. "You'll need to head up towards the bridge, cross it and head down this side of the stream. Then over that wee rise and you'll see the castle. If Shuggie needs us to duck under a bush, we'll do it while you get to us."

Shuggie laughed. "Just walk through some and then that'll do."

"It better," Moss said quietly to Thom as they watched Shuggie jump the stream and Alex struggle up to where the tiny bridge crossed the stream at a narrow and shallow area. "I'm pissed off with this. Do you think your fiancée can persuade anyone to compromise on anything?"

His fiancée? The word gave Thom a jolt. He'd forgotten that he'd have to remind Jan that Moss and Ari hadn't been told the story behind the so-called engagement. But did he have to? Really? Couldn't they make it official?

That gave him something else to think about.

"Oy, Tam, get on wi' it."

Thom jumped at Shuggie's voice. Tam? He gave a mental shrug. It was better than some of the things he'd been called over the years.

"Sorry, Shug. I was wool gathering."

"Well, dinnae."

Thom waved his hand in apology and scowled at Moss, who grinned.

"Come on, Tam, let's get it over and done with. Then we can get back. You to Lois dodge and me to be given the third degree by my ever-loving."

"Why the third degree?" Thom asked, puzzled.

Moss rolled his eyes. "She's a woman."

"Sexist. Better not let her hear you." Arietta would, in their mother's words, have his guts for garters if she did.

"True. There's no way I'd say that to her face, though. Put it this way, she'll be interested to know what we think might happen, and when. Oh, and any more gen on the Lois situation combined with the you-and-Jan-engagement-when's-the-wedding stuff."

There was no answer to that.

* * * *

"Have you ever wondered why you?" Jan queried. *She'd* wondered about that on many occasions, but never voiced the question before. "After all, and no offence, surely she's around a lot of men who are more…more… Oh, stop it." She punched his shoulder and Thom spluttered his glass of wine all over his shirt.

"Serves you right," Jan said. "I was going to say wealthy, richer, maybe more handsome—in her eyes anyway."

"What a good get-out, my love," Thom remarked once he had stopped spluttering. They were sitting in the lounge of Jan's cottage with a well-needed glass of wine after what both of them called their day from hell. "Well saved. But yes, she must do, and no, I do not know why me. I've never been more than politely friendly, if you know what I mean. Shook hands when we were first introduced, treated her to a coffee and nothing more. No knowing looks or winks, no admiring her obvious assets no… Well, nothing. Now if I looked at her like I sometimes look at you…" He twirled an imaginary moustache. "That would be different."

Jan threw a cushion at him, which he caught with annoying dexterity and hurled it back at her. She ducked and it hit the window with a dull thud.

"Oops. Dodgy aim." Thom chuckled. "You need more practice."

"Oops indeed. Children, really." Arietta stood in the doorway and waved a set of keys in the air. "You left these in the lock. I let myself in." She frowned. "Anybody could have walked in and pinched whatever."

"Sorry, Mum," Jan said in a silly singsong voice. "Blame Thom." She accepted Arietta was correct, though. What if Lois had sneaked in and hidden somewhere? *What if… Oh, enough. She's not a bunny boiler. I hope.* "He was last through the door, it's his fault."

Arietta grinned. "It usually is."

Thom scowled. "You pair are ganging up on me."

"Of course we are," his sister assured him. "Friend power works best like that. Which is not why I'm here. I'm on a mission. We just wondered why Lois has told Moss that he might be your brother-in-law but she doesn't have to listen to him. You're the only one that matters and you're in for a surprise."

"What?" Jan and Thom said in unison.

"About what?" Thom added. "Why? And shit, does that mean she's still not got the hint?"

"She must have, surely?" Jan said. "It was given clear enough and plenty of times. When did she say that to Moss?"

"This evening. Once he'd showered, glowered and muttered stuff about sodding films, why did he ever decide to be an actor and should we move to somewhere remote and lotus eat, Moss popped into the hotel to see if you were around, Jan, but Zac said you'd been working here. Moss was on his way out of the hotel when, in his words, she descended like a bat out of hell, informed him about not listening to him and stormed off. He rang me, asked me to meet him here, and here I am."

"That's crazy," Thom said. "She's crazy."

Jan agreed. "I've not seen hair nor hide of her today. It was such a relief, I can tell you. Even Nettie agreed with me and she's never really rude about anyone. She said Lois was a blight on society and needed a good telling off. I was in the office this morning and then came over here to get some peace from people insisting their ideas are the only ones feasible. I wanted to do some phoning without all and sundry about to hear, by accident or design. Came over just after two o'clock, and I saw or heard no one till Thom got home about half an hour ago." She noticed the way she'd said 'home', not arrived, and wondered if anyone else had? If they had it wasn't mentioned by the other two. "It's been chaotic. Everyone saying something different and most of it not a lot of use. Hell, even Sasha popped in." She made miming quotes. "Told me that if it didn't go their way and they didn't get what they wanted they would pull out. I said I'd pass the message on. Zac then started ranting, some old bloke came in and asked if the film lot would protect the ants. No idea where that came from and I told him to get me verified reference of what the problem was. Nettie spilled her cup of hot tea over her hand and scalded herself and had to go to another first aider to have it seen to as she's ours. First aider, I mean. After that lot of woes, I decided I needed a few hours of silence. Or silence when I wanted it. Now there's a stew on the oven, a glass in my hand and my—" She stopped talking abruptly. She'd been about to say and my love by my side. "And I'm feeling a bit more relaxed," she ended lamely. "But not looking forward to tomorrow. What did Moss want?"

Thom winked as he stood up and heat rushed into her cheeks.

The bugger.

"Wine, Ari?"

"Yes please. Moss will be here in a few minutes. It was nothing big, just to see if you'd be around tonight if we popped in. You weren't answering your phone. I brought the buggy, he's nipped home to grab something." She didn't say what.

Jan raised her eyebrows. "Very mysterious. I'd switched my phone off. It was sending me demented. Zac knew where I was if he needed me."

Arietta laughed. "Not really much of a mystery. I came out in a rush, mainly because Moss was worried Lois was on her way here to make more mischief and we wanted to call anyway."

"No Lois. Not so far, thank goodness. We can live in hope she's given up, but I'm not holding my breath."

"Hm."

Arietta sounded doubtful.

A bit like Jan herself was. "Everything crossed, then and breathe deeply."

Thom handed Arietta a glass of chenin and waved the bottle in Jan's direction. She shook her head.

I'm fine. I'll wait until dinner. She did a swift calculation in her head. There would be enough stew for four if Arietta and Moss wanted to share. She'd deliberately made enough to freeze some. "Want to share the stew?" she asked as the doorbell rang and Thom headed to answer it.

Arietta grinned. "After that gorgeous aroma I can smell, I thought you'd never ask."

She looked at her husband, who sat down beside her and nodded his reply to something unsaid before he answered her. "That sounds good, if that's what I can scent in the air."

"Well, it's not my perfume," Jan said dryly as Thom gave a tankard of beer to Moss then plonked himself on the other half of her settee. "Nor Thom's aftershave. So unless one of you two are responsible, yes, it's the stew. Leek and lamb and yes, there's enough, yes of course it has potatoes and other veg in it and no, it's not ready for another half an hour. Plenty of time to enjoy a drink and a chat. Or a moan or whatever else springs to mind after the Lois-in-your-face crap."

"She's out to make trouble," Moss said grimly. "I hope you don't mind that I've put some feelers out as to just why she's so determined to, well, to be crude, have Thom. You know, after she gave me a mouthful earlier on, I was certain I'd seen her before this filming started. Then I remembered I met her years ago when I played a tiny bit in one of Alex and Sasha's early films. She was altogether different then. Happy, quite shy and never in your face. Sporty, and I think played netball quite seriously. Mind you, she didn't work for Alex and Sasha then. I've a feeling she was at college doing photography or an arts-related course. Sorry not a lot of good or very specific, but it was a fleeting encounter. Something is niggling me about her. Perhaps a comment I've heard? I dunno, sorry." He looked frustrated at his lack of memory.

Jan made haste to reassure him. "Don't think about it and it will probably come to you," she advised. "That usually works, often in the weirdest of places. Or at a strange time."

Moss barked out a laugh. "On the loo or in the middle of a church service?"

"More than likely."

Thom coughed to get everyone's attention. "All that apart, why did you need to see us? Not that I mind seeing you, and I'm sure Jan feels the same."

Jan nodded.

"But," Thom went on, "I've spent all day with Moss, we're both knackered, Jan is fed up of the bitching and backbiting and, Ari? How was your day? How's the latest book going?" Arietta wrote romantic regency thrillers – amongst other things.

"Not too bad." Arietta took a sip of wine and put her glass down. "We've decided you need an engagement party. To show you mean business. We thought next week, before Jan heads off to wherever and...well...what do you think? And should we invite Lois?"

Jan gulped and Thom pinched her waist in warning. "What a nice idea," he said as he tried to decide how to answer.

"We decided to keep it all very low-key," Jan replied. "I hate being on show and let's face it, we're only just getting used to the idea. Could we leave it for a bit? I haven't even told May or any of my Hong Kong mates yet. I want to – "

"Savour it?" Thom said as he admired Jan's aplomb. "Get used to it and enjoy only a few of us knowing. I agree, I am so not ready for all the 'about time', and 'when's the wedding' and 'can we have a big party' comments."

Jan shuddered. "That's the last thing I want."

"Oh." Arietta appeared disappointed. "What about a wee party?"

"Very wee," Jan said.

"Definitely wee," Thom added. "Wee as in just us four?"

Moss nodded. "Ari and I thought you might say that, so instead, here's a wee engagement present, and let's have a glass of fizz and say this is the very low-key party."

Thom chuckled. "What a lot of weeing going on. Anyone who doesn't understand the dialect will think we've all got weak bladders, instead of talking about tiny things."

"Trust you." Jan made a silly face. "The *wee* party sounds about right, thank you. Fizz and stew, proper engagement food. Yes, love?" She appealed to Thom, who hid his grin.

He might have known she would get what they both wanted without upsetting anyone. "Sounds perfect."

"Good." Moss stood up and disappeared into the hall before returning holding an insulated bag and a small box. "Champagne and cake. There'll be enough to take some into the office tomorrow if you want."

"What sort?" Jan asked and got out the champagne glasses that came with the cottage. Thom took the proffered bottle and proceeded to open it with a soft pop of the cork and expertly pour the wine.

"Nicely done," Jan said as she took her glass. "I better go and turn the stew off or it'll be burnt offerings. By the way, you never said what sort of cake it is."

"When did either of you give me a chance?" Arietta asked. "It's lemon drizzle. I know you both like it and the bakery in town is renowned for their version."

Jan opened the box and laughed. "Very well done. Look, Thom."

Thom stared into the open box and chuckled. Written on the top was a T and J and 'engaged at last'. It might not be true yet, but he wasn't going to say that, and he could tell by the amused look on Jan's face she agreed with him.

"Nice one, sis, thank you." He kissed Arietta and raised one eyebrow at Moss, who put one hand out to ward him off.

"No kisses, thanks. You need a shave."

"Do I?" Thom appealed to Jan, who stared at him for a few seconds until he began to sweat. It had only been a passing comment so why did it take so long to answer?

Finally, just as he wondered what she might say, Jan smiled. "Well, I like it, and so far I've not had whisker burn, but each to their own. A bit different from the clean-shaven you of Hong Kong."

Tom gave an exaggerated *whew*. "That was for then, this is for now. You had me worried for a moment there, my love. I need to keep the stubble for a while, at least until the next bit of filming is over. We can't all look like male cover models." He grinned at Moss, who did an over-the-top twirl. "Not like Mr Smooth there."

Arietta and Jan both laughed. Moss put on an affronted expression. "Hey, some of us have it."

"And thankfully some of us do not," Thom riposted.

"Boys, enough." Jan stood up. "Time for stew. Thom, if you could set the table please, let's make it all festive. Just in case." She didn't say in case of what, but Thom reckoned they all knew what—and who—she meant. He nodded and headed for the drawer where the cutlery was kept as Jan, followed by Arietta, left the room.

Lucky for Thom the cottage was identical to the one he'd been given, so there was no fumbling about, no need to ask where things were and make Arietta ask questions. Thom was certain both she and Moss were, if not convinced it was a real engagement, going to act as if it was.

"Shove these on the table, will you please? I'll get the table mats." Thom passed the cutlery to Moss, who obligingly began to set the table, before opening the next drawer and finding a set of almost brand-new raffia mats. These were also passed to Moss.

"I just love watching men at work." Arietta came back into the room and put a wine cooler down. "Makes my little heart go pitter pat."

"We aim to please," Moss drawled, and Arietta stuck her tongue out at him.

"And you call me and Jan children." Thom tutted and laughed when his sister gave him the finger and stalked off. What else did he need?

Candles. It might not be dark yet, but it would create the right atmosphere, surely? Did Jan have any? That was something he didn't know. Thom opened the sideboard and almost sighed with relief. Several large pier candles in holders and a box of matches were right in front of him. He passed them to Moss as well.

"I like a candlelit meal," Thom remarked as he lit the candles "Be it a bacon sarnie or a full-on tasting menu. Or of course, stew," he added as Jan put a large casserole dish on the table. The aroma was mouth-watering. "My love, that smells divine."

Jan grinned. "Hope it tastes as good. It's got enough wine in it to add to it I hope. Now once Moss actually hands round the champagne he brought we can dig in."

"I'm on it."

Within a few minutes, each had taken a sip, and all four of them were tucking into the lamb stew.

Thom savoured his first mouthful and sighed in delight. "Just what the doctor ordered. Or in other words, bloody spot on."

* * * *

Sometimes, Jan thought, the simple things in life were what counted most. The evening with Moss and Arietta, the food, the wine, the chat and laughter had been perfect. Now tucked up in bed, snuggled in Thom's arms, she couldn't think of a better ending to what, before the evening, had been a crappy day.

She wriggled and Thom grunted. "Woman, what's up?"

"Nothing, nothing at all. I've just realised how happy I am and what a lovely evening we've had. No unwanted interruptions."

"That was a bonus." Thom rolled over. To settle them more comfortably, she assumed. Jan gave herself a hug before hugging him.

"Thank you." Thom was silent for a moment before he carried on. "I know you've been forced into this position, and it's all down to me."

"No, it's not," Jan pointed out. "It's all down to Lois the Octopussy leech and her determination to get her own way in everything. She's a menace, and even if she didn't appear tonight, I can't say I'm sure she won't again at some point. Probably when I'm trying to show everyone's position in this sodding filming stuff." She bit her lip. "It's still a shit-fest."

"Love your choice of phrases."

Jan began to scowl and changed it to a chuckle. "Honestly, I still have no idea why I'm here. The legal stuff is correct, tight, and can't be changed unless every party agrees to it, which they won't. The rest is a lot of he said, she said, throwing the dummy out, my way or no way. I reckon Zac knows it as well."

"Uninterested third party?" Thom asked. "Covering his back."

"Probably, but it's a waste of my time and his money." Jan sighed. "Ah well, it's got me back to Scotland earlier than usual, it's his money and works time and I'm getting paid for it. Win-win for me, not for half the other people involved. Plus, I'll be on holiday soon."

"Yeah, and I'll be clambering up mountains and picking twigs out of my hair."

He didn't sound enthusiastic.

"Aww, poor thing." Jan blew him a loud kiss and he laughed, somewhat reluctantly, she decided.

"Love your sympathetic outlook, hon."

"I'll think of you as I sun myself by my pool, shall I?"

"You're all heart." Thom kissed her gently, then with increasing passion.

Passion Jan reciprocated. As he slid into her, she forgot everything else. Nothing mattered more than the scent of him, the way they were skin to skin. How hands stroked, and words of love were whispered.

They climaxed together, and still held each other as Jan slipped into sleep.

* * * *

She woke just as it was getting light.

Silly o'clock then.

Jan contemplated the patterns the sun made on the ceiling where it showed through the slightly open slats of the blind. It didn't seem to matter whichever way she closed them, light still filtered through. She'd never prescribed to the 'you need total darkness for a good night's sleep' theory, so the blinds were fine as they were. She'd checked no one could see in, with or without the room lights on, even as she'd felt slightly idiotic as she'd done so. Jan was relieved no one had seen her. It would have been embarrassing to be accused of being a Peeping Tom in her own accommodation.

Peeping Tom? Jan grinned in the semi-darkness. She wouldn't mind a peep *at* Thom!

Beside her the man in question stirred, muttered something she couldn't interpret, rolled over, slung his arm around her waist and snored.

How romantic. Jan bit back a snigger and wondered whether to get up and make coffee or try to go back to sleep. It was nice, stretched out next to Thom, hearing his soft breathing. And occasional snore and snuffle. With his arm across her, it wouldn't be easy to move and not wake him, would it?

That sorted her dilemma out. She'd stay put, at least until it wasn't quite so early, or Thom rolled over.

* * * *

She had no idea how much time later it was when the mattress dipped and she woke up with a start.

Wha…" She rubbed her eyes as someone pressed a kiss to the top of her head.

"Ugh, what's going on?"

"The coffee maker and the toaster as soon as I get into the kitchen."

Jan opened her eyes fully and feasted on the sight in front of her. Thom stood by her side of the bed, naked and, as her nan might have said, in all his glory, as bare as the day he was born.

She swallowed, her mouth dry. "Wow, now that's a great sight to wake up to. I'll take that any day, much better than the newsreader on the TV. What time is it?"

Thom grinned and did a twirl that made a certain part of his anatomy move in a very interesting manner. "Half seven, not too late, but I thought I'd make a drink and a bite to eat for us before we both got stuck into whatever today decides to hit us with."

Jan blew her hair off her face. "Sounds great. Have I got time for a shower?" And to clean her teeth. She hated the sensation of badger breath and unbrushed molars. "I'll make it fast."

"Yeah, wish I could say let's shower together, but I know damn well it wouldn't be quick and we both have things to do. I won't start anything until I hear the shower switch off. How's that?"

"Perfect." Jan scrambled out of bed and headed showerwards. She'd got the two-minute shower, including a hair wash down, to perfection and didn't see any reason to prolong it. Not when she was alone, anyway.

Three and a half minutes later, she entered the kitchen. Her hair was only towel dried, but the aroma of coffee and the lure of drinking it hot was more important at that moment than perfectly dried and coiffed tresses.

"Just in time," Thom said cheerfully as he popped some bread in the toaster and poured out two mugs of coffee. "Jam?"

"Just butter, thanks." Jan took a sip of the steaming brew and sighed in appreciation. "Perfect. Thank you."

"My pleasure. Two slices?"

That sounds good." Jan glanced out of the window at the blue sky dotted with tiny fluffy clouds. "Think it's going to rain?"

Thom shook his head. "Nah. Well, not this morning anyway. What have you got on?"

Jan thought for a second. "I want to finish sorting all the comments and complaints into those that can be answered sensibly, those I need to find out about and those that are flat-out stupid. Speak to Zac and then all our gods help me; him, Sasha and Alex and hopefully not Lois, but I'm not holding my breath there."

Thom looked thoughtful. "Not confident of a successful outcome?"

Jan didn't need to consider her answer. "Not at all. Because however people might try, you can*not* alter the legal contractual facts. Not without everyone agreeing to a new contract. And that, I reckon, is as likely as me walking a tightrope. As in never."

Thom shrugged. "Is this where we say you can't win 'em all?"

Jan wrinkled her nose. "Where whatever we say will be wrong for some people." She ate the rest of her toast and swallowed the last—not almost cold—dregs of her coffee. "Right. I better dry my hair, dress to impress, or not as the case may be, and head across to the Dung Heap."

Thom looked confused. Which, Jan reasoned, he might well do. "The what?"

"Dung Heap. The old stables where the offices are. Nicknamed due to the proximity of where, when horses lived there, so did the Dung Heap. The ones who have rooms on that side of the building swear the aroma still lingers, especially on hot days. Officially Effie Barnet House, but I bet if you asked anyone for directions to there they'd look at you with a blank expression." Jan laughed. "Unless it was that Mr Donaldson. He appeared quite proper. I mean, his email even had my degrees after my name and I didn't put them anywhere. Now where are my briefcase and handbag… Ah." She saw them where she'd left them—on the side table—the night before. "Right. Must dry my hair and make myself presentable. When I see you later should it be here or where?" She held her breath.

"Oh here I think, don't you?" Thom said, "Best place, and I do so want to get my feet under the table, or on you in bed if it's cold."

"Just as well it's summer then."

"Four seasons in one day, remember?" Thom said, and chuckled as Jan shivered in a most exaggerated manner.

"Don't remind me. At least no hottie"—she paused and licked her lips—"bottles are needed tonight." It was warm without more than a gentle breeze.

Damn. Where's a cold night when you need one.

Just round the corner, Jan yawned. "I'll be ready for bed."

Thom winked and she giggled, a most unladylike noise that astounded her. "Someone kept wriggling. I'll need sleep."

Her mobile rang and she glanced at the screen and groaned. "Hold on, it's Zac. Hi, what's up?" she asked then listened briefly. "Yeah, wonder what it's about. Right, thanks, yes I will." She scowled. "I'm up and once I'm dressed and ready, I'll head to the Dung Heap,"

Thom raised one eyebrow

Jan smiled and high-fived herself. "Day off. The Chengs have nipped—I say that euphemistically—to London, back tomorrow. General meeting still scheduled for day after. But with no Alex and Sasha to confer with, I'm not hanging around in case Lois is about. I'm going to play hooky. Want to come?"

Thom tilted his head to one side. "Would love to. However, Moss and I promised we'd take Shuggie to the wee cave. To be specific, the not much more than a dent in the hillside cave, if you want to stretch it a bit. I could be free from around two?"

Jan ran through her options. "Okay. Meet you in the cosy coffee shop in the village round say half two, three? Tea and buns on me."

"Brilliant. I'll cut and run now, and if I'm ready earlier I'll let you know." Thom kissed her in the way Jan had come to expect and enjoy. Deep, long, lingering and with feeling. It always gave her a wanted and cherished sensation.

She returned it with fervour. When they finally broke apart, they were both breathing heavily. Jan took a shuddering breath. "As ever, wow."

"Wow indeed. I love you, Jan. I hope you believe me."

She'd never noticed such an intense expression on Thom's face. Plus what? Hope? Worry? She couldn't decipher it. She could reassure him, though.

"I do. I still do." She stopped speaking and thought over her words. "Not still, not really. More I've discovered a new and stronger love. How's that?"

Thom beamed. "Perfect. Okay, I'm off. Will sail through this morning on a cloud of happiness and see you later."

Jan laughed as he bowed. "Make sure you Lois dodge."

Thom groaned. "Hmm. Everything crossed she's gone to London but I'm not holding my breath."

"Nor would I."

Chapter Eleven

"All right then, which way?"

Moss worried his lip as Thom narrowed his eyes. Thom ignored him and bit back the pithy words he would like to say. How many times did they have to point the sheep track out? He waited for Moss to explode.

"Up there for about a mile." Moss waved vaguely in the direction they needed to head. "Like we said before."

"Ah, I know, but you're so easy to rile." Shuggie grinned and ducked as Moss pretended to swipe at him. "Let's get it over and done with, eh? There's a pint of Tennent's with my name on it. To say nothing of a wee dram. Hillwards!"

The last thing Thom felt like doing was clambering up the damn hill again just to show Shuggie how he and Moss could be camouflaged under gorse and broom, behind trees and underneath the overhang of rock the locals called the Pixies Cave. Said to be the meeting folk for pixies, or the Wee Folk, it wasn't much more than three or four feet deep and just a little higher and wider. However, the way the rock overhung at the front gave a little more leeway inside, and as long as Moss and he were careful they shouldn't end up with sore heads.

"I agree, Let's get it over and done with," Moss muttered as the three of them started up the track at a pace most people would complain about. "I've got a hot bath, a good book and a single malt with my name on waiting for later. The mood I'm in, later can't come soon enough."

Thom was in total agreement. The faster they did the necessary the better it would be. He'd want a shower before he headed to meet Jan.

"Lead on, MacDuff."

Moss grinned and pointed up the hill. "Into the breach and all that."

"Never mind any breeches," Shuggie puffed as they skirted a wee lochan. "I meant tae ask. Did you hear aboot yon Donaldson mannie." His accent increased as his tone became amused. "He telt Zac Whoosit that nae mair choppers should be allowed aroond."

"No helicopters?" Moss asked as Shuggie did some filming. "Golfers have always flown in and out."

"Aye, but he's saying the fillumin will be too mony and scare thon animals. And Ernest Donaldson? He's in deadly earnest." He hooted at his own bad pun.

Thom groaned. "Argh, enough, please."

"The man's a bloody menace," Moss grumbled. "Though he does have a point. The number of choppers will be monitored. It's just his attitude that gets up my you-know-what."

"I can think of a fair few people whose attitude does that to me," Thom remarked as they continued to the cave.

Moss and Shuggie laughed.

"I bet," Shuggie said. "What's all this about you and Lois and the lovely Jan? Sounds kinky."

Thom stopped dead in his tracks.

"I beg your pardon. What on earth have you heard?" He listened to his harsh tone and winced. "Sorry, Shuggie," he apologised in a more temperate manner. "That woman is the bane of my life. Lois, not Jan. Not to put too fine a point on it, Lois is akin to a stalker."

"Aye, ah did wonder." Shuggie got to the cave entrance and looked inside with interest. "This looks braw for what we're wanting."

"Good. What did you hear about Lois, me and Jan?" Thom prompted as Shuggie began to film.

"Ah, that you and she were almost if not already engaged and then Jan did or said something and you ditched Lois for her." He was silent then began to tell Thom and Moss what he needed from them.

Thom accepted that until their work at the cave was completed to Shuggie's satisfaction, there would be no chatting. He was all businesslike, which, Thom allowed, was how it should be. He closed his mind to everything but the job in hand.

****

An hour later they were halfway back down the hill and Thom returned to asking about what Shuggie meant. "So," he said as casually as he could, "there is not and never has been a Lois and me scenario. Where did you hear there was?"

Shuggie shot him a sideways glance as Moss slowed so Thom was now nearest to Shuggie. "It was in the canteen one lunchtime. I think it was one of the production team she was talking to. I just heard her say that some woman had appeared and begun to attach herself to you. How it messed up your and hers' relationship. Then someone else chimed in, ah, one of the makeup lassies it was. She said she'd heard you were engaged. Lois went sort of white and said you were hers and went on about being ditched. That was it until later when I was asked if I knew you and Lois had almost been engaged and you'd chucked her for Jan. It was hinted it was all a bit mysterious."

Thom slipped on a wet, muddy, grassy tussock and stood in something slimy. "Shit on a brick. What did you say?" He moved his foot gingerly and somehow only ended up with one boot in a tiny burn, where the water appeared crystal clear. The state of his footwear clouded the water for a few seconds.

Shuggie guffawed at his predicament. "I just said I dinnae know anything and thought I'd ask you when we were up here. Straight from the horse's mouth. Nae offence meant to you or a horse."

Thom laughed at Shuggie's hasty addition to his explanation. Moss whistled.

"No offence taken, mate, and no mystery at all," Thom replied shortly, his mind whirring as he wondered what else could happen to upset his life. "There never was and still isn't a Lois and me, except maybe in her mind. Goodness knows why, I sure don't. She came on to me, I rebuffed her, she got more and more in my face. I ended up telling Jan about it in more detail that I had before." He thought quickly how to intimate he and Jan had been engaged longer than people assumed. "We've known each other for years and been unofficially engaged for a while. With all this going on we decided we'd better make it official. Sadly, Lois still seems to have problems accepting the situation."

He raised his shoulders and dropped them. "I don't know what else to do or say, except she's a pain in the arse and something has *got* to be done or said. If not, and she's still around and being a nuisance, I'll not be signing any more contracts, success or not."

"He's not the only one," Moss added in the grimmest tone Thom had ever heard him use. "Neither will I."

Thom was stunned. That was the first he'd heard of it. He turned to stare at Moss, who raised his eyebrows. "I mean it."

Thom opened his mouth to protest, but Moss shook his head. "Do not say a word. I've discussed it with Arietta and she agrees. I'll be formally telling Alex and Sasha when they get back from wherever. Not up for discussion."

The rest of the journey down the hill and back to the hotel was made in silence.

* * * *

Jan had watched Thom as he grabbed a jacket and headed for their buggy, which someone had thoughtfully brought up from the hotel. She reckoned he'd head to Moss and Arietta's place and he and Moss would meet Shuggie. That meant Thom wouldn't be alone for long and, as he'd said, safety in numbers in case Lois was around. The woman was so unpredictable, the less time she could catch Thom alone, the better.

Arietta! Jan suddenly thought that if she was having time away from the hotel maybe she should see what her friend was up to? She sent a brief text rather than phoning. Once on the phone and they were chatting, time just slipped away from them. She didn't still want to be getting ready to head out at lunch time. The reply to her, 'day off, not meeting Thom till later, want to catch up?', came swiftly back. It was also short and sweet. 'Damn and blast. Sorry I can't—got an appointment. Tell you all when I can. Enjoy'.

That was that then. Jan got herself ready, headed to her car and by ten o'clock was on her way down the drive. She had no intention of hanging around.

The day was one of those rare summer days where it was warm and not even a hint of rain in the sky. The sort of day which, Jan thought with a wry smile, made you think there was nowhere better to live. Sadly, they rarely lasted for long, and grey, overcast and dreich weather made you wish you were elsewhere. Even so, Jan realised now that she was back in Scotland how much she missed it when she was elsewhere. If only she could split her time between Scotland and Hong Kong.

I wonder if I could persuade the Powers That Be it would work. It was something worth considering when the stint at Romansa Castle was over.

If I still have a job. Jan scowled. *Oh, for goodness sake, enough already. Get a grip. And get on with getting out before the phone rings and calls you back.*

As if on cue, her mobile rang. Even though it was hands-free, she ignored it. If it was important whoever it was would leave a message or get back to her. She'd check when she stopped in town.

She parked in a side street where a tiny car park had enough space for about half a dozen cars and was only half full. As she'd noticed there was a market in the town square, it was probably unusual to find a space so easily. Jan got out of the car, checked the ticket machine and realised why. Most car parks in the area were free for a four-hour maximum, this one was a park all day one but now it charged after half an hour. The fee was modest, but Jan reckoned a lot of people would avoid it on principle. That suited her just fine. Principles were all well and good, but not if you had to waste petrol driving around before you found somewhere free of charge.

She paid the money—no parking app in sight—displayed the ticket and checked her mobile. An unknown number and no message. That solved that problem then.

Jan headed to the market for a nose around. It was bustling and cheerful. Fruit and veg stalls stood next to each other, vying for customers. The fresh fish van displayed various types of fish and seafood on a bed of ice, and next to it Fred McSporran, butcher, bellowed out his 'best price' deals.

Raucous and it enticed the customers. His banter was funny, insightful and a lot of it regarding things very local. Jan noted with interest how his customers gave as good as they got.

It might not be a big market but it had all the necessities. In many ways it was so different from the markets in Hong Kong, but in others, very similar. Jan wandered around the dozen or so stalls, gave in and bought a box of strawberries and another of raspberries along with some home-made meringues and a pack of scones. With regret she gave the clotted cream a miss.

As the day was still warm she doubted she'd get it home unspoilt. It was a pity, there was nothing quite like a cream tea whether you put the jam on first or the cream.

The stall keeper smiled at her. He'd obviously realised her dilemma. "I can sell you a cool bag and some cooling blocks if you want." He winked. "I always have them cold in my chiller. You'd be surprised how many people want cream and forget sommat to put it in. A fiver and cheap at the price."

Jan relented. She bet he sold a lot of them each summer. "Go on then, better give me one of the big tubs of cream." She had a feeling Thom would make inroads into it when he saw the goodies it would complement. She handed her money over, accepted her purchases and a paper carrier bag to hold them and, after proffering her thanks to the stallholder, finished wandering down the row of stalls.

At the far end, tucked into a corner, she saw some pottery that immediately drew her attention. It wasn't quirky like some she'd already looked at. It wasn't chunky, or funny coloured. It was, she decided, classic. If only she had somewhere to use it.

"I like that, shall we get some?" Someone spoke in her ear and she jumped and spun around as Thom caught hold of her, steadied her and kissed her. In that order.

"Whoa, Ms Spinaround. It's only me." He grinned at her. "I thought you'd seen my manly presence."

Jan glared at him. "No, you didn't, you sod. You meant to startle me and I bet you were hoping I'd jump."

Thom spread out his hands. "What can I say? It's a fair cop, gov." His accent was pure B-movie baddie.

It was a struggle, but Jan managed not to grin. "What would you have done if I'd fallen onto the stall? Smashed the lot? Or dropped my bag of groceries?"

"Checked you were all right and kissed any sore bits better. Paid for the breakages, picked up the groceries and replaced anything too mangled to rescue," Thom said promptly as the stallholder laughed. "Said sorry and took you for a recuperative drink. All which I intend to do after we choose what we want. Everyday or special?"

The look he gave her kept Jan from saying anything that could be misconstrued. "Or both?" she asked in a saccharine voice.

Thom winked. "Great idea, hon. You chose the special and I'll pick the everyday. Then we can see if we both like what we've picked."

The stallholder grinned. "I like your style."

So did she, Jan had to admit as she picked out a full dinner service in a pearly, almost translucent colour—or non-colour. She glanced across at Thom, who was obviously trying to decide between pale blue or green. As she liked either, she'd be happy with whatever he chose.

Why am I getting so excited about crockery? How do I even know if I'll get to use any of it? Their relationship seemed as if it was really on again, but Jan reckoned that until the Lois stuff was well and truly over and done with, she wouldn't know. Or would she? There was no point in wondering any more. She would just keep going round in circles. As long as she knew what her answer would be if he did reiterate a Jan and Thom together forever scenario was his intention. One they both wanted for no other reason than they were in love and couldn't face the idea of not spending the rest of their lives together. Yes they'd both said that, but not really sat down and explained what each other meant by it.

Thom wandered over to her and casually gave her a hug under the watchful eye of the stallholder. "

"Earth to you, love."

"Eh?" Jan realised she'd been staring at a dinner plate for ages. She put it down with care. "Damn. Sorry, in a daydream. Have you decided? I have."

I think I'd like the blue for every day. That okay with you?" He picked up one of the pearly plates. "This is spot on. The whole shebang?" He waved his hands and gestured at the service. "For heydays and holidays?"

Would her credit card stand it? "Why not."

"Then if," Thom turned to the stallholder, "this lady here will box the lot, we could pay for it, nip and have a coffee and pop back in, say, an hour?"

"Sounds good to me." Jan glanced at the stallholder and judged that by the look on her face couldn't believe her good luck. Then the woman's expression became speculative as she stared first at Thom then at Jan.

Jan held her breath and waited for the questions to start.

Instead, the woman nodded. "Of course. What name shall I put on it?"

"You'll recognise us surely?" Jan said in as sweet a tone as she could manage. "It's only an hour."

The woman blushed. Jan had never seen someone react to something so fast.

"Oh yes, but, ah, well I might not have been here," she mumbled as both Thom and Jan reached for their credit cards. Thom put his hand over Jan's.

"My turn, love." His eyes narrowed. "You paid for the last lot of stuff."

I did? What was he playing at? It wasn't the time or the place to argue or contradict him. Jan smiled as she mentally promised to ask him later. "Of course. Well, we'll enjoy using it, eh. Whoever pays for it."

Thom grinned. "Same account anyway."

What is he doing? Jan watched as he handed his card over, saw the woman's eyes widen even farther if that was possible, and swore. Of course she'd see his name on the card, put two and two together and make goodness knows what about it all.

Should we just cut and run?

* * * *

"I think the pub rather than the coffee shop," Thom said as he draped his arm over Jan's shoulder and they wove their way between the stalls and across the road. "I could do with a pint."

"More likely a stiff drink," Jan said. "But a glass of wine and a ploughman's will do. What was the lovey-dovey stuff all about?"

"I'll explain when we're not dodging kids on bikes and babies in buggies." They swerved around a couple of both. "I forgot it's Scottish school holidays. Was it always like this?"

"Worse," Jan said promptly. "Not so many foreign trips so more time at home causing havoc. Market days were the best, especially once the market ended and the stalls were being taken down. The bin men wouldn't have been, and anything left out for the bins or stuff leftover was fair game for us. Rotten fruit was a great find. It's amazing what an old slimy peach or apple can do when you ride your bike over it."

Thom chuckled. "I bet. And were you one of the riders?"

"Of course. It was a rite of passage. First you got to be lookout, then finder, then chucker, and then once you got a two-wheeler and could sit on the saddle and touch the ground with your toes, you got to be the rider." Jan gestured towards the pub door. "The Twa Doos?"

"Why not? Though why anyone wants to call a pub the two pigeons is a mystery."

"No, it's not," Jan said as they entered the old building with '1803' carved over the entrance. "It's an old coaching inn and two pigeons refers to people a couple of old gadgies—blokes—used to try and play cards with. Travellers who would stop for the night maybe, and move on. The old men intended to win by cheating. Called the travellers pigeons for the plucking. In local dialect of course."

"Wow. I'm impressed with your local knowledge. You know all this how?" Thom asked as they sat down at a table in a window alcove.

Jan tapped her nose.

"Oh go on, spill the beans. Don't leave me in suspense."

"Ms Google and Ms Social Media." Jan laughed. "I did a bit of research at school and then did a bit more when I knew I'd be back in the area. Mum and Dad moved away years ago, so I've not been back for yonks. Then the other day, I came into town and met an old schoolfriend. She said she fancied you and Moss." Jan grinned as she remembered Cally's comments. "I won't go into any more details."

"Spoilsport. Did you tell her I was taken, as well as Moss?" Thom glanced at Jan's mischievous expression.

"No, don't go any further. I want to drink my pint in peace. So you fancy a ploughman's and what? White wine?"

"Definitely a ploughman's, please. With ham as well if they do it. Just soda water to drink. I'm thirsty."

Thom picked up the menu and glanced at it as he wandered to the bar and put in their order. He decided to have the same food. The barman stared at him as he poured the pint. "On holiday?"

"Couple of days. Nice area, hope I get to come back for longer next time."

"Aye, it's nae bad. Grub in five. Put these on your tab?" The man put the pint down and went to get the soda.

"Yes, thanks, a tab will be fine."

Thom wove his way around a couple of empty tables and handed Jan her soda. "I think I must be getting clocked as I keep getting stared at. Sorry. Are you okay with it or should we just pay and go?" He waited as Jan downed her drink and put the glass back on the table.

"I'm hungry and I'm okay with it if you are. It's part of life for you, I guess."

Phew. He didn't realise how churned up he was until he had heard her answer. "Not a lot, to be honest. I must have an instantly forgettable face. But the stallholder will see my name on my card and I guess some people other than those at the castle must be in the know about the possibility of us filming around here." He shrugged. "Goes with the job. I'm not that well-known, though, so I'm rarely bothered."

"You soon will be." Jan waved a copy of the local paper under his nose, just missing swiping him with it. "Oops, sorry. But there's an article in here about the castle and the film. Which I should have been informed about and I wasn't. Someone has messed up there. It even says no one was available for comment from the castle."

"May I look?" Thom scanned the article and grimaced. "Our estimable Ernest at it, I see." It had a quote from Ernest Donaldson in it, emphasising all the negatives. He stared at the grainy photos of him and Moss. "Bad pics. I look like a monster from the depth of a loch." He folded the paper carefully. "Is this yours?"

Jan shook her head. "Either someone left it or it's the pub's. I'm assuming it was left, so I can appropriate it and wave it under Zac's nose when I see him. How the hell could no one be available for comment? The paper came out this morning. It talks about the meeting. Well, Mr D mentions it, so it's his version. Therefore, why wasn't their query passed on to me?"

Thom guessed she'd find out and there would be fireworks. "Want a stiff drink?" he asked.

"*Do not* tempt me. I would down it in one. Nope, I need a clear head. Ah, here comes lunch." A tow-headed teenager put their plates in front of them and stared at Thom, who stared back.

"That looks lovely," he said. "Thank you."

"You're welcome. The chutney's home-made by Ma. It's a wee bitty spicy." The lad bobbed his head and backed away. Thom saw him chat to the barman then disappear through a swing door. Resigned to the fact he'd been noticed, he turned his attention to his food. He'd told the truth to Jan when he'd explained to her he was rarely recognised as an actor and hardly ever bothered for autographs or photos. It might change after the film, but if it did he'd cope. Thom had long decided there was no point in worrying about things he couldn't change, but to do the best about things he could if need be.

"I wonder who said no comment," Jan asked as she picked up a piece of crusty bread and a chunk of cheese. "This looks great."

"I always thought you didn't like cheese?" Thom remarked as he forked up some pickle. The lad was correct it was a wee bitty spicy.

"I don't like some, but have begun to eat others," Jan said and sniggered. "I have also been known to ask for a pizza, no cheese. It's the smell of cooked cheese I really don't like. Turns my stomach."

"How do you cope with cheese on toast? Best snack ever invented."

Much to Thom's amusement, Jan shuddered. A better shudder than he reckoned he could have achieved.

"I don't," she said in a you-better-believe-it manner. "Never ever. You want it, you cook it, eat it *and* wash up before I go near the prep area or you."

Thom grinned. "Point taken. I will make a note. Things to keep Jan way from. Anything else I don't know?" He was intrigued. They had been a couple long enough before that something as everyday should surely have been mentioned? But then, he remembered, she hadn't gone near cheese at all. The one time they'd headed to a deli that had a dedicated cheese shop next to it, Jan had stayed out and well away.

"So?" he prompted. "Next surprise?'

"Hmm, can't think of anything off hand. What about you?"

"Tripe," he said promptly. "Lois. Big spiders. Dentist's drill."

"I know most of those. Never knew about the spiders, though." Jan ate a slice of apple with a crunch. "You kept that well-hidden."

"Too true. You wouldn't have known. I did my best to hide my scaredy side from you. He-man and all that."

"Even he-men have foibles. I knew a man, no, not like that, you rotter." Jan nudged his arm as he leered at her then laughed.

"Sorry," Thom apologised. "Go on."

"Nope." She ate another crunchy slice of apple.

"Aww, go on." Thom cajoled her. "I'll behave." He picked up his last chunk of cheese and added the remains of his chutney to it.

"Nope. You blew it." Jan folded her arms. "Too late, buster."

"I'll tickle you."

Jan sighed very ostentatiously. "That's a low blow. He hated orange pith."

"Can't say I'm keen on it myself," Thom remarked. "But hate? Really hate? That seems a bit OTT."

"If you saw his reaction you'd know what I mean. If there was even a speck on his orange, or anyone's in the vicinity, he'd stomp away. His wife was used to it, but really? It was a very weird reaction. His excuse? It left a funny taste. Which, okay, yes, but no need to leave a restaurant about it." Jan wiped her mouth with her napkin and finished her soda water. "I was ready for the food. As Gran would say, I was fair clemmed."

"Not heard that expression for hungry for ages. Nowt so queer as folk, eh?" Thom drained his pint. "Your gran and the bloke. I'll away and pay. This is my shout, yours can be the next one."

Chapter Twelve

Thom headed to the bar before Jan remembered she wanted to ask what the joint account stuff was all about. They'd not even begun to talk about crockery, lovey-dovey affection in public, or what they would do next. The article in the newspaper had seen to that. Jan gathered her parcels and belongings together and saw Thom laugh and sign something other than the credit card slip.

He walked back to her and took one of the shopping bags from her. "Yes I was recognised, and I signed a napkin," he murmured as they left the pub. "Said I was having a few days around here and confirmed I was stopping at Romansa Castle with you. The young lad, Freddie, is a fan of that old TV series I did around here a few years ago. He thought it was me. The barman thought I was someone else entirely. A weather forecaster called Tom Wannaker or Warrender or something. I didn't catch it exactly. Any ideas?"

"Not a clue," Jan admitted cheerfully. "It's a long while since I've had time to watch the weather on TV. However, nice to know you have a memorable face, even if not for the person you are, eh?"

Thom rocked on his heels as they waited to cross the road. "That's a convoluted sentence if ever there was one."

"Oh, you know what I mean." Jan stuck her tongue out. Heat rushed into her face as someone nearby tutted and muttered. "Now look what you made happen," she hissed as they headed back to the market. "That woman tutted at me and said something about setting a bad example. I'll be shoved on the wall of shame if I'm not careful. How mortifying would that be?"

"Is there one?' Thom asked as they neared the pottery stall and the stallholder looked up and saw them.

"No idea but if there was… Ah, hi, we're back," she added as the woman in front of them beamed. Behind her three other women appeared to be doing their best to pretend they weren't rubbernecking but browsing. The way one nudged one of the others made it apparent they were there to be nosy and see if it was Tom.

"Here's your parcels all wrapped up carefully," the woman said, and glanced from Jan to Thom. "Who's going to carry them?""

Thom laughed. "Me. I'm the designated pack horse today."

Jan snorted. "You'd think we tossed for it. I'm the driver so I get to carry the lighter stuff. Fair division of labour." She took the carrier Thom had held since they were in the pub. "And then if anything gets damaged it's not my fault." If Thom was intent on promoting them as a pair she wasn't going to stop him. "Plus," she added with a wicked grin on her face—or so she hoped—"next time he's the driver and I get to choose where we're going. I'll pick a nice pub."

The stallholder sniggered and one of the other women let out a laugh she tried to change to a cough.

"Sounds perfect. Well, thank you for your custom. Er, I've got to ask. Are you the Thom Clare who did that TV series around here a couple of years ago? If you're not, you're his double."

Jan waited to see if Thom would use the get-out clause he'd just been handed. He gave her a sideways, querying look and she returned it as bland as possible. It was up to him.

"That's me," he agreed and one of the watching women squealed in excitement. Just in time, Jan remembered not to roll her eyes. The woman was fifty-ish, not fifteen.

However, Thom took it in his stride as someone held out a mobile phone and another a felt tip. Which would be first and where did the woman want the pen to write?

It was a new experience to Jan, to watch how it all played out.

"Do you think we could have a photo?" The phone holder asked. She pushed by Jan, who grabbed hold of the stall for balance. "Maybe your PA could take it?"

His who? The woman was looking at Jan. *She means me.* Jan bit her lip to stop herself giving a pithy reply.

"I don't have a PA," Thom said in a neutral way. "Who do you mean?"

The woman who had pushed by Jan gave her a long hard stare. "If you're not a PA, then what are you?"

How rude. Jan glanced at Thom. He frowned, shook his head slightly and took hold of Jan's hand. "Oh, you mean my fiancée. Darling, would you oblige this lady?"

The woman's jaw dropped and she swallowed heavily. Thom hadn't sounded exactly friendly.

"I, er, oh…um, sorry. I got it wrong."

Didn't you just.

"Congratulations," one of the other ladies said. "How fab. Dare I ask your fiancée's name?"

"You dare, of course," Thom said with a grin as he passed the mobile phone that had been thrust at him to Jan. "It's up to her if she chooses to share it. Your choice, my love."

Gee, thanks. What do you want me to say I wonder. Argh, what the hell. They'll find out easily enough if they try. Jan schooled herself to smile. If this was the new norm, she'd need to get used to it.

"I'm Jan," she said in a pleasant way. She held her hand out to show her ring. "And over the moon."

"I bet," someone said in a voice full of envy. "I tell you, when your beloved wore a kilt in that series I almost swooned."

"Nice legs, eh?" Jan said with a wink. "Just as good in a pair of boardies as well."

Thom groaned. "Enough, ladies. Leave me with some…ah, secrets. Right, Jan, love, can you take the photos and then we better head off."

Jan glanced at her watch. "Yikes! Only half an hour before the car park ticket runs out." *Bloody hell, yikes. What next?*

Next was five minutes of taking photos and obligingly posing with Thom for one as well and a quarter of an hour of idle chit-chat. By the time they got back to the car, with a few minutes to spare, she felt like she'd run a marathon. Backwards in a penguin suit.

"*Phew*! That was a, well, I don't know what. Baptism of fire or something. Is it going to be like that every time we go out and you're recognised?" If it was, she'd need to get a more positive frame of mind about it. Jan hated being on show if she wasn't aware of everything that was happening. The last hour had shown her that side of her more than ever.

"Nah, that's not usual. Most people gawp but don't do anything more. Actually, let me be honest, most people don't recognise me at all. Why should they? I'm no megastar. Even Moss, who lives around here and *is* a lot better known, says he's hardly stopped and asked for photos and stuff. But if he is or I am, we both do what's needed with good grace. They pay our wages, so to speak. This thing today is probably because we filmed around here for a good few weeks, and Moss and I stopped at his when we could. It's the nearest town to the castle and to where the filming mainly happened, and I guess we spend a fair many hours here. A pint with the crew, who took over the caravan site on the other side of the river for a month or so, shopping in the wee supermarket, eating in the Italian and Chinese restaurants. That sort of stuff. And of course people go up to the castle for lunch and golf."

"But not for the pool or gym," Jan said as she put the car into gear. A thought struck her. "Um, where's your car?"

"I wondered if you'd think of that," Thom said. "I left it at the castle and got one of the courtesy cars to drop me off. I was hoping you'd take pity on me and bring me back with you. Mind you, I was going to shout you tea in the café before we headed back."

"No need," Jan said with a smug expression. "You can take me out and pay another time. I have a cream tea for two in the carrier. In a cool bag sold to me with it by the very enterprising stallholder. Good eh?"

"Bloody perfect." Thom sat back. "I haven't had one of those for ages."

Jan waited for a few minutes. She couldn't believe he wouldn't add or ask more.

She was correct.

"What would be a perfect tea then? Better than just good."

Jan laughed. "Oh Thom, how predictable. Cream tea as a tea, a Scottish high tea as my dinner. Spread over two meals. How anyone can manage a full-on cock a leekie soup, fish supper and cake in a oner I have no idea, but I know people do."

"True. I have." Thom was silent for a second. "Mind you, I was comatose for three days after. A lethal combo. I have a feeling someone tried to get me to sign up for a family I'd support but I already do one, so must have said no dice. Or if I was well gone, no dieth."

He was silent for a moment. "Why am I rambling?"

"I have no idea, why are you? And what family do you support?" Jan was intrigued to hear about his life other than work. She turned onto the single-track road that led to the castle and expertly dodged a sheep that seemed to be on walkabout. None of the fields nearby had sheep in them. Wherever it had come from, she hoped someone would see it and return it. She turned her thoughts back to Thom. "A family how?"

"Oh, via a charity. It's no biggie. I send the money, get a lovely letter from them, and hope I'm helping a bit."

Thom wriggled uneasily. He hated talking about himself if it sounded as if he was bragging. *This is Jan. She knows me better than that.* Or he hoped she did. He searched for a way to change the subject. "Ah, what do you think we should do with the pottery?"

Jan indicated to turn up the drive to the castle. "What do you?" she asked him. "And what's with the joint account stuff? You said you'd explain and then we both forgot."

He'd hoped she wouldn't remember. What imp had caused him to say it? The fact he wished it was true? Thom admitted to himself that was probably at the root of the statement, but was Jan ready to hear it? They really did need to sit and have a proper talk about their future.

"Spur of the moment devilry," he said mildly. "I just thought it would sound good, and who knows, we might one day." That was as far as he was prepared to go while Jan was driving. He cleared his throat. "When you've got all the castle stuff over, I thought we could go away somewhere for a few days and talk about what we both want? I've got a week's filming over on the coast starting next week, and then I'm off for around a month. I could fit in with you."

He waited anxiously to hear Jan's reply.

"Sounds like a plan," she answered as she drew the car up outside the cottage. "My feet ache, and I need the loo and a cuppa."

"You head in and put the kettle on and go to the loo," Thom said as he opened the boot of the car and began to get bags out. "I'll bring the stuff in and find plates and so on." His tummy rumbled. "The cream tea is calling to me."

"You're on."

Before he'd got the second bag out, Jan had disappeared, leaving the cottage door open for him.

It took three trips to get all their purchases inside. Thom shut the car boot, found the keys in a bowl on the hallway dresser and used them to lock the vehicle. The castle might be in the middle of nowhere and considered safe, but it paid to be cautious. He whistled as he put the cream into the fridge, salivated at the sight of the fresh fruit and the scones he saw, and hummed to himself as he switched on the kettle and warmed the teapot.

How domesticated.

His phone rang as he made the tea. Swearing under his breath, he covered the pot with a tea cosy made of various tartans—very twee and not to his taste—and fished his phone out of his pocket.

Zac! *Strange.* "Hey, what's up." Thom cringed. *Not a very original greeting.*

The sigh Zac sent down the phone was enough to make the leaves on the tree outside rustle it was so long and loud. Enough to set Thom's nerves on high alert.

"That bad, huh?"

"Worse," Zac said in tone that more than hinted of doom and gloom. "I've had a bloody reporter around."

"Only one?"

"If you've ever met this bugger, you'll know one is enough. He's been chatting to dear Mr Donaldson and says no one from the castle will speak to him. Why hasn't Jan? And why is she not answering her phone?"

"Whoa, slow down." Thom could feel Zac's fury. "Give her a chance. I reckon she's not answering because she's in the loo. You know it's not easy when—"

"Okay, that's graphic enough," Zac broke in. "But why didn't she talk to him?"

"You better ask her that," Thom said grimly. "I know she's spitting fire about an article we saw today in the local rag saying exactly the same thing. No one has contacted her, at all, so if someone has rung the castle the phone call hasn't been passed on." He heard a toilet flush then Jan's footsteps. "She's here now. Hold on." He held his phone out to Jan, who raised her eyebrows in query.

"Zac, About the no one available for contact thing."

"Ah." Jan took the phone. Thom leant back on the work surface and waited for fireworks. If only the phone was on loudspeaker!

For a few seconds there was silence from Jan. Thom could hear the sound of Zac's voice but not make out the words. A pity.

"Then someone has cocked up and it isn't me," Jan said in as harsh a voice Thom had ever heard her use. "We better find out who. No, that is not the royal we. It's we as in you and me."

Zac said something else Thom couldn't make out.

"Right," Jan said flatly. "Give the man my phone number. You have it?" She cocked her head to one side. "You what? That's wrong. One number out. Where did he get that from?"

Thom poured the tea, put her cup down next to her and tapped her shoulder to show her. Jan gave him a thumbs-up, pointed to the phone and changed the gesture to a thumbs-down.

"He did, did he? Okay. Can you ring him back, give him the proper number and arrange for him to come and chat to both of us, say, tomorrow afternoon. We need to talk, just the two of us first. Right, see you in the morning." Jan ended the call and handed the phone back to Thom.

"Well, now then, what a piece of work that woman is."

"Lois?" Tom guessed, though he had no idea how she could be involved in Jan's business.

"None other. Zac had the foresight to ask the reporter what it was all about. Funny enough I think I actually used to know the bloke. I've an idea he's the brother of a mate I was at school with. He got my phone number from the bloke who wrote that article. Who had been given it from someone from the film company. Evidently when they first tried to get some info, the person on the switchboard knew I was out, it was just after the first meeting, so put them through to the film crew. A lady called Ms McDonald helped him."

"So now the fifty-million-dollar question is, did she give out the wrong number by accident or design?"

"Yup. And why not pass the message on, either verbally or by a note? Hell on wheels, I know she's got it in for me, but does she not realise how much damage it's doing to the film company as well?"

Thom shrugged. "I never understand how other people's minds work, especially hers. Anyway, now you know what's going on, how are you going to handle it?"

"Smooth things over as best I can. Explain we are working hard to find a way forward that is acceptable to all parties. Not to say I personally do not think there is a snowball's chance in hell of doing it. That is for my mind and so far your ears only. I expect Zac has a good idea, though."

It was much as Thom had thought. He didn't envy Jan one bit. Whatever happened, there would be a fair few unhappy people round, and Jan was the obvious scapegoat. She might say that was part and parcel of her job, but it wasn't a part he'd care for. "Let's have some cream tea and forget about it for now." Not that he thought she would be able to. He certainly wouldn't. "It might not solve the problems, but it will help."

Jan sighed. "Or try to. Yeah. Argh, sod it, sod her, sod the lot of them. Cream tea here I come."

****

Several hours later, Jan admitted defeat and accepted she wasn't going to get back to sleep in a hurry. She squinted to see the time on the luminous dial of her watch.

Three forty-five a.m.

Argh. Why oh why did she have to wake up in the wee small hours, need to go to the loo then find herself unable to get back to sleep? She'd crept back to bed after using the bathroom in the hall—then the flush wasn't so loud in the bedroom—and discovered Thom had rolled over and now hogged most of the bed. A gentle shove to his shoulder had made no difference. A harder one had. He'd grunted, muttered something incomprehensible and moved to give just enough room for her to get in. But not enough to go back to sleep.

Rather than wriggle and wake her now snoring bedfellow, after thirty or so minutes Jan gave in and headed for the kitchen. People told her ad nauseam that coffee at night kept you awake. She'd never found that, but just to be on the safe side had begun to make a cup of instant decaf if she woke up and couldn't return immediately to her slumbers.

Once she was curled up on the comfy sofa, she sipped her drink and began to think about the day ahead. Had Zac found out where the no comment had come from and why? Surely nobody connected to the hotel would want to show the place in a negative light?

But if whoever had phoned the hotel, who on earth else could have answered? The girl on the switchboard had to connect calls to whichever extension was asked for. If there wasn't one, surely she'd know how to enquire who might be the best person to answer?

That question went round and round in Jan's brain until she finished her coffee, washed the cup up and returned to the sofa.

* * * *

She was shaken awake a couple of hours later.

"Whaa…?"she stuttered as she opened her eyes and looked up into Thom's worried face. "I was dreaming about you," she said as she put one had on his neck to tug him closer for a kiss. "And here you are."

"Here I am," he agreed. "I woke up to a cold other half of the bed and no Jan to caress to wake up and then make love to. I was bereft. Why are you out here and asleep, not in there awake with me?"

Jan rubbed her eyes and tried to arrange her thoughts. Not easy. "I went to the loo and when I got back someone was hogging all the bed. I slid in but didn't even have room to turn over and I couldn't get back to sleep. So I got up, made a drink and, it appears, I dozed off here." She kicked off the light throw she must have draped over herself at some point and swung her legs to the floor. "Dammit, I would rather have been in bed asleep cuddled up to you, not a cushion." She glanced at the clock and yawned. "I'll have a shower and make coffee after. I need to get a move on. What about you?"

Thom shrugged and reached behind her to present her a mug, its contents gently steaming. "Coffee awaits. I'm off to meet Moss and we're heading to meet someone about something I can't talk about. Mainly because I don't actually know anything other than he thinks it's a good idea. Tomorrow we'll be back around here but if we will be filming I haven't a clue. The idea was to do a bit in the forest that will go in the film. But who knows. Not me, that's for sure. I seem to be in the dark about most things these days. Toast or a bacon sarnie?"

"Eh?" Jan collected her thoughts. "My hero. I'd love a sarnie if that's okay. I'll only be five minutes." She scrambled up and headed to the bathroom. If someone was cooking her breakfast, she'd make her usual brief and sweet shower even faster than usual and be all business.

She took her coffee with her.

It was seven and a half minutes later when she followed the scent of cooking bacon and headed to the kitchen. As she put her coffee mug in the dishwasher, Thom slid three crispy strips of bacon onto a crusty roll and handed it to her.

"Sauce on the worktop."

"You are an angel." Jan added some brown sauce and took a generous bite.

"Delicious," she said once she'd swallowed it and wiped brown sauce off her chin. "You are now appointed chief bacon cooker."

Thom grinned and rubbed her cheek. "You missed a bit of sauce. How on earth do you manage to get it from your roll and onto most of your face?"

"It's an art," Jan said as she screwed her nose up. "Perfected over many years of sauce on sarnies.

Strangely never if the sauce is just on a plate. It's the way I squidge the bread together that does it."

Thom laughed. "Each to their own."

"True. So what's your dodgy habit food wise?" Jan wondered what he'd admit to.

"Salad cream on shortbread biscuits."

That rocked her. "Sal... You're kidding me. It sounds disgusting."

"It was and I guess it still is. I was thirteen at the time, out for tea at a mate's house. He had a sister who had a French penfriend visiting and boy to Malc and me she was hot stuff. A year and a bit older and shapely. She had breasts. Most of our peers hadn't. I tell you, we lusted as only young adolescents could." He rolled his eyes and did a swift caricature of a love-struck teen. "Anyway, I was so nervous that after our ham salad, when there was a plate of biscuits and cake, I picked up a biscuit and smeared salad cream on it. Michelle-Marie, the exchange visitor, asked me if it was a quaint Scottish habit, and I said it was in my family. Thank goodness the other two had taken our plates into the kitchen, so I was able to eat the thing before they came back and took the mickey. Years later, Malc and Donna admitted they'd see and heard it all, but decided not to rag me but to save it up." He smiled. "Funny, I hadn't thought of that for ages. I wonder what they are all up to now? Last I heard Malc was in the navy, and a high heid-yin, and Donna had married a farmer and emigrated to New Zealand."

"And Michelle-Marie?"

Thom laughed again. "I have no idea. We reckon she should have been a model, but then, that was based on the ideals of randy thirteen-year-olds."

Jan giggled. "We should look her up on social media."

"Sadly, I can't remember her surname."

* * * *

"So where are we headed and why?" Thom asked his brother-in-law as Moss drove his top-of-the-range four-by-four down a bumpy track at what felt like breakneck speed but was well under the speed limit you found in towns. "You've been very mysterious about it."

"That's because I want you to listen to what's said with no preconceived thoughts."

"Fair enough." Thom glanced out of the window in time to see a magnificent stag stare at him from a few feet away. Behind him a few does grazed, seemingly oblivious to the now mud-splattered vehicle passing them. "I promise I have no ideas about whatever it is."

Moss laughed. "You'd be hard-pressed to. Hour and a half-ish and we will be where we're going." He navigated around a stray pig that appeared to be intent on hogging the road. "That hog is a hog."

Thom groaned. "Cheesy."

"And that's all the cheese you're getting, mate. If you're good, you might get a burger later."

With that Thom had to be content.

* * * *

Where they were heading still wasn't clear when Moss turned into an industrial estate on the edge of a fair-sized town on the coast. Thom looked around with interest. Lots of units of various sizes, well-kept and with a buzz around the place. "We going to be building a house or sommat?" He'd noticed several units sold doors and roof struts and one announced an architect's office. "A classy designed for you or whatever one? If so shouldn't Ari be with you, or is it a surprise?"

"You know your sister. It wouldn't be the sort of surprise she'd be happy about. Nah, that's not it. You might want to soon, though?" Moss shot him a sideway glance. "If you and Jan are going to take the plunge."

"If and when we plunge will need a bit more discussion," Thom said slowly. "As in, where do we live? How do we live and who sacrifices what? We've been down that route once and I have no intention of cocking it up again. And Jan's with Ari on surprises. It would be more than my life's worth to make a major decision without her input. Where to live would be a very major decision."

Moss whistled. "You've thrown me there. That was something I hadn't considered."

"Well, believe me, I have. A lot. And once this crap at the castle is over we intend to sit and talk about it." Thom intended to anyway. He didn't know if Jan had come to any conclusion yet. "But as it's irrelevant and you've brought the car to a stop, do I now get to find out what this is all about? Or are you going to blindfold me and leave me here to find my way home?"

Chapter Thirteen

Zac peered at Jan over the top of his specs with an expression of weary exasperation. She did her best not to grin at him. He always did the peering thing when he wanted to give himself a few seconds to think before he spoke. She sat back in her chair and contemplated the picture of a misty loch which hung on the wall beyond his head. It wasn't a brilliant picture, no old master – or even a young one – but it captured some of the stillness of an early autumn Scottish morning. Jan would be happy to discover who the artist was and see what else he or she had produced.

"Oh, I discovered what happened about the no comment stuff," she said casually. "I wasn't around, I'd gone into town. Marina went home sick, the fire alarm went off. Nothing major. It was a faulty plug in one of the treatment rooms in the spa. The hotel switchboard was for some reason playing up, and the reporter who rang decided not to hold on or call back. Arsehole. I've sorted that out, though. An apology is to be printed. No doubt in tiny letters and buried next to the obituaries on page forty-four, but hey ho." She hadn't even known about the problems, as no one had thought them worth mentioning to her. It hadn't impacted anyone apart from one user in the leisure complex. She'd put that erroneous decision straight as well. Then of course Lois had handed the wrong phone number over. By accident or design and *when* Jan hadn't been able to discover. She doubted she ever would, unless by accident.

Jan glanced at the picture again. She really must find out who painted it.

Zac coughed and Jan brought her eyes back to study his face. "I'm awake," she said. "Wondering who painted the picture behind you. I like it and wouldn't mind one by the same artist. Just waiting for your observations."

"I painted it, you can come and choose one after we've sorted this all out. You know what my observations are," he said grumpily. "There's no agreement on everything, so it's up to each...each group, I guess, to see what they would accept."

"That's what I've said all along," Jan said with a patience that was fast running out. "In a nutshell, the residents can't stop the film company staying in the hotel as guests, or filming in the areas of the estate that are not exclusively for their use."

"Like my own private land."

"Exactly. The film company, however, cannot close anywhere to anyone that is normally open to them. Like the pool and gym. However..." Jan grinned as she watched Zac scribble on a notepad. No doubt he'd then ask her what she said as he couldn't read his hasty scrawl. "I discovered that those areas are only open from six a.m. to ten p.m., correct?"

Zac nodded. "Yeah. So we can do cleaning and maintenance with as little disruption as possible."

"So that unusable time could possibly be utilised by the film lot if, and it's a big if, they could guarantee not to disrupt the maintenance schedule and be out and everything cleared up before the pool and the other facilities reopen." She tapped her pen on the desk. "Personally, I'm not sure I'd trust them, but thankfully that's not my decision to make."

Zac let his breath out in one noisy gust. "*Phew*. Okay, so that's a maybe. Next?"

"You aren't owed any money by the film company nor do you owe them anything if the arrangement can't go ahead."

He nodded. "That's good. Mind you, if they had asked for the money they paid to explore the possibilities I could have told them to take a hike. I did check it was paid for service rendered." His lips twitched. "Blimey, that sounds a bit iffy, doesn't it?"

"Just a bit." Jan sniggered. "It's as well I know what you mean. So now, onto some more concerns put forward by Mr D and others." She glanced at her laptop screen and scanned the bullet points she'd made in her document. "They can be assured that hotel guests will not park outside the residents' cottages or to the best of your ability in residents' parking spaces at the hotel or leisure facilities. I've even added that the road markings would not be affected and if they were, they would be repaired, not at the owners' expense."

Zac rolled his eyes. "Ye gods. Some people."

"Each to their own, I guess. As it states in their deeds, they can't sublet, but you can rent out the cottages owned by the hotel as you do now." Jan picked up her rapidly cooling mug of coffee and took a few sips.

"To be honest," she went on, "I've spent all this time, on your behalf, merely rewriting what you and they know. Condensed it perhaps, but it's nothing more than what could be found just by reading contracts and so on." She scanned another page. "The film lot were told right back at the beginning that their demands were highly unlikely to be met, but they persisted. That's their prerogative. The residents made their feelings known, ditto. You let them and listened. I've collated it. I'll have paper copies of all this printed and everyone can have one to read. It'll also be available as a PDF and emailed after the meeting." She sipped some more coffee and waited for Zac to reply.

He grinned. "Let's be honest, I didn't expect any more, but as you know, it's not just me who owns the place. This way no one can say I didn't take due diligence or explore every avenue to get an outcome, whatever it will be. I suspect there will be a few more arguments and then we'll go on as before. The film lot can stay here and film on my land, which is between here and Moss' house. If they don't want to… Ah well, I'll chalk it down to experience. Talking of Moss, any idea why he maybe wants to have a meeting with me and your beloved day after tomorrow? It's all flipping meetings at the moment. I haven't managed a good game of golf for ages." He let out a short bark of a laugh. "Going around the course with you and Thom doesn't count."

"I bet it doesn't, and I haven't got a clue."

* * * *

"Well?" Moss fixed his eyes on Thom and sat back in his chair. They were sitting side by side in a pub not far from the industrial estate, each with a half pint and a sandwich in front of them. "What do you reckon?"

Thom chewed his cheese sandwich as he thought over the last hour. "In principle I think it's a great idea. The office we've just visited would be perfect. But I'd need to know more before I could commit. We've both got stuff on and I've got another TV show to film which will start in a few weeks. Might be earlier now to all intents and purposes the film is finished for me. I've got a few days off and one more day or so, I think. So far anyway. And hope it will all be Lois-free. She's been very quiet lately. May it last." He'd got very little else to do in the film and would be called back if need be. "So, the building," he continued. "New, well thought out. Space to do all we need, space for storage and even, dare I say it, space to do some filming. But, A, could it all be done there, B, how much money would be needed, Cc, what does Arietta think, D, isn't it a lot for us to undertake, E, what—"

"Whoa, hold your horses." Moss ate a few crisps that were part of the garnish on their plates. "One thing at once. I have discussed it with Ari, of course I have. It's something we both want, and therefore most of the money will be ours to put in. If you and Jan come in with us, we negotiate how much you need to donate if you like." He grinned. "Donate, waste, invest, who knows. We've talked it over with our financial advisor, accountant and solicitor and we can sort out a partnership. The building we checked out would be perfect for now. We're not going to be big, just a nice wee Scottish production team specialising in what we want to do. I drove you here the pretty way. It's less than an hour to drive if we come the boring but better roads. You've said often enough you'd like to spend more time here, get on with finishing doing up your cottage, and well, here's your chance." He picked up his drink. "Plus I have an idea in mind for a TV series that I think would work. If you read it over – I'll get a copy to you when we get back – tell me what you think and then, well, that's another area to work on."

"Another carrot to dangle in front of me?" Thom asked wryly. He really did have a lot to consider.

Moss smiled. "If you like to call it that. Anyway, have a think, chat with Jan and let me know. If you're for it, then I'll speak to Zac as well."

Thom nodded. He loved the idea, but would Jan? "I'll talk to her when we get back and see what she says. I know…" He hesitated. "Look, you know how we ended up splitting last time. Over both of us wanting different things work-wise and not able to compromise. Well, I wasn't. Hell, Moss, I don't want that to happen again, it was sodding awful, childish and well…you know. That means we do need time to discuss this as well as other things. And it's the 'bloody not a cat in hell's chance of compromise' meeting tonight that she needs to chair. I'm not saying anything until that's over and done with. If you need a fast answer, I can't give you one." What it would mean to him and Jan needed careful thought.

"That makes sense. I've asked Zac to be available the day after tomorrow. If that's not time enough, I'll push it back. I've got the option on the building for a month anyway." He grinned. "I paid the rent. If we go for it, we can rent or buy."

"If you fell in a midden, you'd come up smelling of roses."

* * * *

By the time she had to get ready for the meeting, Jan was on tenterhooks. She'd heard nothing from Thom other that, 'all okay, see you before the pistols at dawn' stuff. By that she knew he meant the meeting which he'd also called duelling people-groups. She personally decided there were a lot more names for it, including 'who would spit the dummy out the most'. Really, a lot of those involved were acting like spoilt babies. They needed to put up, grow up and not act up. If only she could say so. Instead, it would be more of a 'here's the summary, over to you' speech, and…And what Jan had no idea. There really wasn't an answer to satisfy everyone and she failed to see how that wasn't apparent to them.

Jan changed out of her comfy multicoloured leggings and oversized sweatshirt into a pair of smart trousers and a silky shirt, put on some makeup and decided she would do. She wasn't looking forward to the next couple of hours, but once the meeting was over and done with, she'd be about finished at the castle. Then Portugal?

That was something she wondered. If Thom and she were to be a couple, a proper couple, would she go? Would he be able to join her? What would happen when it was time to go back to Hong Kong? Could they have a long-distance relationship and make it work?

So many questions.

Blast and damn. Before she could even start to think about how to solve them, for now, the meeting had to take priority. Satisfied with her appearance—businesslike but not too formal—and as ready as she would ever be, she left the cottage and swung into the buggy to head to the conference room booked for the evening.

It was ready and set out as she'd asked. Groups of comfortable chairs sat in semicircles around coffee tables where refreshments would be put nearer the time for the audience to arrive. If they were an audience. Jan wasn't sure what she should call the attendees. In her mind she might think of them as punters or protagonists or even the bloody-minded lot, but officially? Perhaps attendees *was* the correct expression.

She put the paper copies of her findings on the tables, set up the video for the results to be screened and grabbed a coffee from the lone pot on the long sideboard. Put there, she knew, by Zac, or on his request, so she could have a drink whilst she arranged things. It would sustain her more than the water already on each table.

Half an hour to go.

The main door swung open and Arietta walked in. Jan smiled at her. "Hello, stranger, where's the men?" She'd thought that Arietta would come with Moss and more than likely Thom would accompany them, seeing as he'd been out with Moss, she assumed, all day.

"According to the text I just received they'll be here in about ten minutes," Arietta replied. "Anything I can do? "

"Grab a coffee if you want one. There's nothing else to do except wait. The rest of the refreshments will be brought in later. I'll deliver my verdict, wait for the ruckus to subside, if it does, then the bun fight can begin."

"Not literally, I hope. Be a waste of good buns."

"Who knows. Ah, I hear footsteps." The door swung open again and Ernest Donaldson entered with another three owners. They were followed by Alex and Sasha then Zac.

No Lois? Could we be so lucky?

The door opened again. *Sod it.* Lois walked in, dressed very casually for her in a long skirt and a floral top that she tugged at every few seconds. It was obvious she wasn't very comfortable in it. Jan wondered why. It might not be as clear cut in line as a lot of her usual clothes but it suited her. Without looking to left or right, or acknowledging her sister and brother-in-law, she sat beside an empty table, poured a glass of water and downed it in three gulps. She glanced around as she put the empty tumbler back on the table, saw Jan, paled and bit her lip. Then swallowed, turned and began to study the folder in front of her.

What was that all about?

Zac wandered across the room, and must have noticed Lois, because he stiffened, gave her a slight blink-and-you'd-miss-it nod, and headed to Jan.

"All set?" He didn't allude to his attitude to Lois, so neither did Jan. It was nothing to do with her unless Zac told her it was.

Jan scanned the room and was about to mention it appeared everyone except Thom and Moss were there, when the two men entered. After a swift glance round they headed to the table where Arietta had seated herself—and very carefully made sure anyone who approached her knew the empty seats were reserved. She'd even made sure there was one for Jan and one for Zac, if they got a chance to use them. Jan hoped they would, even if it was only to grab some of the food that would be offered. It had been a long while since she'd had lunch and that had merely been a mug of soup and a slice of crusty bread. She'd been too churned up to eat after that.

Jan smiled at Zac. "As ready as we'll ever be. Waste of time, you reckon?" she said out of the corner of her mouth, having made sure no one would be able to lip read—or overhear her words.

Zac shrugged. "You've done your best, no one can do more."

Jan walked to the front of the room with him, and stood back a little as Zac tapped on a table to get people's attention.

"Thank you for coming."

Jan zoned his voice out, curious to watch peoples' reactions to what she was damn sure they had either just read in the files given to them, or guessed. As Zac spoke, she watched Moss nod, Ernest Donaldson scowl and Alex stare stony-faced at no one in particular. Lois didn't lift her head and appeared to study her fingernails.

Wondering if they're long enough to scratch someone's eyes out? Bitch is me. Wonder what's wrong with her, though?

The wondering didn't last long, as she vaguely heard Zac begin to sum up what had been covered and brought her mind back to the present. No doubt she would now have questions to answer.

She did. A very disgruntled Ernest went on the attack immediately.

"Why didn't Miss Fraser there say all this? Why did you? Just so you could gloat and say really we are worth nothing?"

Jan took a step forward and gave Zac a warning glance to tell him to keep his mouth shut.

"Mr Moncrieff spoke because he, like you, is involved. He gave you my findings. I'm here to clarify anything you wish me to." They had discussed whether she or Zac should speak first. He'd chosen to, though Jan hadn't been sure it was wise. Now she was certain it hadn't been, but it was too late to do anything about that.

"I think it's clear what can and cannot happen. There is nothing in my findings to denigrate you, or indeed any owner, visitor or casual passer-by. What is and is not contractually allowed is set out. Whether anyone wants to avail themselves of any of those options is up to them. If the film company choose to stay here as guests, that is their prerogative. Ditto if they chose to use such facilities available to guests. Whether they want to is up to them. They know what is permissible, as do you. It's in black and white in front of you." She pointed to the screen, where the salient details were in bullet points. "And in your files."

She smiled and bet it didn't reach her eyes. What was it with the man? Did he think he'd been thwarted and therefore was about to have a hissy fit? If anyone should react that way it should be Alex, surely?

"*Harrumph.*" Ernest sat down.

Jan hid a genuine smile. She'd often wondered if people really did go *harrumph*. Now she knew they did.

Alex got to his feet. "Thank you," he said to both Zac and Jan. "It is indeed very clearly set out. I will consider what I wish to do, if anything, within the limits." He sat down again and whispered something to Sasha, who nodded.

"We will be in touch," she said flatly. "I also say thank you."

There was silence. Jan glanced at Zac, who cleared his throat.

"Refreshments will be brought out any moment. Meanwhile, if anybody has anything else to say or wishes to ask, Jan and I are here."

"And don't I wish we weren't," he muttered as he sat down. "Why do I have an itch down my spine? As if someone is going to throw a poisoned dart at me. I tell you, I'm over it. I took on running the place as a favour to my dad who couldn't persuade his company it was a good investment and he thought it was. Mind you I love it, always have. Sadly since I took over, I've had nothing but grief. It's a bloody shame. It's a fabulous venue, I love the castle, I want it to succeed and be on a par with any of the big venues in the country. It's got everything anyone could want to enjoy a break but—"

"Like every Eden it has its serpent?" Jan suggested.

"You got it," Zac replied. "This Eden seems to have more than one at the moment. Here's one coming."

Jan twisted in her seat to see Lois walking towards them.

Oh, shit, what now?

"Lois," Zac said flatly. "What can we do for you?"

She ignored him and turned towards Jan. "I wish to speak with you," she said in a small voice. "Alone." She cleared her throat. "Please." The word appeared to be forced out.

Jan reckoned it hurt her to plead. She waited until she was certain Lois didn't intend to say any more. "Why?" she asked bluntly.

"I, er, I wish to ask you something, to tell you something, but not with him around." She gestured to Zac, who snorted but didn't speak.

All of a sudden Jan was weary. She couldn't deal with Lois at that moment. "Tomorrow?' she said in a take-it-or-leave-it way. "I'll be in my office in the Du…Effie Barnet House until around lunch time." She'd almost said the Dung Heap, but had stopped herself in time.

"Then may I come around ten?" Lois asked, still in the same small, uncertain voice. "I would appreciate it. It, ah, well, I wish to apologise and explain. But in private."

Jan nodded. "Ten it is." She had no intention of starting the clear-up until later in the morning. She needed that to regroup and clear her mind. Now she might not get the clear mind, but with luck she would get clarity about the Thom and Lois situation.

Lois bobbed her head and walked out of the room.

"She can't think much of the refreshment then," Zac said. "Or the company."

Thom stared at Lois' straight back as she made her way forcefully but, he thought, with dignity out of the conference room.

What was that all about? He'd noticed her approach Zac and Jan then ignore Zac in a definite manner. Ready to go over and intervene if he thought she was harassing Jan, the body language he thought he'd interpreted had been interesting. Zac had seemed to be incensed about something, he thought it involved Lois. Jan had listened without any expression to what Lois was saying—asking—he wasn't sure which, and had appeared to concede to a request?

Damn if he didn't want to march over and discover what. However, he'd wait. With luck, Jan would tell him of her own accord. If not, then he would ask and see if she was prepared to tell him.

And if she wasn't? He'd have to suck it up.

"Wonder what that's all about?" Arietta asked. "I thought the unlovely Lois wouldn't go near Jan in case you went apeshit. And Zac looked about ready to spit tacks." She stopped speaking as a waitron delivered a tray of nibbles and a bottle of wine to their table. "Oh, food and wine. Perfect, thank you."

"Zac asked me to say he and Miss Fraser are on their way so, and I'm quoting here, please don't scoff the lot." The waitron grinned. "I do have another plate coming."

Thom laughed. "Zac's the scoffer." *In more ways than one, usually.* "Thank you." Once the man had left them, Thom pointed to one of the plates. "How I'd love to hide that from Zac. He's said often enough he could make meal out of prawn vol au vents. Sadly it's too late."

"What's too late?" Jan asked as she and Zac sat down at the table. "Ohh, prawn vol au vents. I love them."

"So does Zac," Thom said. "Let's all grab a couple while we can."

"Unfair," Zac said in a pseudo-aggrieved voice. "Anyway, I've asked for plenty so I imagine there will be another plate soon. I'm starving. It's been one of those awful days."

"Get stuck in then." Thom took a sandwich, waited until everyone had some food—not just the vol au vents—on their plates, then touched Jan's wrist. "Okay?" he asked quietly. "No major issues?"

She gave him a look that indicated she understood damn well he was fishing.

"Define major issues. Nothing I couldn't handle or, I guess, predict. The meeting went just as I thought, right down to the fact Mr D took issue I didn't speak first. Mind you, he'd have complained about something else if it wasn't that."

"*And* that was my fault," Zac interrupted. "Sorry, Jan, I'm not eavesdropping but I couldn't help hearing that. He's a tricky sod, and if you'd have stood up I reckon he would have said, was I not man enough to share the information you'd collated. Or something. Anything and everything would be wrong for him."

"Not to worry," Jan said equably. "It's over and done with now. Except, of course, to discover what Alexa and Sasha intend to do about filming. That's still in the air."

She still made no mention of Lois.

Thom made his mind up. Jan must know the interaction had been noticed. It would be strange if he didn't remark on it.

Arietta got in first. "What did the unlovely Lois want?"

Beside Jan, Zac scowled.

Ah, so he knows and isn't letting on? Interesting. Thom waited to see who would reply to his sister.

"No idea," Zac retorted. "Nor do I want to."

"Nothing important," Jan said in the sort of voice that told you it was a warning not to dig further. "Just… not a lot."

And that, Thom had to accept, was all they were getting. "Fair enough, if you say so."

"I do say so. Pass the chicken wings, please. I'm like Zac. I've not had anything to eat since half a mug of soup at lunchtime. How was your day?"

It was a definite change of subject.

"Tell you about it later."

* * * *

They walked home to, as Jan said, digest the food and stave off indigestion. The buggy could be collected the next day. Neither of them said a word for several minutes. Thom was happy just to be arm in arm with Jan and enjoy the warm summer evening.

The scent of flowers vied with the scent of midge repellent as they sauntered along the path to their cottage. Jan sniffed and laughed.

"It's one of those immediately recognisable aromas, isn't it? Repellent and flowers. So reminds me of home. Of growing up, long evenings and having to play indoors or be bitten to death. Now tell me, how was your day? It sounded oh-so mysterious."

"It was interesting. I'll go into details properly when we get home. It's a bit complicated and I want to be able to explain it properly."

"Fair enough, and before you ask about Lois she just asked if she could speak with me tomorrow so I said yes. No idea what it's about, no, you cannot be present and yes, I promise not to clout her with my umbrella unless severely provoked. Plus, before you ask, yes, Nettie will be within yelling distance if I need rescuing. Okay? Have I covered all eventualities?"

He guessed it would have to be enough. "Yes, with reservations."

Jan gave him what could only be called a strange look.

"Reserve away."

There was not a lot he could say to that. Thom grunted as they reached their cottage and went indoors.

* * * *

"Now," Jan said as soon as they sat down. "You go first. Your whatever-it-was that you've done today happened before my chat—if you can call it that—with Lois. I'm all ears. *Ow*!."

Thom grinned. He'd tugged on one of her ears. "Normal-sized I'd say. So not all ears at all."

"Hmm, men. Smart aleck, or rather, smart Thom." Jan rubbed the ear he'd pulled. "You know what I mean. And if you're not careful I'll call you bug-a-lugs."

"That is nasty. Really mean." It was an expression used in Jan's family for someone who was always bugging you. She'd mentioned it to him years before and he'd remembered her saying how much she hated it. "I'll think of something even worse."

"I bet. Okay, no more scoring points. Just please put me out of my misery and tell me what you've been up to. I need to hear something other than about the castle, Mr Donaldson's complaints—both valid and not—and Zac's worrying about something called the sodding demesne's haha's lack of ha. Which I worked out to be the sunken bit of ground round the land closest to the house is filling in with weeds or rubbish. I think he thought I would need to ask him what he meant, but I suggested he got the head gardener to check it out and see if it could be cleared by hand or if he'd need machinery to get the ha back. It almost raised a smile, but not quite. He's been in a right mood all day, and I don't think it's just about the film stuff. Goodness knows what it is, but if he doesn't snap out of it, I'll be snapping at him."

That was interesting. Thom knew Moss hadn't mentioned his ideas to him, so what was wrong? Zac was usually one of the most easy-going men he knew. However, as he couldn't do anything about it, he'd forget about Zac for the moment and explain his day to Jan.

Then what? He didn't have a clue.

"Right, are you sitting comfortably?" he asked in the manner of someone about to read a story to a child. The way his mum had told him a children's radio programme started.

"As I'll ever be."

"Then I'll begin. Once upon a time—"

His phone rang.

"Damn and blast, what does Alex want now?"

Chapter Fourteen

Her mind full of what she and Thom had to discuss—his phone call had had him haring off to the hotel.—Jan began to plan exactly what she thought of everything she knew. Which she decided was not a lot. There was no point in worrying, though. She'd wait to hear what Thom had to say, offer her opinion, tell him what things she had to share and see where they went from there.

However, by the time Thom returned, saying he'd have to film in the morning and they'd need to have their discussion later, Jan was drifting off and content just to go to bed, snuggle and slumber with him by her side.

He'd left at some early hour and, unable to sleep after he'd gone, Jan had headed for the Dung Heap early, tidied her desk and waited for Lois to appear with as much patience as she could muster.

Three coffees later and after a mental note to buy some more decaffeinated roast, exactly at the appointed time, Jan heard a knock on the door. Rather than shout come in and sound officious, Jan opened it and stood back to allow Lois to pass her. She gestured to the settee.

"Take a seat, I've made coffee and there's pastries on the table. One of the perks of working in a top-class hotel."

Lois half smiled, sat and arranged her skirt around her legs.

As if she might get it dirty? Oh, enough, I mustn't be bitchy. Yet.

"Thank you." Lois accepted both and after a nibble of pastry and a sip of coffee put both down. "I didn't expect such kindness."

"Oh, I can be kind if I think it warrants it. And sometimes just to be courteous." She had no intention of enlightening Lois as to which of those times it now was.

Lois reddened. "I guess I deserve that."

Why do I now feel like I've kicked a kitten? Darn it, she'll have me feeling sorry for her in a minute. Give over and let her have her say.

"Nope, it's me being a bit—" Jan shrugged. "You know."

"Oh yes, I know. So, I expect you are wondering why I am here," Lois began and stopped suddenly to eat a piece of pastry. Then she began to cough. "Some crumbs," she gasped, her eyes streaming. "Wrong way."

Jan grabbed a bottle of water from the minifridge, twisted it open and handed it to Lois. "Here, little sips."

Lois did as instructed. "Thanks, and thanks." She took the tissue Jan gave her and wiped her eyes. "Better now."

"Take a minute," Jan advised her. "I've waited this long, I can wait a bit longer. Then you can explain." She might be willing to listen, but Jan was in no mood to make it too easy for her. Lois had said she wanted to apologise, so apologise she would.

"I… Damn it, it is so hard to explain without sounding a whiny child, but it does go back to when I was younger," Lois said hesitantly. "Or the need to behave as I do—did—does."

How can she say that and not get tongue-twisted?

"I'm listening."

Lois nodded. "My parents were…at first controlling, and then when Sasha became a teenager their attitude switched. I was basically left to do as I pleased and all their attention was on her. At first it was bewildering, then annoying and then…" She shrugged. "Then it meant that by the time I was sixteen, I thought, they do not want me, I will find someone who does." She wrinkled her nose. "He was called Alfredo, eighteen years old, had several tattoos—or so I thought, until I discovered they were all temporary—and he drove a motorbike. It was all innocent, not even a fumble, merely a kiss or two, but my parents were convinced I had gone off the rails. Even though I was a good student and got excellent grades, I was sent to boarding school. It sounds like some old-fashioned story, doesn't it?" She sighed. "If only it was. I passed all my exams, left home and went to university. I studied photography, love it and worked hard. Once I was of age communications between us were few and far between. Mainly my parents issuing demands that I do or didn't do something. So—I married without telling them. A musician. Still sounds like a story, doesn't it?"

"Have to agree there, but it's a good one," Jan said. "Carry on." She paused. "Actually, I do believe you." It was too far-fetched for anyone to make up and explain it so simply. No embellishment. "And did you live happily ever after?"

The answer Lois gave astounded her. She'd expected a sob story. A lot of hand wringing and crying and poor me.

She didn't get it.

"We did for several years. I was his secretary, I suppose you could say. He worked as a builder, to help make ends meet. I took care of our finances, paid the bills, sent out invoices. We weren't well-off but we did okay. It was the happiest time of my life." She paused. "I was wanted and needed. Or so I thought. Then one day, he simply disappeared.

"I got a note saying he was sorry, he'd gone to find himself. That building no longer fulfilled him. He needed to immerse himself in music. The next thing I get is divorce papers and a demand, albeit a very polite demand, for half of our money. He explained that he felt he couldn't stay married when he had no intention of returning to me." She smiled wryly. "A lot of crap about how he still loved me but we had grown apart. Actually," she said in a reflective way, "that was true. We had very little in common. Anyway, half of not much is very little, but I handed it over. Our flat was rented, so I stayed in it. I went back to my love of photography and began to sell a little. Started to play netball again—I'd played for my county when I was younger. Started to get on better with my parents. Worked for Alex and Sasha as a gofer on occasions and, well, life went on. Then my ex appeared and insisted he needed to use my expertise to continue to find himself. Basically he wanted me to run his life for him so he could relax and not worry about anything. Of course, older if not much wiser than when we had been a couple, I said no and he stormed away, telling me I'd be sorry. He headed to my parents' and it appears he told them some rubbish about me. They never said what it was but it meant once more we were not on speaking terms and now rarely meet. They just demand I settle down with someone responsible, who will not expect me to be their banker. After a few months my ex sent an apology, and then…" She shrugged.

"I am here. They're still demanding I be a good and dutiful daughter and do as they say. My photography didn't pay enough for me to live. I got a job in an office, was made redundant. They nagged. I had no idea what to do. I am me, and I cannot be someone I am not. Sasha and Alex insisted I work for them again, and begged me to try conform to our parents' ideas. I cannot. We thought if I worked for them it would help. It hasn't. My parents insist I should be married. It is crazy."

In spite of herself, Jan was intrigued. She suspected it was a very abridged story, but it was fascinating to hear. "Your parents think filmmaking is conforming?"

"It appears so."

"Did he find himself eventually? Your ex."

Lois laughed. A proper happy sound. "Well, if driving a tourist coach is finding himself, I guess so. I saw him not that long ago driving into one of those big soulless chain hotels with a coach full of ladies. Guess his tips should be good."

Jan was fascinated but decided it was time to go for the nitty-gritty.

"So why did you stalk Thom?"

Lois opened her mouth, shut it and spluttered. "Stalk, I didn't… I just thought we would be good together." She swallowed hard. "Stalk is a harsh word."

Jan was now in no mind for niceties. "What you did to Thom was harsh. Why oh why?"

"He was nice to me at first." Lois swallowed hard. "Bought me a coffee, was pleasant. My parents…as I said, think I am a loser. Sasha and Alex feel sorry for me. They took me on again when I had no employment, no money. Must have decided I was a sad person and needed looking after. I suspect Alex made up my job for me so my parents would help me out to find somewhere to live. To give me a better standard of living. Alex and Sasha have been so kind."

Jan had to butt in. "You repaid them by pursuing Thom."

"When you put it so succinctly like that, I feel terrible. Truly, I did not see it that way. Mama wants me to marry someone sensible. She goes on and on. Sasha had told him how lucky they were to get you and Moss to star in the film. Moss is married, Thom is not."

Lois lifted her shoulders and dropped them, something Jan noticed she did a lot when she seemed stressed.

"Go on," she said in a gentler tone. It couldn't be easy baring her soul to someone she'd recently seen as a rival.

"Our parents approved of him, they nagged and I…" She held her hands up as if in defeat. "Okay, I stalked. Honestly, I didn't see it as that. I reckoned if I showed him how interested I was he would notice me. I even put air fresheners into his apartment that were similar to my perfume. How stupid is that?"

"Very."

Lois bit her lip. "Thought I needed to be around at every opportunity. He would notice me more. However, not in the way he did."

"I was told you groped Martin as well." Jan decided she might as well add that into the conversation.

"What?" Lois sounded incredulous. "I did not…oh. When someone pushed past me and I ended up with my hand on his, well, you know. I was mortified. No one believed it was the accident it was."

"Strange though it may seem, I do." Why she had no idea, unless it was the way Lois was being so frank about everything else.

"Thank you. I hope one day Martin and Peggy will too. I did try to explain but—" Lois shrugged. "I cannot blame them for not believing me. Not the way I acted. No more, though. I have had enough of meddling parents and men. And filming. I have resigned." She sat back in her chair, drank some more coffee. And made a face. "Urgh, this is cold. May I have a refill, please?"

"Help yourself."

"Would you like some more?"

How ultra-polite we now are. Wonder if it will last?

"No thanks, I'm on caffeine overload." Jan waited until Lois had made herself a fresh cup of coffee and returned to their conversation.

"You've resigned?"

Lois nodded. "As of next week, I'm going to work in a craft shop. I have rented a one-bedroom flat in town. And I am looking forward to it. I have decided it is time to be me. I love photography but have hardly taken a picture this last year. I am going to start again. I might even see if there is a netball team around."

"Where did you say you were going to work?" Jan was certain Lois hadn't mentioned anywhere specific and Jan was interested. She'd ask. After all, the worst Lois could do was tell her it was none of Jan's business and to butt out.

"Is it Cally's Crafts?"

"Yes. Why? Do you know it?" Lois sounded astonished. "The lady who owns it had put a note on the door saying she needed help. It's not full-time, but it will be enough for me to live on."

How nice to be able to say part time would be enough to live on.

"I went to school with Cally," Jan said affably. "She is nice. Congratulations."

Lois stared and her lip trembled. "It's a long while since anyone congratulated me."

* * * *

"And that was that. We agreed to draw a line under it, and she would like to apologise to you properly. But not today. The rest of today is for us."

Thom nodded. "Then here we go..."

* * * *

Was it rude to press your ears to see if you really had heard properly? Probably. Jan decided she better not but instead go over in her mind what Thom had explained to her.

"I think I've got it straight," she said cautiously. "Please shout out if I haven't. Explain to me where I've gone wrong."

"I won't shout, that's rude," Thom said in a prim voice, then smiled. "Go on, tell me what you think, please."

"Right then. Firstly, Moss has asked you to go in partnership with him and maybe someone else—if you agree—to set up your own production company?" To

Thom's obvious amusement, she ticked that off on one finger. "Set in Scotland but open to working where you think is right. Yes?"

He nodded. "Correct so far."

"It would mean you spending more time here."

"Also correct."

Jan frowned. Something was niggling her.

"You say you want us to really be together, but if you are here and I'm in Hong Kong, won't that be hard?"

"It will but, if we really do want to be a couple, *and I do,* we could sort something out I'm sure. In fact," Thom got down on one knee, "I've intimated I'd be based in Hong Kong—if you agree to me sharing that part of your life with you. You see," his voice was serious, "I love you and want us to be together. Will you marry me? Or at least think about it?"

Pardon? Did I hear that correctly? Oh my. Her mouth became dry, her heart missed a beat and her pulse became erratic. *I've got all the signs of shock.*

"I'll think about it," she said in a cautious manner. Stared at him, saw a cloud of what—Hurt? Worry?—flash through his eyes and realised she was being idiotic. It was what she wanted. Why on earth was she being so stupid? Talk about a Victorian maiden. She might as well have fluttered her eyelashes, twisted her hands together and done the 'oh my, this is so sudden, I have no idea what to say' routine. Then fainted and needed reviving. *With a kiss?*

"I've thought about it," she said, and grinned. "Yes, please. When?"

Thom got up, pulled her to her feet then swung her around before kissing her soundly. Jan returned the kiss with enjoyment and increasing passion. When they finally drew apart her breath was choppy, she was hot, sure she was flushed, and her skin tingled.

"Wow. Kissing is much better when you're properly engaged." Jan flapped her hand over her face, laughed and gave Thom a quick hug.

"I've got news for you as well." She tugged him to sit on the settee and snuggled beside him. "Just before I went across to the meeting I sent an email to May, my boss. I said that after careful consideration, I might be able to accommodate their suggestion that I spent more time in the UK as their European representative. I was going to see ask you what you thought of that suggestion."

Thom stared at her. If only she could work out what he was thinking. As ever, when he wanted it to be, his expression was blank.

"But you adore Hong Kong," he said. She'd be happy to leave it for months? "It's not fair asking you to move elsewhere."

"You didn't ask, love. I suggested it," Jan said with a happy laugh. "To be precise, the company did before I even got here, and at first I said a flat no, which is why I hadn't mentioned anything about it before. They are amenable to me keeping on the house in Sai Kung as long as I spend part of the year there and part here, in Europe. And, if I need it, they'd give me an allowance for a house here as well. What do you reckon?"

"I reckon you are remarkable," Thom said hoarsely. "We could swing between here and there as the mood—or the jobs—take us. Do I take it you think I should say yes to Moss? It will be hard work, but I'm not bothered about that. I'll be a bit short of spare cash, but I have enough saved to put in for our startups. He's got some ideas on what we should do first, and now I can put him out of his misery and say yes, I'm in, we can decide what to ask of the other person we think might be interested."

"What about the TV series of this film?"

That had been one of their niggles. That and Lois of course. Plus, he was certain Jan was curious who the mysterious 'other person' was. If he had been free to divulge that, he would have done.

"I thought that was next?"

"If it goes ahead I'll see, I'm not contracted or anything." Thom held his hands up in a 'who knows' gesture. "At the moment I reckon it's very up in the air. As in, I can't see anything happening with it. This filming is just about wrapped up, no talk of more as yet. I'm lucky, I do have another job lined up. I've got a month before I start it." He grinned. "I play a convict who has just got out of jail and heads to a deserted croft to think over what next. Gets mixed up with poachers, the polis, the local lady laird. It sounds weird but the script is fabulous. It's supposed to be a one-off, but I'm not so sure. Anyway, time will tell. Coincidentally, it's set in Scotland."

"With a croft in it I did wonder." Jan laughed. "Good planning?"

"Good luck more like," he said honestly. "And between you and me, I'm in the running for a part in a new drama series set in Hong Kong. Keep everything crossed for that."

"Everything," Jan assured him. "And you won't need to hunt for digs. Mind you, except for the Lois perfume, that apartment you had was bloody great."

"But you weren't in it with me. Sai Kung is preferable. Oh, and about where to live here, I have a suggestion. Have you got tomorrow morning free?"

"If I hadn't I would have now. Why?"

"Wait and see."

* * * *

The following morning Thom hauled Jan out of bed as soon as it was light. "Early start today. I'll make coffee." He smiled at her thoroughly rumpled, thoroughly loved appearance. "You look like a sleepy dormouse."

"Thanks for that. Proper thanks for coffee. Give me ten minutes."

"You can have twenty."

* * * *

"I'm all a-wondering where we are off to." Jan wriggled in her seat as Thom headed down the drive. "You going to give me any clues?"

"Nope." He tapped his nose. "Patience, hon, not too long to wait. Twenty, thirty minutes max." He'd borrowed Moss' sturdy, larger-than-his-own four-by-four vehicle for the journey. It wasn't that far to go, but the distance could be cut by a third if they used a couple of tracks and single-lane roads. "That's a clue."

Jam huffed. "If you say so. The coast? The ben? The town?"

"Not saying. Hold on, this is going to be a wee bit bumpy but it cuts the corner off, so to speak." Thom turned onto a rutted track which, by the looks of it, had recently seen cows driven down it. "This is on land owned by a friend so we can use it. Not that there is a law against trespass here. I could have taken you along roads but thought this would be more fun."

"Fun… Ah, okay." Jan held onto the door handle as Thom braced himself to drive over one of the deeper ruts.

Damn it, he'd known it would be bad but after no rain the ruts were rock-hard and deep. It was lucky it only went for a few more hundred yards. "Half a mile of hell to save five," he said as they reached the end of a lane and turned onto a minor road that also had evidence of cows' presence. "Then only about ten more miles. No points for guessing."

"Okay I won't guess Easter Archraig, then."

Thom laughed. "What makes you think there, clever clogs?"

Jan grinned smugly. "You always said if you could live anywhere that's where it would be. I'm having a wild guess here, but I'm sort of thinking there might be a house for sale and we're off to see it. It's not too far from the airport or shops and it's a village that has all anyone needs."

Thom laughed. He'd had a bet with himself he wouldn't be able to deceive Jan. "Almost but not quite. We *are* going to see a house there, but it's not up for sale."

"Not? Then why? *Ahh.*"

Thom saw the moment Jan got his drift.

"You have one there? Wow! Where? What's it like? Is it—"

"You'll see in five minutes." Thom broke into her myriad, bullet-fast questions. "I bought it several years ago and I've been doing it up as and when I had the time or the money. Now I've got a bit of both I thought, if you liked it and we agreed it could be our Scottish base we could get some workmen in to finish it. I've enjoyed the bits I've done but some things needed and still do need professionals. It's been rewired, new water pipes put in and a new bathroom. They're all professionally done and to the required specifications of course. I'm no plumber. Putting a washer on a tap is about my limit. The house needs a better kitchen, that was next on my agenda. A Welsh dresser, a press, a sink, fridge and Aga aren't really enough. The press makes a good larder, and I've added an old bookshelf to use as a sort of pantry for now, but it needs doing up."

"It sounds like it." Jan wriggled and bounced a little. "Exciting. Can't wait."

"You don't need to." Thom turned off the main road—if it could be called that—and drove up a narrow side street until the road opened out and circled a tiny duck pond and a patch of grass. He pulled up outside what he'd call a traditional Scottish cottage. One-and-a-half stories, with the bedrooms in the roof. "This is it. Two old farm cottages knocked into one. That means we get two good-sized bedrooms and a smaller one. That gives us space for two bathrooms, one of them is en suite. Downstairs there's a large open-plan living-kitchen-diner, separate lounge or snug or whatever you want to call it, and a broom cupboard for an office. Gah, I sound like a seller singing its praises."

"You do sound like an estate agent. A broom cupboard?" Jan got out and stared at him over the bonnet of the car. "Seriously?"

He shook his head and grinned at her mock-scowl. Or he thought it was put on. Hopefully. "Small but not that small, big enough for a desk and cupboards and so on. Earmarked for you, if it all works."

"What about you?"

"There's a really not much bigger than a broom cupboard room off the hall. I think it was originally a place for storing coats and outdoor stuff. There's a porch for them now. It would do me for all the times I'll use it. The cupboard, not the porch. Anyway, instead of talking about it, how about us going in and you can see?" He was both curious and concerned to hear what Jan thought. "Give me your honest opinion." He loved the place and had poured a lot of time and effort into it, but if it wasn't to Jan's taste then he would think again. It was only bricks and mortar and hard graft already completed. In the past.

Jan was his future.

A sudden sharp spatter of raindrops made him grimace. "Let's make a dash for the porch." Once there, he took out a key and unlocked the door to usher her in.

There was a loud pitched ringing. Jan looked at him with alarm. "What the?"

"Security." That's what came from being gallant. He had forgotten all about it. "Give me a sec." He punched in the security code and there was a blessed silence. "All fine now."

She let out her breath. "*Phew*. Good. You had me worried for a bit. I had visions of us being carted off to explain who we were and what we were doing. Crazy. How long did you have to turn it off?"

"Long enough. I've never actually discovered that because I always until now remember about it. Anyway, as you are now in my parlour, so to speak, have a wander and let me know your thoughts on what you see." He'd never felt so anxious in his life about anything. Not even passing his finals at uni, or his driving test. "Take your time and be nosy and I'll wait in the kitchen, make coffee and bite my nails."

Jan nodded. If she was on her own and hated the place it would give her time to compose herself and think of a pleasant way of saying it wasn't her cup of tea *and* to try to find an alternative. "Can I look in there first, though? The kitchen."

"Love, you can look where you want whenever you want. Unless it's the loo and I'm in there." Thom rolled his eyes. "My time then."

"Fair enough." She grinned. "I prefer privacy there myself. Which door? Not the loo, the kitchen."

Tom pointed towards a door. "That one. To the left."

Jan opened the door he indicated, gazed into the room beyond and gasped. She'd never expected to see what she stared at. "Oh my! This is something else. It's gorgeous." It might not be finished, but the potential for an amazing family room was there. "Love the colour scheme."

Behind her she heard Thom chuckle. "It's not bad, is it?"

"Not bad?" Jan turned away from viewing the delights ahead of her and glared at Thom. "Understatement there."

His smile nigh-on split his face. "A four-door Aga with a stove attached that gives out constant heat. That fabulous fridge in mint green, and *ohh,* a plate rack. For some weird reason, I love plate racks, even if you do need to keep washing clean plates to be able to use them."

"Eh? You've lost me."

Come to think of it, that doesn't make sense. "Because if the kitchen door is open, there's often a bit of dust floating around. Plates are out, so it can land on them. I once saw a plate rack behind glass doors. I think that's a good idea. But seriously, this is amazing. All that gorgeousness to be played with? What a brilliant start to a viewing."

"Don't forget the Welsh dresser and a vast expanse of emptiness," Thom added. "One sort-of-comfy chair and a wee table with a wobbly leg. All home comforts."

Jan swatted him with her scarf. "Don't be negative. That vast space is perfect. You know as well as I do it has so much potential. You wouldn't have bought it otherwise." She wandered across the half-empty room and visualised where she, *if* she did end up living there, would put a settee or two and a big dining table. *The settees to take advantage of that glorious view of the garden.* The window was south facing, and the view from it encompassed the good-sized garden and the hills beyond. *Perfect.*

At one time, she thought, the room must have been the whole downstairs area of one of the cottages, and she could imagine the garden was one of the advantages of living there.

Thom cleared his throat and she turned to look at him with her eyebrows raised in question.

"You stood still and silent for so long I wondered if you were all right," he said. "Asleep on your feet or turned into a pillar of salt."

"Cheek. Like Lot's wife, eh? I was admiring the view. You sit in the sort-of-comfy chair and let me carry on my nosy." She didn't wait to see if Thom complied but went back into the hall to continue her walk around.

There was nothing about the cottage she didn't like, Jan decided as she wandered from room to room. Yes, it still needed a lot of work doing to it, but on the whole it was perfect for them. Thom even had a super-king-sized bed…and not much else in what she assumed was the main bedroom. It was certainly the biggest, anyway, and had the en suite he'd mentioned. As he had also mentioned, the main bathroom had been refitted, and the plain white loo, basin and bath were totally to Jan's taste. So was the walk-in rainforest shower. She itched to try that big-enough-for-two space out. The image of her and Thom in it, naked and making love, was hard to dispel. Jan shook her head at her wayward thoughts and moved out of the room at a smart pace. There was no time for those thoughts at that moment. *Later, maybe*!

It didn't take her long to check out the rest of the cottage. The other two bedrooms were a decent size and cried out to be furnished. She'd have fun doing that. Would Thom mind her saying how his house should look?

He said it's ours. Nevertheless, Jan made a note to remember to suggest and discuss, not state how things should be.

Back downstairs she could hear voices coming from the kitchen. Did that mean visitors? *Damn, I'm not in the mood for socialising. I want to finish looking around, then tell Thom yes please and talk about what we do next. Not make polite conversation to someone I probably don't know.* She stood outside the kitchen door, uncertain whether to go in or not, and listened intently.

It was a radio or TV, which meant Thom must have either been listening to something on his phone, or he'd got either of them hidden away in the dresser. She moved on.

It didn't take long to check out the other few rooms. He'd been right about the so-called broom cupboard. It wasn't spacious, but it would work. Jan accepted without compunction she'd let Thom have that and she'd go for the smaller of the other two rooms as an office, leaving the other room to be their snug.

She went back into the kitchen with a grin on her face.

"I love it," she said as Thom looked up quizzically from studying his phone. "When can we move in?"

He wiped his brow in a very over-the-top manner. "*Whew*. Thank goodness. When do you want to?"

"Tomorrow," Jan said promptly. "However, I accept that's maybe a bit premature. As soon as we can. I've all but wrapped up at Romansa Castle, which I've decided is well named, and I've got a month or so before I have to go back to work in Hong Kong."

"I'm all yours."

Tom leered. "Oh, that sounds good."

Jan batted him with her fingers. As long as he was all hers as well. "I hope it is. So, what do you reckon?"

"I thought you were off to Portugal?" Thom said. "When do you go there?"

"That's the beauty of it all," Jan replied, her heart full of joy at how things had turned out. "I've not got a flight booked yet, because I had no idea how long I'd need to be at the castle. Accommodation is sorted. Mum and Dad have had a house in the Algarve for years. It's rented out when the family don't want to use it, but it's been left free this summer so any of the family can go there. Ten minutes' walk to the sea and vacant for me. Or us. Good, eh?"

"More than," Thom replied. He rubbed his chin. "I'll be glad when I can either grow a beard or shave this stuff off. It's at the itchy stage."

Jan glanced at the dark stubble on his chin and upper lip that he'd grown for the film. It suited him. Dare she say it made him look a bit off a ruffian? A hard man, but with a heart of gold? *Nope, it sounds stupid.* "I think it suits you. Is this a change of subject because you don't like the idea of stopping here? We can always nip to the house in Portugal as well. Didn't you say you'd got a few weeks before your next job?" Was she assuming too much? He actually hadn't said he'd like to accompany her.

"It wasn't, it isn't and if it sounded as if it was, damn it. It was me saying what else was on my mind. I'm glad you like it, it still itches and yes, I have a month off. I think, if it's okay with you, we should have a week here. Mind you, it would mean roughing it. No proper bed."

"We can still stop at the castle. Zac is happy for us to hold onto the cottage for a couple of weeks." Jan had checked that when she hadn't been sure what her plans were. She hadn't wanted to be left without any accommodation.

"Perfect. Then not so much roughing it after all. We shop and see what we want to buy then order it. Maybe head to Portugal for a couple of weeks, come back to sort out the cottage and then I guess you need to head off and I need to work. It's only a short job, four or five weeks at the most. Then...well, I've no idea what then. Except I want to be with you."

"And I want to be with you. We'll work something out," Jan said firmly. "With a bit of luck I'll be able to work where I am around where you are. The joys of working from home. Or homes. We'll manage it this time, Thom. I'm sure of it. Older, wiser and more in love than ever."

Thom gave her such a look of love, Jan's heart fluttered.

"That we will, my love. That we will."

Want to see more from this author? Here's a taster for you to enjoy!

The Scots and the Sassenachs: The Duke's Lost Love

Raven McAllan & Cassie O'Brien

Excerpt

By the light of a flaming flambeau held aloft by Sydney, page and general dogsbody to the Armstrong household, Mrs Evanna Percival-Smyth walked home. The moon was on the wane and that, added to the heavy cloud obscuring the stars in the night sky, made his illuminating assistance to guide her footsteps a necessity. A trip, with its likely consequence of a twisted ankle, was high on the cards otherwise.

Her house was cloaked in near darkness when she arrived. No servant would be up waiting. She was not meant to be there, but rather at Denny House, where she'd accepted an appointment to chaperone the Lady Cairstine McColl during her visit to Corbridge.

Circumstances had led to this unexpected return.

Of course, if she chose, she could wake the household and have people ready to do her bidding immediately—or almost immediately. It would mean they would have to dress and hurry, probably bleary-eyed or yawning, from their various rooms, and Evanna was more considerate than to ask for that. She valued her staff. Why should her unforeseen homecoming disturb their slumber? In her mind they got little enough respite as it was.

Plus, she had a lot to think about and didn't want anyone to see her agitation. Sydney, bless him, did not count. His intelligence was not of the highest, but he was always willing to please.

At her front door, she opened her reticule and passed her young escort a silver sixpence. His eyes widened.

"Cor, Mrs P. Thank you."

She patted his shoulder and smiled, even though, with her knees all a tremble after seeing Cairstine's father, Nathan, for the first time in over twenty years, it was the last thing she felt like doing. She wanted to run and hide. Be alone.

Think things over.

Sydney stared at her, a slight frown creasing the space between his eyebrows. "You all right, Mrs P? You looked a bit strange just then."

Bless him. "You're a good lad, Sydney. I'm fine, just tired I suspect. Run along now. I imagine there will be plenty for you to do tomorrow. Is your bed ready?"

He nodded. "Course it is. I's been mekking it tidy every morning like what you told me to."

"Good boy. Take the flambeau to guide you but be sure to extinguish it in the water bucket when you get home."

He nodded and dashed off.

Evanna watched him disappear and reached into her reticule, which along with a quantity of small change also contained her door key. She let herself in and sighed in satisfaction at the familiar scent of her own home—lavender and beeswax. Her housemaid had obviously not skimped on either the elbow grease or the furniture polish while she'd been away. An oil lamp, its wick turned down low, lit the interior and saved her fumbling about in the dark. It took but a second to pluck it from a small consul table and make her way up the stairs to her boudoir. By the lamp's absence her servants would know she had returned.

Her thoughts were all over the place as she considered the events of the evening just gone. A large sherry to calm her agitation was in order, she decided. Once it was poured, Evanna settled back into her chair and thought back to when it had all started. Her first and only visit to Edinburgh…

* * * *

Before

The excitement began when she overheard her father's dour tones followed by her mother's firm but snappish retort from the other side of a not-quite-closed door.

"It would cost a small fortune. I'm nae made o' money for you to fritter away on female foibles and frolicking, woman."

"It's got nothing to do with frolicking or frittering, Angus Kerr," her mama retorted with a hard edge to her voice that Evanna had never heard her employ when addressing Papa before. Forceful. That was it. Intrigued, she continued to listen.

"Evanna is the prettiest of our girls as well as the eldest. Just give me five hundred pounds to take her to Edinburgh…"

Evanna held her breath, hardly daring to hope.

"And I'll practically guarantee she'll catch herself a well-to-do husband. Then she can sponsor each of her younger sisters when they are of marriageable age.

That's four for the price of one. Consider it an investment. After all, it's not much more than you spent on that gelding last month."

Her father fired back, "At least the gelding crossed the finishing line first and brought home the prize fund."

"An aberration no doubt." Her mother sounded less than impressed. "Let's face it, it's about time one of your stable achieved a positive result. Your racehorses cost more than all of we females do put together. The gelding's winnings should meet the majority of the expenses I'll incur in Edinburgh."

"But…but…five hundred pounds," her father said glumly. "Would fifty nae do?"

"It would not, now wheesht or I'll be demanding a thousand. You think on my words, Angus. You fathered them and you have a responsibility to see your daughters respectably established."

The rustling of stiffened petticoats warned Evanna it was time to move. She picked up her skirts and hurried away.

* * * *

Now

Nathaniel, Duke of Glenard sank gratefully into the padded comfort of a fireside chair and accepted the balloon glass of brandy offered to him by his daughter, Cairstine. The concern in her eyes mirrored the tone of her voice as he took his first sip. "You look quite knocked up, Papa. Drink this and we'll talk in the morning. There's no rush now the letter has been destroyed."

Knocked up, knocked sideways and thoroughly knocked off kilter. Nathan could only manage a nod. One image filled his mind to the exclusion of all else. There was no room for more.

Evanna... My love...

Cairstine smiled softly and walked to the door. If she was disappointed at his lack of response in not enquiring as to her own part in the affair of the treasonable letter that had brought them all hotfoot to Corbridge, she didn't show it. He would make it up to her in the morning. Ask all manner of questions about her adventures over the last few weeks. Tell of his own and express his happiness at her marrying the very man he would have chosen for her if she had not already done so herself – Duncan, the Earl of Callander. But for tonight he needed some time alone with his thoughts.

Evanna...

About the Author

After 30 plus years in Scotland, Raven now lives near the east Yorkshire coast, with her long-suffering husband, who is used to rescuing the dinner, when she gets immersed in her writing, keeping her coffee pot warm and making sure the wine is chilled.

With a new home to decorate and a garden to plan, she's never short of things to do, but writing is always at the top of her list.

Her other hobbies include walking along the coast and spotting the wildlife, reading, researching, cros stitch and trying not to drop stitches as she endeavours to knit.

Being left-handed, and knitting right-handed, that's not always easy.

Raven loves to hear from readers. You can find her contact information, website details and author profile page at https://www.totallybound.com

Sign up for our newsletter and find out about all our romance book releases, eBook sales and promotions, sneak peeks and FREE romance books!

www.ingramcontent.com/pod-product-compliance
Lightning Source LLC
LaVergne TN
LVHW091033080826
845145LV00002B/473

9781802505313